Loving Josephine

Book II

Waters of the River Red Series

SUSANE LAVALLAIS BOYKINS

Sun Red Books, LLC

Dallas * Texas

This book is a work of fiction. Any references to historical events, real people or real places are used fictitiously. Other names, characters, places and events are products of the author's imagination, and any resemblance to actual places or persons, living or dead, is entirely coincidental.

Paperback: ISBN 978-0-9985221-2-8

Printed in the United States of America.

DEDICATION

For David Wendell, Chantelle and Lisa

ACKNOWLEDGMENTS

The love and support of my family plays a significant role in my life. I wouldn't have been able to complete my second book without the unwavering encouragement of David Wendell, Chantelle and Lisa, my three grown, industrious children. They helped me brainstorm ideas, plan events, both professionally and personally, and was a general ear when I needed one.

I owe a debt of gratitude to my friends, too numerous to name, who kept me motivated to keep going by asking me, "When was the next book coming out?" Whenever I got stalled, that was the push I needed to get me back on the right track.

To Tonya Nash, my daughter from another mother, thank you so much for previewing and critiquing my book. Another set of eyes is invaluable and you did an excellent job.

Also by Susane Lavallais Boykins

Waters of the River Red – A Novel

~ CHAPTER 1 ~

Marksville, La.
September 1934

Her large brimmed straw hat shielded her eyes from the blazing sun and bobbled up and down, as she scurried down the gravel country road. Drops of sweat ran down her medium brown, complexioned face and large wet spots were visible in the armpit areas of her husband, Luke's, large over shirt that she'd worn to protect her arms. Even though she had shoes on, the hot rocks that protected the cars and wagons from getting stuck in the Louisiana red clay during the rainy season, were hurting her feet.

Twenty-eight-year-old Josephine Ford, known to her friends as Feen, was deep in thought, because she'd awakened that morning with a feeling she couldn't explain. A feeling something terrible was going to happen that day. However, she'd needed groceries for supper, so she'd put her misgivings aside and taken this two-mile walk to Donay's store, anyway.

The peacefulness and splendor of the countryside didn't soothe her thoughts and she attempted to calm her spirit by humming a gospel song. Gospel songs always set her back into the right frame of mind.

She was near home and should be there before her seven-year-old daughter, Laura, arrived from school.

"Feen," a familiar female voice called from a porch of a nearby house. It was Clarice, the sister of her best friend, Teresa, standing with one of her hands raised in a wave. Clarice lived with Teresa, and Feen wondered why she wasn't in the fields. She'd probably snuck off, as was her habit of doing.

"How do, Clarice. Don't have time ta talk now. Tryna git home." Feen answered in her strong creole accent that most of the older less educated blacks spoke with. She didn't slow her pace or wave back.

"Okay. Guess I'll see ya at church, Sunday," Clarice hollered back with her voice showing disappointment because Feen hadn't stopped to talk with her.

At the store, she'd exchanged two dozen eggs her hens had laid, along with her last dollar, for two links of sausage, two pounds of rice and one pound of sugar. She carried this in an old fabric flour sack, tied at the top and flung over her shoulder.

The houses were spread far apart and between them lay pastures of lush green grass, fields of cotton, corn, potatoes and rice. Sprinkled along the sides of the road were trees displaying the coming of autumn with leaves of different shades of orange, rust and gold.

She'd passed another house before she heard her name called again. This time it was from someone behind her on the road. She turned to see Wickliffe Francisco running to catch up with her.

"Feen," he said, once he was walking beside her.

"Hey Wickliffe," she said. "Where ya come from?" She usually traveled back and forth to the neighborhood store and never saw a soul. Today she'd run into two people.

"I was over at my cousin's house and saw you pass by. Hadn't talk to you in a while, so I thought I'd catch up so we could talk," he said.

"Why ya not at work today?" she asked.

"I left early to help my cousin fix a fence. What are you thinking about? With your head down, walking fast."

"Tryna git home 'fore Laura," she said. "I'll see ya at church, Sunday. Tell ya mom and dem, I ax 'bout dem." With that dismissal, she hoped he'd catch the hint she didn't want to talk right then.

Wickliffe was a handsome, tall colored man with a smooth dark brown skinned complexion. He worked at Marksville's largest sawmill. Hauling and stacking lumber caused him to be trim and muscular. Most of the colored girls in town thought he was "just the cutest thing." She'd once thought so herself. But now, she had eyes for only her husband, Lucien, nicknamed Luke.

She knew Wickliffe was still a little sweet on her and the way he looked her up and down right then, irritated her. Her light blue shift-like dress with one of Luke's long-sleeved shirts that was way too big for her, was not the least bit sexy, so why was he acting like it was. Sometimes, she'd had fun with him and flirted back. Today, she was not in the mood for that kind of playfulness.

So, when she reached Perret's Path, she turned onto it and expected him to continue straight. Instead, he'd followed her and she'd let out a huge sigh.

"What's the matter?" he asked. "You act like you don't want to talk to me or something. Why?"

"Taint nothin', Wickliffe. Jus' got a lot on ma mind. S'all."

The path was small with tall grass and bushes on each side of it. She walked with her head down to make sure she stayed on it. The footpath was used a lot by people in a hurry, not usually two people, socializing, because the chance of encountering snakes or other varmints made the road a better place for conversation.

They came to a familiar place, a clearing under a large pecan tree they'd played under when they were children. A place with a lot of pleasant memories and the shade gave blessed relief from the sun. She put her sack down and wiped the sweat from her face with a handkerchief. This was an excellent time to find out what it was he wanted to talk about, so maybe he'd go on about his business. She took a deep breath and looked squarely in his eyes.

"Remember when we went to the parish fair that time? What a good time we had. Remember that?" he asked.

Nodding her head, she said, "Yeah, I 'member. We did have a good time. But, dat a long-time pass." She emphasized long to make her point. "Dis a diff'rent time. We's chirren den. I'm twenty-eight years old now."

His eyes ran quickly over her plump lips, large brown eyes and smooth brown complexion.

"You know, you still look good, Feen. Mighty good."

"Well, tank ya Wickliffe. Ma husband tell me dat all the time."

He rolled his eyes in his head and said, "Yeah, I bet he does."

She rolled her eyes in response. "Look, I gots ta go, and I know ya got sometin' ta do, and I don't wanna keep ya from it," she said.

He caught her by her left arm and she jumped. Her head jerked toward him and her eyes opened wide. "Whatcha doin'?"

"Aww, c'mon now. I just want to talk awhile."

His facial expression was serious and his eyes had a darkness about them. She believed he'd never understood why she'd chosen Luke over him. He'd finished high school and Luke had only gone to fourth grade. He read a lot of books, spoke well and talked about things the rest of them didn't know anything about.

"I already done tol' ya, I gotta git home."

"You can talk a little while. Because if you didn't want to talk, you wouldn't have turned down Perret's Path." His voice had a low thick sound to it.

"What?" she exploded. "Perret's Path go by the back a ma house, Fool. Ain't nothin' ta do witcha. Jus' tryna take a shortcut." She was tired, frustrated, hot and her temper exploded faster than normal. "I got a husband, a good husband. I don't need ta bring nobody down Perret's Path ta talk. Or nothin' else."

She shook her arm out of his grasp and turned to walk away. His eyes dimmed and he grabbed her arm again. Stronger this time.

"Hold on a minute. Just hold on a minute," he said.

"I done tol' ya, now. I ain't got time," she said in a low hissing voice as she jerked her arm away.

His arm flew out and his fist connected hard on the back of her head which caused her to stumble forward.

Ya hit me," she said in a loud voice with her eyes wide.

The contact hurt her, but more than that, it surprised her. For as long as she'd known him, she'd never seen him act aggressively in any way. Her anger was more than she could contain.

She slapped him back with all her might. She was quite strong, due to years of hard work and his head rotated with the lick.

When he faced her again, his eyes glistened and his lips curled above his teeth. He lurched forward, caught both of her arms with each of his hands and pushed them behind her back. This forced her body next to his and he attempted to kiss her. She wrestled with him, and her face moved from side to side to avoid his lips. When he seemed to be unmoved by her attempts, she spat in his face.

His head flinched and his eyes widened. He released her left arm and hit her on the left side of her head with his fist. As her head swayed with the force of his punch, it exploded with pain and her knees buckled.

He pulled her back to him. His arms and body kept her from falling. She was now leaning on him and he tried to kiss her again. Her disgust was so great an involuntary reflex made her spit in his face again.

This time, he leaned back and threw a punch and hit her, squarely, on her lips.

Her head lurched back, her neck popped and she screamed in pain. Blood and mucus drained from her nose and lips. Her legs were wobbly and her body rested almost entirely on him. She strained with all of her might to pull away.

"Why ya doin' dis ta me?" she whispered.

"Oh. Now, you want to talk, huh? I guess you're not as bad as you thought, huh?"

From somewhere, strength came and she stepped on his right foot as hard as she could. He yelled in pain and his arms released her.

She turned to run away, but because of her weakened condition, she was slow and only made it a few steps.

He recovered fast and jumped on her from behind. As his body brought them both to the ground, they brushed hard against some thorny limbs of blackberry bushes. The broken limbs came down with them and some landed under her. The weight of him crushed her chest, making it difficult to breath, and the thorns underneath her, tore into her flesh.

Breathing heavily, he turned her over and slapped her across her face. Fighting for her life, she clawed him across his face and arms.

"Goddamn you, Feen," he said, and backhanded her. Bells rang in her head and a loud sob flowed from her lips.

"Lawd, help me," she said.

Still wrestling beneath him, she kicked him in the groin, but her strength was nearly gone and it didn't have enough force to stop him. It only served to anger him more. He made a fist and hit her so hard in the stomach that blood flew from her mouth. As the swoosh of air escaped from her lungs, it took the last of her resistance with it.

She had no strength left. She tried, but could not raise her arms. One of her eyes had swollen shut and her mouth was filled with blood. Air rushed against her legs as he raised her skirt and despair overcame her as the sound of his pants unzipping reached her.

She said, "No, no. Gawd, please help me."

His hand touched her thighs and she said, "Wickliffe, please. Please. No."

She tried to keep her legs together, but he forced them apart.

The bands of her underwear tore into her skin as the fabric gave way.

"No. No."

Now the helplessness of her situation seemed to be overwhelming and she needed to remove herself from that place and time, if not in body, then in spirit. His face became a blur. His movements and speech sounded in slow motion.

"Why you had to fight me?" he uttered as he worked to complete his assault.

The pain and the smell of his cologne made her stomach heave. It was the same brand she'd bought for Luke last Christmas. The odor she'd loved so much that she'd saved every extra penny she could, to get it, now nauseated her. His heavy breathing, grunting and nasty sentiments degraded her to her soul. She wept, softly, until he was finished and she heard his final groan.

He lay on her for a second, then arose and she heard him as he adjusted his clothing, then the sound of his zipper again. There was quietness for it seemed like an eternity. Her eyes were closed as his hand touched her face. She lay very still as she waited for him to hit her again or for his hand to move to her neck to choke her. All her strength was gone. She was at his mercy and sure he was going to kill her.

His sob broke the quietness. She was puzzled and tried to see what was happening, but one eye was swollen shut and the other was brimming with tears.

His anguished voice said, "Oh my God. What did I do? What did I do? I'm so sorry. I didn't mean to hurt you. It was a game. You know the game we play. It was a game that got out of control. Please God, forgive me."

His voice seemed far away and as he spoke, the volume of it gradually diminished. She went into blessed unconsciousness.

~ CHAPTER 2 ~

A buzzard hawk flew overhead and circled. Ants flocked and made streams of lines as they crawled upon Feen's legs and arms. The stings from their bites awakened her, and she groaned. Her whole body, including her head, had a dull throbbing pain as though, she'd fallen off a cliff. Her side throbbed like a rib might be broken and she was on fire and itched from the ant bites. Tears coursed down her face, silently at first, but slowly turned into big gaping wails that caused her ribs to pulsate with pain and she winced.

She struggled to swat the ants away, but the agony prevented her from being successful. Her left arm was injured. In fact, she could not lean on it to get up. She tried once more to brush the ants away, but began to lose consciousness, again. She fought to stay awake.

"Oh, my God. What happened? Miss Ford, who did this to you?" she heard a surprised, concerned voice say.

"Aah," she mumbled. "Git 'way."

She wanted to say it more forcefully, but did not have the strength. She wondered if Wickliffe had sent someone to see if she was alive, and if she was, to kill her.

"Lemme be, please," she begged. "I never done nothin' ta nobody ta deserve dis."

"Miss Ford, it's me Adrian, Azalea Fonteneau's boy. You know me. I see you and Mr. Luke at church all the time. Don't be scared. I'm not gonna hurt you."

Through the fog of her pain, the voice was not one she knew. It was not the rapist's voice. It was a young voice. A teenager's voice. She'd understood him to say his name was Adrian. She cried anew. She wondered if her skirt was still pulled up. Could he see what had happened to her? Shame consumed her. As painful as it was, she tried to smooth her dress down to cover herself. The humiliation was just as agonizing as the pain coursing through her body.

"Git 'way from me. Git 'way. Please, git 'way."

"What happened, Miss Ford?" His voice brimmed with concern and disbelief. "Let me help you," he said, as he leaned down to her.

"No," she said and tried to pull herself into a fetal position, but every move was so painful. "Git way, I say. Git way from me."

"I have to get close to you to help you," he said in desperation. "Let me put my arms around your back and waist to support you up. Let me help you home."

Home. He'd said the word home. Home seemed to have been the magic word. It created hope within her and her tears began to subside. Home. Sweet Home. A place so different from where she lay, in pain. Pain from an attack. Pain from ants. Pain from probing eyes and questions. As her mind envisioned her bed, the image of Luke also appeared. She would have to tell him. There is no way to hide it. The shame. Oh, how the shame consumed her. Her heart was heavy and her eyes closed, wishing somehow this whole situation would go away.

"Miss Ford, I need to come close to you, so I can help you up."

She didn't have a choice. She had to either let him help her or stay where she was and get stung to death by ants. Luke would come and find her body and know what must have happened. Just not by whom.

"Okay. Alright," she said, still sniffling.

He took his handkerchief out of his pocket and wiped the ants from her legs. At his touch, she jumped.

"It's alright, I'm just trying to get these ants off you," he said as he worked. It was difficult to do with just a small handkerchief because the ants got on the handkerchief and traveled to his hand. He'd wipe them, throw it to the ground and stomp on it until the ants stopped moving. Shake it out and look for other ants. He did this until he didn't see anymore. "How long have you been here?"

"I dunno. I tink I pass out."

He'd seen the sack of groceries under the tree. He walked back, picked it up and came back to her.

She cried out as he raised her to her feet. The left arm, which was the arm Wickliffe had held onto was either broken or sprained bad. She couldn't lift it; thus, he moved to the right side of her and hugged her as gingerly as possible, so he could support her.

"It's okay. Lean on me. I gotcha," he said as they slowly started home. Even though she did not know this young man well, she'd always thought him to be polite and of good character. Now, the softness of his voice told her he was kind, too.

"Who did this to you? Do you know?"

"Yeah," she choked. "I know who t'was. I cain't talk now, though. It hurt too much fur me ta talk and walk at the same time. I hurt sometin' awful."

She knew she would have to when Luke saw her, because he wouldn't let it go. Especially when he found out who it was. It took all her strength just to walk. They walked in silence, except for spontaneous utterances of pain by her. Every now and then, Adrian would say something encouraging like "we're almost there."

Feen could see the small unpainted gray house, stacked firewood, the barn with their horse, Star, fowl, the hen house, chicken coop, their cow, Sophie, the small fenced pasture where Sophie grazed, her vegetable garden, and the field between her and her sister's house. She also saw the last tub of clothes she'd washed, hanging out on the clothesline.

When she wasn't helping Luke in the fields, Feen was a washerwoman, a laundress, as some called her. She washed clothes on a rubbing board in a tub in her backyard over a fire pit. For twenty-five cents per tub, she cleaned, starched and ironed clothes for rich white folks all over Marksville. She usually laundered one customer's clothes a day. But around holidays, when people either traveled or had a lot of company, they had more clothes to have cleaned. To keep up with the demand, if the weather were right, she'd do as much as she could in one day. Those days she worked from early in the morning to late at night.

As she looked at the clothes on the clothesline, she realized she'd promised Mrs. Frank her clothes would be ready the next day. She'd washed two tubs that morning. "Oh, Lawd, ham mercy on ma soul," she said in an agitated tone.

"What's wrong?" he asked. "We're almost to your house."

"Miz Frank comin' ta pick up her clothes tomorra evenin' late. I cain't iron all dem clothes by den. Even if I kin git dem iron, I cain't face her. Not like dis."

Relief entered her senses as Adrian unlatched the back gate. Her chickens came to greet her, probably thinking she was going to feed them. Her back door, which had once seemed so far away was now very close. There had been times during that walk when she'd wanted to stop and lay down wherever she was.

As they inched toward the back door, they heard a loud jolting sound. It burst open, hitting the wall behind it with a loud bang and bouncing back and forth two times. Feen jumped and emitted a shrill squeal. There stood Luke, his six feet one-inch frame blocking the door, his face red with rage, his legs spread apart as if ready for battle, his hands made into fists and his eyes glaring down at them.

~ CHAPTER 3 ~

Luke had come home early to surprise Feen before Laura got home from school. She'd told him that morning she had to go to the store, but he was surprised and more than just a little irritated when he arrived home and she wasn't there. She should've been home by now. He was in the mood for some quiet time with her before Laura got home. Anxiously, he'd looked out a back window and his heart propelled forth into a rapid beat, when he saw a battered Feen leaning on another man. He ran to the door and swung it open with such force that it made a swooshing sound.

Luke was a hardworking, tall, light complexioned handsome man with straight black hair. His eyes blazed at the young man holding his injured wife.

"What the hell goin' on here?" he hollered. He hurried down the steps to help her and repeated, "What the hell goin' on?" His eyes never left Adrian's face.

Feen cried softly with her head down and did not answer.

Adrian answered in a nervous voice, "Found her in the pasture by Perret's Path all beat up, and I helped her home. That's all I know."

"Ya sho dat all ya know?" he asked. He pushed Adrian out of the way and situated himself between them. She shrieked when he squeezed her arm as he embraced her to help her up the back steps.

"Baby, I'm sorry. What happen?" he asked. Not wanting to sound too harsh, he tried to calm himself.

Her soft cry became huge sobs.

"C'mon, lemme help ya in the house." He looked at Adrian, "If ya wanna help, go git ma sist-in-law, Rae. She the next house, a lil bit up the road."

"Yeah, I know where Miss Rae stay. I'll go get her."

Luke helped her through the small kitchen into their little bedroom. The furniture in the room consisted of a bed on the far wall, a chifforobe with a mirror on the opposite wall, and a picture of her mother dressed in a white frilly dress on an adjacent wall.

He seated her on their bed and carefully removed her outer shirt. She winced and cried out.

"I'm tryna be as gentle as I kin be," he said. "Don't mean ta hurtcha."

She nodded.

Kneeling in front of her, he assessed her battered face. His gaze took in the swollen eyes, bloody nose and mouth. As his eyes came down the rest of her body, he saw her arms and wrists were swollen and bruised, and everywhere were scratches, punctures and swollen red bumps. His breathing increased and his frown deepened as he continued to look down her body. He blinked his eyes as he observed drops of blood near the bottom of her dress and his heart sank as he wondered what else was hurt. Her dress and the parts of her legs that were visible were dirty with small drops of blood on them.

Once his eyes had passed her face, she'd closed hers, tightly. She could feel his eyes boring into her. She pressed her lips tightly together as agony and shame consumed her.

Luke's heart swelled up with empathy as he gently touched her face, which caused her to open her eyes as much as she could. His feelings were a strange combination of love for her, rage at whoever had done this and loathing for himself, because he had not protected her. He was her husband and wasn't it his job to keep her from harm?

"What happen?" he asked.

She put her hands over her face and shook her head.

"What happen? Did he…?" His voice betrayed that he was losing his patience.

"Oh, Luke," she sobbed and nodded. "He beat me and he rape me."

Silence, except for her sobs.

"Who?" His voice was deadly calm.

Feen didn't answer. She began to rock back and forth as she continued to cry.

"Who?" He repeated as his voice raised a little and as the anger burned profoundly in his chest, he could hardly stand it.

They glared at each other and the front door opened, breaking the tension. Adrian was back with Rae, who came to the door of the bedroom, took one look at the scene and went into the kitchen to boil water. Adrian stood in the doorway and Luke stood up and joined him.

"Tank ya, Man. Sorry if I 'cused ya wrong."

"It's okay. I understand. How's she doing?"

"Tryna git the name of the low life …," he stopped in frustration, then continued, "dat done dis ta her."

Rae returned, sat by Feen and gently embraced her. Feen's whole body relaxed against her. "It alright, ma chere. It alright. Ever'tin' gonna be alright."

Luke was surprised by Rae's tone. She was someone who could be depended on in time of trouble, but her life had been hard and her usual demeanor was not one of gentleness, tact or patience. He sensed she understood this was a time to be tender.

Leaving Adrian at the door, Luke bent down in front of Feen again. He took her face into his hands and said gently, "Ever'tin' gonna be alright. Ya home. Ya safe now. Butcha gotta tell me who done dis ta ya?" He paused and his hand left her face and gently rubbed her arm. "Baby, who done dis?"

She avoided his eyes and did not answer.

"Is he White? Is dat why ya 'fraid ta tell me? Ya tink I'm gonna go afta him and git maself kilt. Is dat why ya not ans'rin'?"

She shook her head violently. "No," she said. "He not White. He Colored."

Luke's eyebrows shot up. "Den tell me. C'mon, Feen," still talking soothingly. "Tell me."

Silence.

She shook her head in disbelief. "It Wickliffe."

His head jerked back and he frowned. "Cliffie? Dat don't make no sense. Ya sho 'bout dat?"

Luke's world spun around him. Wickliffe was his cousin. They'd played together. In fact, they were more like brothers than cousins, because Luke had lived with Wickliffe's family after his own mother had passed.

He'd known of the romantic feelings between them, but that had been long ago. Could she have led him on? He quickly dismissed that from his mind. He saw her looking at him through her one eye and suspected she'd guessed what he'd been thinking. They knew each other that well. Over the years, Luke had still been a little jealous of Wickliffe, because of their past relationship and because Wickliffe was more educated.

"I promise ya, Luke, I ain't done nothin' fur him ta tink I wanna do dat."

"I know ya didn't. I know better than dat."

15

Rae went into the kitchen and returned with a towel and water in a wash pan. "I need ta tend ta her so's she don't git no 'fection. Y'all gone outside."

"Alright. Call me if ya need me," said Luke.

His hunting shotgun was stored under the bed and now he wondered how he could get it without Feen and Rae seeing him do it. He left the room and closed the door behind him.

He tapped Adrian on the arm and said, "C'mon wit' me outside fur a minute."

Once, they were on the porch, he put his hand out to him. "Tank ya, Man. Ya name Adrian, right? Well, I'm mighty grateful, Adrian. Look, sometin' else I be mighty grateful 'bout. Dis need ta stay 'tween us. Ya know what I mean. Jus' 'tween us."

"No problem. I don't see any reason to say nothing to nobody."

"Not even ta ya mom and dem."

"Nobody. I won't tell nobody."

Luke nodded his head. "Good." He wasn't sure if he could trust him. He measured him for a second. Adrian was a tall, skinny, light skinned, teenager with curly hair and hazel eyes. His family was hard working Christian people.

Luke took a deep breath and exhaled. He didn't have a choice. He had to trust that Adrian would be discreet. There was no way he could control what Adrian said once he left his sight.

Hearing Rae in the kitchen, he decided this might be a good time to get the shotgun out of the bedroom. He turned to go into the house.

"Where are you going?" asked Adrian.

"I gotta check on ma wife," he said.

"Okay, I'll wait 'til you come back."

Luke paused for a second. He started to tell him he could go on home, but he thought better of it. He didn't want to upset him. He nodded and went inside.

Rae looked up at him when he came in.

"How she doin'?"

"She quiet down some. But Luke, he beat her up real bad. I jus' wouldn'ta thought dat a him."

"Me neither," he said.

"I bandage up her arm real tight cuz it sprain and I clean her up real good, pad her wounds with spider web, give her some aspirin and rub her arm wit liniment fur the pain, and so's the ant bites and briar scratches don't git 'fected. Some a dem briar scratches pretty deep. Gonna wait 'til tomorra ta see if she take a fever. If she take a fever, we might hafta take her ta a doctor."

"I sho hope we don't hafta do dat. I know she don't wanna answer lotta question," said Luke with a scowl in his forehead.

"Well, I hope not either. I fix her tea so's she kin sleep. She 'sleep now."

"I need ta git in the room ta git sometin'. Ya tink she wake up."

"She might. But I don't tink she git up or wanna talk. So jus' be quiet, and git whatcha want."

He tiptoed into the room. Her breathing was low, so he believed she was awake, but she did not stir. He kneeled by the bed and reached under it, took the shotgun and shells from underneath and left the room.

Rae's eyes got big when she saw what he had and followed him outside. "Whatcha gonna do wit' dat gun? Please, don't do nothin' crazy, Luke. Ya cain't go ta the pen now. Ya got a wife and chile ta take care of. Please, Luke." Her voice showed her desperation.

Luke did not answer her. He was looking at Adrian, who was eyeing the gun in his hand.

"What you gonna do with that gun? Your sister-in-law is right. I know you mad, but this ain't the way, Man."

"I'm gonna go down ta his house. I cain't jus' do nothin'. I gotta look him in the eye and ax him why. Why he do dis ta ma wife? Why? I hafta git some kinda understandin'. Why her? He know her all his life. Dis not makin' no sense ta me. Ya hear me? Jus' don't make no sense."

"I understand what you're saying. But you too mad right now. Nothing good can come of this."

"I gotta go."

"Well, I'm going with you," said Adrian.

They faced each other as Luke weighed the trust issue again, because this was still a boy, with a boy's judgment. He didn't want to take him thinking he could depend on him, then find out at a crucial time he couldn't, and get both of them hurt in the process.

"You just want to talk with him, right? Well, he's got lotta brothers. You're gonna need somebody to watch your back."

Luke's hands went up in front of him. "Wait a minute, now," he said.

"I'll take the shotgun, but I'm not gonna point it at nobody," Adrian added, quickly. "Nobody. It's just to give you a chance to talk. In case things get outta hand."

"How old ya be?"

"Nineteen."

"Ya jus' a boy."

"I'm a man. I'm old enough to go in the Army and die for my country. Old enough that my paw say it's time for me to be on my own."

Luke's eyes examined Adrian up and down. He didn't think he'd be much help in a fight against his cousins, but he did need someone to keep him calm. He hesitated another second, took a large breath and exhaled.

"Alright. Ya can come wit' me." Then handed him the gun.

"Tank ya, Jesus," said Rae. Both men's head spun around to look at her. They'd forgotten she was standing there. "Please, don't git ya self kilt. 'Member ya got a fam'ly."

"I reckon I know dat, Rae," he said, impatiently. "Dis why I gotta do dis. I cain't let nobody tink they kin do dis ta ma fam'ly and git 'way wit' it. What kinda man dat make me?"

"Maybe so. But, a dead man ain't no good fur nobody. Ya betta hear what I say ta ya," she said, emphatically, wanting to have the last word.

~ CHAPTER 4 ~

As they started down the gravel road, they were both very quiet, deep in their own thoughts. His aunt also lived near the river, but in another section, so they walked away from the river to a road that led back to the River Road.

"Ya know," said Luke, "Feen was Wickliffe's gullfriend first, when we's young."

"Oh yeah?" said Adrian.

"Yeah, she was. She was a pretty lil gull. Prett'est gull in Marksville. But I never pay no 'tention ta her, cuz a dat. Cuz she ma cousin gull."

"Hmm. I see," said Adrian. "What happen? What changed your mind?"

"Well, Cliffie call hisself a lady man. Ya know, even young as he was. Cuz lotta girls like him and he start talkin' ta 'nother gull and Feen find out 'bout it. And she git mad wit' him."

"So, what happen?"

"Well, I passin' by her momma house and she haulin' two bucket a water, one in each hand, from a pond near they house. And I run and help her." He paused. "Man, I tell ya, when she turn dem big pretty brown eyes on me, I lost ma breath."

"Really?" asked Adrian.

"Yeah, really. She didn't want me ta help her cuz she tink Wickliffe sen' me. I tol' her he ain't sen' me. Dat I jus' wanna help her. Den she lemme bring the water ta they house. When I left, she smile at me and tank me agin. Man, I tell ya, I was hook."

Adrian smiled imagining how Luke must have felt. He understood the magic of those eyes himself. Even though she was what they considered to be old, most of Adrian's young friends thought Feen was attractive and would look at each other whenever she passed at church.

"Was she hooked, too?" Adrian asked.

"I dunno if she hook right den or not."

"What did Mr. Wickliffe think about you being with his girl?"

"I ax him 'bout her. I wanted ta know if he still like her or not. He say yeah, he still like her, but she mad at him, and he not gonna change. He say he too young ta jus' talk ta one gull. She ack like she not gonna git happy, so he not worry 'bout her no mo. If I want her, I kin have her. So, I kept comin' by her house and help her haul water and help her wit' other stuff too, like feedin' the chicken, workin' in the garden, jus' plain help her. She got lil sisters, but they at school and Teresa married by den. Her and her momma like how I help dem. I don't have a lot ta offer a gull like dat. But when I ax her ta be ma gull, she say yeah."

"So how did Mr. Wickliffe take it when he found out?"

"At first, he ack like he don't care. I don't tink he b'lieve she stay wit' me. I tink he b'lieve he kin git her back anytime he want." Luke shook his head. "But he couldn't. Later on, he try, but once she wit' me, she stay wit' me. But I kin tell when she 'round, he cain't take his eye off her. But she don't look at him no mo."

"And so it was over between them?"

"Yeah sir, it was. Ya know sometin', Adrian. I still feel the same way 'bout her now. There are times when I look at her and she take ma breath away."

"Wow," said Adrian. "Really?"

"Yeah, really."

A bird flew overhead and caught their attention. "Birds are beautiful. They God's creatures." He paused. "Miss Charlawt, Feen's momma, raise a lot of chickens, ducks, guineas, turkeys and even a few pigeons. Po' as they was, they didn't eat the pigeons or the guineas. Miz Charlawt like how the pigeons look and how the guineas sound. She said guineas made a lot of joyful noise in the yard and pigeons added beauty. Doves are jus' like pigeons, jus' smaller. Did ya know dat?"

"No, I didn't know that," said Adrian.

"Well, they is. Pastor preach 'bout doves one Sunday in church. He say Noah turn loose a dove afta the flood ta find land and it came back wit' a olive branch. A sign a life afta the Flood and land was near."

"Um hmm," said Adrian

"And he say a lot of other stuff too, but the part I 'member best is 'bout dove's eyes. Dove's eyes kin jus' focus on one ting. They gotta turn they whole head ta look somewhere else. Most kind a doves mate fur life. They cain't and don't wanna look at 'nother dove as a mate."

"Very interesting."

"Yeah, one wife fur life. Don't want no other. Dat's what they mean wit' doves eyes. Only fur one dove or one person and dat the way I feel 'bout Feen. I know he still like her, but I know he like to run 'round, too. And she deserve betta than dat. She should have someone wit' dove's eyes fur her."

"Dove's eyes, huh? I like that."

"Yeah, we say we got dove's eyes fur each other. In the end, he 'cepted it. Him and me never have a bad word 'bout it."

They walked on a little further in silence.

"Ya know," Luke said. "He my cousin. Raised like brothers. Hard fur me ta reckon he woulda done dis ta me or ta her fur dat matta."

Luke turned his head toward Adrian waiting for a reply. Adrian did not make a comment.

"Raping somebody is not 'bout the sex, it 'bout hurtin' and controllin' somebody. Why he wanna do dat ta Feen?"

Still no answer.

"Spent ever holiday together, either at ma grandma, our house or they house. Learnt how ta hunt and fish together."

"Your aunt's a nice lady. She was my teacher in school," Adrian said.

"Yeah, she was most people teacher if ya come from here," said Luke. "And yeah, she a nice lady."

They turned on the River Road and his heart started thumping in his chest as he neared the familiar home.

"Sure am glad we finally got here," said Adrian. "After walking all this way on gravel roads, my feet hurt."

"I'm sho I'll feel it tomorra, but today never even notice it," said Luke.

The large white house sat back from the road. On the other side of the road was the levee and on the other side of the levee was Red River. It had once been owned by white folks and had served as a trading post and boat landing during the 1800's before there was a levee there. As a child, he'd always been in awe of the house with its massive supports that set the house at least ten feet off the ground to protect it from flooding. The flight of twelve steps that led to the front porch was ten feet wide and was known to tire some people before they reached the top.

Colored people could not afford a house like this, because most of them were farmers or farm hands, which means their work was seasonal. During the off season, money got tight and that's when almost everyone in the family, except the very young, hunted game, fished and worked odd jobs to make ends meet. Being able to save enough money to buy a house and pay it off in one lump sum was impossible and paying a monthly or quarterly note would have been just as difficult.

As a teacher, his aunt received regular pay six months a year when the school was open. She, also, did seamstress work on the side. Julia's husband, his sons and a few other Blacks had been fortunate enough to have year-round jobs working at the sawmill. So, when the place had become available, they were able to buy it and pay it off in quarterly installments.

Three pecan trees graced the front yard and gardenia bushes surrounded the part of the porch that didn't have the enormous steps. A white gate and picket fence encircled the front yard and along the fence lines, were rose bushes.

Because Luke's mother had passed away when he was thirteen, this had become his place of refuge for many years. Looking at the structure now, his feelings were mixed. It felt like coming home with a sense of betrayal all tied together. The walk to the house and the conversation along the way had calmed him some, but he was still very angry with Wickliffe.

Adrian waited by the side of the road as Luke went in to face his aunt and cousins.

As he ascended the steps to the front porch, he was still trying to figure out how he'd tell his aunt what had happened and whether he could keep himself calm to face Wickliffe.

~ CHAPTER 5 ~

L ord, have mercy. Didn't expect to see you today. But, it's so good to see you, Luke," his aunt said as she opened the door for him. "C'mon in here, Boy, and give me a hug."

Looking down upon her plump, smiling face, he smiled back at her. He couldn't help it. He loved this woman. She'd been his mother for years and had always treated him the same as she'd treated her own children. He bent down and hugged her, smelled her jasmine scented dusting powder she'd consistently worn that reminded him of his mother. He relished the feel of her embrace. As she withdrew from his arms, he saw her eyes become puzzled when she saw Adrian standing by the road.

"Good ta see ya, too, Taunt Julia," he said nervously, not meeting her eyes. "I need ta talk ta Cliffie."

The house smelled of stew and onions cooking. He looked around the spacious living room, with a large blue sofa and chair facing an over-sized fireplace on the back wall, high ceilings and beige wallpaper with small blue flowers. White crochet doilies lay on the back of the sofa, chairs and tables. The floors were dark, shiny mahogany with a beige throw rug beneath the blue sofa. This room had impressed and intimidated him as a child, because it was far different than the four room house he'd lived in with his mother.

"Uh huh," she said, still fixated on Adrian by the side of the road. "How's Feen and Laura? Y'all haven't been by for a while. Why don't y'all come for dinner, Sunday?"

Luke wondered how she would handle knowing her son had raped his wife. He continued to avoid her eyes, still looking toward the back of the house.

"They fine, Auntie, but I came by ta talk ta Wickliffe."

"You sure you're alright?" asked his aunt. "You're all red in the face. You know that's a dead giveaway with you, yellow people," she added in a joking manner. Julia was brown skinned, in contrast to Luke's mother, who had been light complexioned. She and Luke's mom had been sisters and talking about the reactions of light-complexioned people's skin color in certain situations always seemed to amuse her. It was always done in a kind manner, so no one ever took offense. He didn't this time, either. He shrugged his shoulder and did not comment.

"Cliffie," she said in a loud voice. "Luke's here to talk to you." She smiled at Luke.

Luke heard footsteps as Wickliffe came through the dining room into the living room. The calmness he'd gotten from his aunt's smile and embrace now disappeared. His body tensed up and his fists clenched.

His legs began to shake, and he fought to restrain himself. He noticed a scowl come across his aunt's face in response to his changing demeanor. Her eyebrows drew up into a deeper frown as they both saw fresh, significant, deep scratches visible on Wickliffe's face and arms. Some of them were deep enough to have dried blood on them. Luke's breath became deeper as the fury continued to rise within him.

Her hand went to her chest. "What happened, son?" Julia said in a distressed voice.

Before Wickliffe could answer, Luke blurted out, "What kinda animal are ya?" Luke walked closer, and the two men faced each other, both with their jaws set and flexing. Hearing the commotion, Wickliffe's younger brother, Julian rushed into the room and stepped between them. Julian faced Luke with his arms outstretched to prevent Wickliffe from stepping around him.

"Hey," Julian said, loudly. "Good to see you, Luke. But what's going on? Why are you coming in here threatening Cliffie?"

"Tell dem why. Why don't cha? Ya big man, tell dem why," said Luke, as he looked around Julian at Wickliffe. Luke's eyes moved from Wickliffe's to Julian's. "Ya wanna know why? I tell you why. I came ta ax ya brother why he rape ma wife today?"

Julia squealed and her hand flew to her mouth and said, "What? What you say? Feen? No, that's a mistake. He wouldn't do that. Would you, son? Tell him you wouldn't do that." She turned from Luke to her son as her eyes surveyed the scratches.

He didn't answer, and they glared at each other for several seconds. Her eyes took in his whole body. The deep scratches, the dirty grass-stained pants and drops of blood on his shirt.

She turned back to Luke, "When you say this happened?"

"Today. In the pasture 'long Perret's Path. Not fur from ma house."

Silence.

"I'm sorry to hear that. What makes you think it's Cliffie?"

"Feen tol' me. She wouldn't lie 'bout dat."

She gave him an unwavering stare. "How you know it was rape? They used to like each other when they were little. You remember that? They liked each other a lot. I can't tell you how many times that little girl came up here to play with Cliffie."

"Taunt Julia, ya don't git swollen eyes and bloody lips and bruises all over when ya wanna lay-up with somebody. She all beat up." His voice rose as he spoke.

She turned to her son, whose shoulders were slumped over with his eyes directed at the floor. "Momma, I didn't do it."

"Where did you get those scratches?" his mother asked in a low soft voice. "You know that I'm not a fool."

Wickliffe's eyes didn't meet hers.

"You're my son and I love you, but, right is right. You don't have no business raping no woman." Her voice was stern. Her hurt was evident in her voice.

His head fell lower. Silence. Finally, he said, "I'm sorry, Luke. I don't know what got over me. I just don't understand it myself. You know I ain't never done nothing like that before."

Luke pushed toward him, but his brother stood steadfast between them.

"I know you're mad," Julian said. "Me, too. I don't understand it either. I like Feen. Even, if I didn't, I don't think no woman deserves that." He took a deep breath. "How about we go into the backyard and you can have a piece of him? Would that help you feel better?"

"Yeah. Maybe. I know I gotta do sometin', Man, ta git dis bad feelin' outta me. Maybe, gittin' a piece a him will help. I dunno. I wanna make him feel like he five foot nothin' gittin' beat up on by a man over six feet tall. I want him ta feel the pain ma wife in right now."

Julia's face turned toward the front door and her finger shot up in the air as realization sat in. "Wait a minute, now," she said. "I taught that boy outside. Adrian. Why is he out there with a gun?" she asked, nodding toward the front yard.

"He jus' wanna make sure I don't get double team, s'all. I tol' him Wickliffe ma cousin. Dat we brung up like brothers. Dat y'all not gonna do nothin' like dat. But he wanna come, so I let him. We not here ta kill nobody, jus' ta git some understandin'."

Julia continued to stare at Luke.

"He not gonna use dat gun, I promise," Luke said.

"Are you sure? Whatever my boy done, I want him to take the punishment. Whether it's jail or what y'all talking about doing now. But I don't want him to be shot."

"No shootin', Taunt Julia. On either side. Y'all got guns, too."

"Nobody here is gonna interfere in a fair fight. But nobody here is gonna let you shoot my boy while he's unarmed. If he," she said, nodding toward the front yard, "or you do that, you're not walking away. You understand what I'm saying?"

"I understand. I cain't promise ya dat dis the end of it, though. Might hafta git the law if she don't heal right. Cuz if dat happen, he gonna pay wit' the law." He looked at Wickliffe, whose head was still hung down. "But, I promise ya, I'm not afta killin' nobody. Neither is dat young boy outside. Alright?"

Julia looked at Julian, who shrugged his shoulders, and at Wickliffe. "Well, Cliffie, what you say?"

He nodded his head without looking up.

Luke followed them through open French doors to the dining room. They passed a long table the boys had made from a large oak tree by the river. They'd stained it and Julia kept it shining. Then through a small kitchen that held a glossy black, iron, wood stove, and on to the back porch.

The back porch had four rocking chairs on it. Two of the brothers sat on two of them. The large backyard was fenced in. The chickens, turkeys and guineas were enclosed together with their hen houses and coops on the far-right grassy end of the yard. Another fenced-in section of the yard, which was behind the chicken yard, had a large barn with horse and cow stalls. The back end of the cow yard was opened to green pasture with cows and horses grazing. That took up the right side of the property.

After leaving the backyard, on the left side of the property, were subdivided lots. There were three other smaller houses with their own separate yards.

Julia walked into the backyard, waved her arm and beckoned the three brothers who lived in those houses to come to her yard.

"What's going on?" they asked once they'd arrived.

Julia walked with them to the far end of her yard where the chicken coops were, where Luke couldn't hear. For the first time since he'd known her, he felt like an outsider. She'd never made him feel that way before. He watched as they all focused on what she was saying and Luke saw heads nodding up and down, in agreement.

He walked to the side of the house where he could see Adrian and signaled him to come around to the back. His aunt and cousins went to the center of the dusty yard.

Both men had seen movies of boxers and took stances with their bodies angled sideways and their arms bent and fists up. They'd done this plenty of times growing up, but always stopped when they had gotten tired or before anyone got hurt. This was not play fight. Everyone was aware of the seriousness of it.

With eyes intent, they circled each other. Luke threw a hard punch and Wickliffe ducked. Luke threw another punch to Wickliffe's head and the sound radiated throughout the backyard as he connected and Wickliffe's head flew back.

His brothers all gasp as though they'd felt his pain. The fighters continued to circle each other and Luke connected another punch, this time to the stomach.

The observers, again, moaned in response. This went on for several minutes, with Luke connecting to the head or body of Wickliffe and Wickliffe not responding. This didn't please Luke at all, because he couldn't fight someone who wasn't going to fight back. That would be as bad as what Wickliffe had done to a woman half his size. He had to make him fight back and he thought he knew how to do that.

"She don't wantcha, so ya rape her."

No response as they continued to circle each other.

"Ya couldn't stand the fact with all ya learnin' and ya big job at the mill, she still don't wantcha. She want me."

No response.

"I's always a better man than ya ever be." Wickliffe took a deep breath and the muscles in his cheek began to flex. "A woman know a real man and ya don't have the sense of a mule. Ya tink she gonna wantcha now? Afta ya hurt her?"

Luke stepped in and did a one-two punch to his stomach and he went down to the ground, lay for a moment and closed his eyes.

When he opened them, he said, "Okay. Okay. You want a piece of me, right? Well, to get a piece of me, you gonna have to give me some of you."

Everyone waited wide-eyed. He stumbled on his way on. Without pausing, he ran into Luke, head first, knocking him to the ground. After they'd both gotten up, Wickliffe threw four punches to Luke's stomach in quick succession. Grunting in pain, Luke stumbled backward.

When they'd fought as kids, Luke usually won. He was the better athlete, while Wickliffe was the better scholar. The determination in Wickliffe's eyes shone through and Luke knew that Wickliffe had decided to make this a competitive fight. He stood back up erect, and they circled each other, and dust flew in the yard as they did so.

Luke swung so hard that when the next punch connected, pain radiated from his fist and traveled up his arm. He heard his own groan and saw the pain in Wickliffe's eyes. Despite his own pain, he took advantage of Wickliffe's stupor and moved in to hit him three more times.

Wickliffe fell flat on his back. Determination was still on his face, however. He rolled over on his stomach and used his hands to help himself stand up. He put his head down and rammed Luke's body with his head, again.

They both fell. Wickliffe jabbed Luke in the face three times before Luke pushed him off. They both lay spread eagle on their backs in the dirt, resting for a while before they got up.

Their faces had grown lax from fatigue and the circling of each other stopped. They stood with their feet planted and exchanged blows. Wickliffe hit Luke in the side. Luke hit Wickliffe in his side. They threw alternating punches that continued to sound off as they landed, until one of Luke's blows descended on Wickliffe's nose.

Luke heard a squishing sound as blood spurted out and Wickliffe groaned, "Aw Man, I think you broke my nose."

His eyes involuntarily darted to his mother as the blood drained down his face making tracks through the dirt stuck there.

Julia made a step toward her son, but Wickliffe waved his hand toward her and shook his head. She stopped in her tracks and moved back to her original position. Wickliffe grunted as he threw a punch to Luke's mouth. Luke tasted blood and his head throbbed with pain. Both men were tired, dusty and bloody.

Luke's legs were unsteady and he was not sure how long he could continue, but he had to work this anger out, and it wasn't out yet. With a groan and all his might, he propelled his body forward with a short jump and threw a mighty punch to the side of Wickliffe's head. He screamed in pain and grabbed his ribs as his whole body spun around and he hit the ground.

Luke looked down at him for a good while, took a deep breath, turned and stumbled toward Adrian.

Wickliffe turned on his stomach and crawled to the fence line near the barn, where a sickle and scythe, long-bladed tools used to cut hay, were propped. He grabbed the sickle, raised the upper part of his body and drew the sickle back, over his shoulder, to throw at Luke's back.

Luke, walking in Adrian's direction, saw Adrian's gun go quickly from pointing to the ground to cocked on his shoulder.

The crowd loudly protested. "No. No."

Only a fraction of a second later, he heard the cock of guns. Luke froze. The very thing he'd feared might happen was about to happen. He whirled around to see Wickliffe with the sickle in his hand, no longer aimed at him, but at his side, and his cousins with their guns pointed toward Adrian. His mouth fell open. He didn't know they'd armed themselves. He didn't remember seeing them get guns.

Julia's hand went up in the air. She said to Adrian, "Don't shoot." Walking over to Wickliffe, she took the sickle from his hand. "I'd knock you silly if you weren't already hurt so bad," she said, looking at him with concern. "Everybody can put your guns down now."

The fact that Wickliffe was going to throw a sickle at his back, an act that would surely have killed him, caused his anger to re-surface and he suppressed a desire to run over and hit him again. Adrian seemed to have read his mind because he said, "C'mon now. That's enough. You need to go home to your family."

Julia told her sons, "Y'all take him into the house. I'll be there in a minute."

While they did that, she walked over to Luke and examined his face, his mouth and eyes. She raised his shirt and gently touched his ribs. He grimaced.

"You're hurt a little bit, but, I think you'll be alright. Luke, I'm sorry for what he did. I know you're still angry. I could've told you that beating him would not soothe your anger. Only time and forgiveness will do that if you let it. Forgiveness is key to the process. If you nurse it and let it fester, it will not go away. It will only get worse. No matter what he's done, he's your family. Just like you, you're my family. I've thought of you like a son since your momma died."

"I know dat, Taunt Julia. I feel the same way. I never thought a Cliffie like a cousin. He was ma brother." He shook his head, and tears rolled down his face, leaving tracks through the dirt on his face. "It hurt real bad, Taunt Julia. Real bad."

She walked closer to him and took his face in her hands and wiped it tenderly with a handkerchief. She pulled his face down to hers and kissed him on his forehead ever so gently.

"I know you don't believe this or understand it, but like I said, forgiving him is the answer for that. Not for him or for me, but for you and Feen." She paused as their eyes held. "I'm going to pray for your family. I pray she heals in body and soul." She hesitated and dropped her hands from his face. "Are you going to call the Law?"

"No, I'm not gonna do dat. Not fur his sake, fur Feen sake. She not gonna wanna sit in no courtroom and tell strangers. Kin ya tell the boys ta keep quiet 'bout it?"

A sigh of relief escaped her. "Yes, I can do that. Look, I cooked a big pot of beans this morning before I left for school. Let me fix some for y'all tonight."

"I tink Rae fixin' us supper, but tank ya." He was feeling light-headed and didn't know how much longer he could stand. "We fixin' ta go."

"Thank you, Son. For taking care of this the way you have. It's the God in you and He's going to bless you for it."

"No need ta tank me, cuz I did what I had ta do. What I really wanted ta do was shoot him wit' dis shotgun," he said, pointing at the gun in Adrian's hands. "But den, what woulda happen ta ma fam'ly wit' me dead or in prison."

He was very unsteady on his feet and had a long walkhome. He wasn't sure if he could make it.

~ CHAPTER 6 ~

It was dusk dark when Luke and Adrian started back down the road. "Do you feel better?"

"No, not really. But I had ta do sometin'. I wouldn't a slept tonight if I hadn't done what I done. Still might not sleep. I jus' felt so helpless. Still do."

"You gave a lotta good blows, but you took a lotta good ones, too. You want to lean on me a little bit."

"No, I'm alright. I can make it. Sorry 'bout all dem guns pointed atcha."

Adrian smiled, sheepishly. "Yeah, that was some scary stuff. All I knew was some of them was going down too." He nodded his head as he looked down at the road. "Ooh Man, that certainly was some scary stuff."

"Well, ya tol' me ya were gonna go in the Army. I gave ya some good trainin'." He chuckled. "I know dem boys. They wouldn't a shot cha. Not long as ya didn't shoot Cliffie."

"Hmm," said Adrian. "You thought you knew Wickliffe, too. You didn't think he would have done what he did, either."

"Well, ya got me there."

They walked a far distance before Luke said, "I tink I'm gonna need some help afta all."

Night time caught them on the road. Both men were used to traveling at night. They hunted, fished, walked back and forth to church at night. Without street lights, darkness in the country when the moon's not out is very dark. The kind of dark that it's hard to see your hands in front of your face. They were fortunate. A full moon was out, so they could see well.

They hooked arms in such a fashion that Luke could lean on Adrian as they continued down the road. They talked and listened to the chirping of grasshoppers and crickets.

When they'd reached Luke's house, he started chuckling, "It's kinda funny. Ya had ta help bof us home today."

"Hmm. I guess you're right."

When Rae opened the door for them, she looked at the dirt and blood on Luke's face, hair, clothes, and the way he was hopping along. Her expression turned to shock. "Oh, ma Gawd! Are ya shot?"

"No. I'm not shot. I'm alright."

"Is he dead?" she asked with her eyes wide.

"No, he not dead."

"Well, I hope ya hurt him good, at least. Cuz he sho hurt you kinda bad," she said matter-of-factly. "

"He hurt good, Rae, worse than me. Don't ya worry 'bout dat. I had ta walk home, 'member?" he said irritated. "Gimme dat bottle a liniment and a towel and the wash pan."

She did as he asked, but when she started to wipe his face, Adrian said, "I have it. You go take care of Miss Ford. I'll help Luke clean up."

And he did.

When he'd finished, Luke looked at him and said, "I was wrong. When I say ya a boy, I was wrong. Ya mo man than a lot twice ya age."

Adrian gave him a wide grin. "Thank you, Mr. Ford."

"Call me Luke." He said with his hand out.

Adrian's mouth and eyes opened in astonishment. He did not know what Luke's age was, but to Adrian he was old. For someone like Luke to want him to call him by his first name was indeed validating his own manhood.

Nodding his head, Adrian took his outstretched hand and shook it. "Okay, Luke."

~ CHAPTER 7 ~

When Luke'd entered the room to get his gun, Feen had heard him moving around, but she'd kept her eyes closed. She didn't want to answer any questions. She'd seen the look in his eyes as he surveyed her for signs of violation. and when he realized who the culprit was. Because she knew him so well, she'd sensed he wasn't sure whether she might've, inadvertently, caused the attack. Now he was kneeling by the bed and she heard him remove the shotgun they kept there. She realized she should stop him, but she wasn't sure she wanted to. Wickliffe deserved to pay for what he'd done to her. But if Luke did it, she might have to live without him and she didn't believe she could survive that. Still, she didn't have the strength to stop him. Stopping him would mean she would have to open her unswollen eye, raise her sore aching body out of bed, look in his accusing eyes and try to persuade him to not put his own welfare in jeopardy. By the time she'd concluded she should try to stop him, he was gone.

She'd heard Rae's voice rise in fear when she'd, evidently, noticed the gun. They'd gone outside of the house, so the sounds were muddled. She tried to turn over and found it impossible to put any weight on her left side. She'd found herself crying again, but despite the pain, she'd fallen asleep.

She's dressed in her black skirt and white blouse she wore to church and Wickliffe was dressed in black slacks and a white shirt. Walking along the gravel road to the church, he said a joke and they laughed as though that was the best joke ever. Suddenly, Wickliffe slapped her hard across the mouth and she screamed in pain, bringing her hand up to her face. He slapped her again, this time with the back of his hand. She tried to run. Her feet were moving, but she was still in the same place. No matter how fast she moved her legs, she stayed in the same place. She felt his hands around her neck and she screamed.

She sat up straight in the bed screaming and Rae ran and put her arms around a terrified Feen. "It's okay, ma chere. Jus' a bad dream. That's all it was. Ya home now. Ya safe now."

Letting out a huge sigh of relief, Feen laid her head on her sister's shoulder and cried. She remembered Luke getting the shotgun and now she hoped Luke would shoot him, but not before he'd done something awful to him, like pulling all his fingernails off. Finally, her tears diminished and she lay back down on the bed.

"Tank ya so much, Rae. I dunno how I woulda made it without ya."

"Ya ma sista, Feen. Dat what fam'ly fur. Ya do the same fur me. Is ya pain gittin' better?"

"Uh-hmm. If I don't move."

"Do ya want me ta rub ya with some mo lin'ment and do ya need 'nother aspirin?"

"Aspirin."

"Well, ya need ta eat sometin' first; otherwise, it make ya sick. I bake some biscuits and some of dat sausage ya bought."

"I'm not hungry," she said forcefully.

"Well ya gotta eat," Rae said, just as forcefully. "Else it make ya sick. Afta ya eat, ya kin have a aspirin. Ya hear what I say?"

"Okay, Rae," she said.

After she'd eaten a little bit and taken the medicine, she went back to sleep.

∞

Once Adrian left, Luke walked into where Rae was standing in the kitchen washing dishes.

"How she doin'?" he asked.

"She had a bad dream. She gonna have dem fur awhile. Time and prayer is what it gonna take fur her ta git better." She walked closer to him and whispered, "You gonna hafta leave her be fur awhile."

He said, "Okay."

Rae said, "I mean, don't try ta git on her, ya know. It gonna bring it back too clear. I know it not gonna be easy fur ya, but kin ya do dat fur awhile?"

Luke thought he comprehended what she was saying. It sounded like she didn't want him to make love to his wife. Of course, he was going to let her heal. He wasn't an animal. He wasn't sure how he felt about it right now, anyway. He was having certain kinds of feelings about the whole thing. About Wickliffe touching her. About how his touch had made her feel. About what was going on when it happened. About how she'd let it happen.

"Don't worry. I'm not gonna touch her," he said.

"Dat's not what I say. I didn't say don't touch her. She gonna need understandin' right now. She gonna need ya ta touch her. Touch her, hug her like someone who care 'bout her. Not like a husband who wanna have his way with her. Do ya understan'?"

"Rae, I say I'm not gonna touch her. I understood whatcha meant the first time. Whatcha tink I am? I kin see what she went through. Ya tink I don't have feelin'?"

"No, I don't tink dat. I jus' wantcha ta take care a ma sista, s'all. Take care her in the right way. Ya hear me?"

Luke held his temper. He was not in a mood to be lectured right then. He was disappointed, hurt and tired. His eyes dimmed as he looked at Rae and he could see the soft-spoken Rae who'd comforted her sister was gone. The "Ya hear me" Rae was back.

He took a deep breath and said, "I hear ya, Rae." Looking around the room, he asked, "Where Laura?"

"I sent her ta ma house. I didn't want her ta see Feen right now. She gotta see her 'fore she heal, but Feen gotta git herself together first. She kin see her tomorra when she come back from school."

"Okay, if ya tink so. I cain't tink straight right now. I'm gonna sleep in her room tonight. Dat give Feen room ta turn over without bumpin' inta me."

"Yeah, cuz bof y'all hurt," she said with a tiny giggle he barely heard.

He gave her a stern sideways look to let her know there was nothing amusing about the situation.

"Alright, den. I be back early in the mornin' fore I go ta the field ta pick cotton. Be back agin tomorra evenin' late afta I feed ma fam'ly."

"Much obliged, Rae."

After Rae left, he opened the door to their bedroom and Feen was asleep. He closed it back, gently, and went to Laura's room.

All of today's emotions had taken a toll on him, and he understood he still had a long road ahead of him. He was still worried about Feen and mighty hurt his brother/cousin had betrayed him. One thing he was grateful for was he wasn't going to worry about it tonight.

As he lay on Laura's bed, being sore at work passed through his mind. It was going to be a hard day. Also, he planned to ask Feen to tell him what happened between her and Wickliffe. He didn't finish that thought before he went to sleep.

~ CHAPTER 8 ~

Rae awakened earlier than usual and turned over to see Mose asleep. She could smell the odor of old rotten liquor emanating from his body. He'd changed over the years. The once vibrant man full of hope and dreams was now regularly hung over from being drunk. She steadily looked for the good, dependable man who still existed inside of him. Lately, he'd been drinking a lot, even during weekdays. She suppressed the urge to wallop him.

"Mose, wake up," she shouted.

She threw the covers back and got out of the bed, turned around and said louder, "Git up, I say."

He moaned and turned over.

Rae was five feet eleven inches tall. She'd worked in the fields and done farm work all her life. Her body was firm and her hands hard. When she moved, it was usually with purpose and now she walked toward his side of the bed. It was if he detected her coming in his sleep, because his eyes opened and his feet swung to the side of the bed.

"I'm up," he said.

"Good. Cuz I got plenty ta do today and we need ta git started. Gotta drop some biscuits off at Feen's and den I'll be in the field with y'all."

"What wrong with Feen?" he asked.

"None ya bidness," she answered as she went into the kitchen to boil water for the family to wash up.

"Time ta git up," she called out to the rest of her house.

As the four kids ate their breakfast of biscuits and syrup, she kept watching the bedroom door for Mose to appear. When he did not, she returned to the bedroom to find him and discovered he'd gone back to bed.

Shaking her head, she said under her breath, "Worthless piece a sh…"

Anger overtook her as she walked to the edge of the bed and looked down at him. "Worthless."

With her right hand balled up in a fist, she struck him hard on his jaw and he screamed and jumped out of bed toward her.

"Whatcha do dat fur?" he yelled with his hand raised poised to hit her.

"Cuz ya act like ya don't hear me." She pointed her finger at him and said, "Ya betta be glad ya didn't hit me." She stood with both hands on her hips as their eyes met and held like two opponents ready to go into battle. Mose was wiry and tall, while Rae was the same height, but stout. "Ya heard what I say. It time ta go. I need ya ta go with these chirren ta the field. I done tol' ya dat. Ain't got time ta be tellin' grown people sometin' over and over. Now git ret ta go."

Still staring at each other, Mose slowly let his arm fall. Rae could tell his anger was boiling over, but she didn't care, as long as he did what she said. She was fed up with his drinking and she was on the verge of putting him out, anyway.

"Ya keep pushin' me, Rae. Ya ought not do dat ta a man. Ya dunno when ta quit."

She turned around and walked out of the room. She didn't have time to explain to a man with a family, why he needed to be up and going to work.

~ CHAPTER 9 ~

Coming out of a deep sleep, Feen heard footsteps in her room and screamed.

"It me, Luke."

"Tank ya, Jesus. I'm at home. Tank the Lord. I'm at home," she said, with her hand on her chest, still trying to catch her breath.

He sat on the edge of the bed, put his hand on her shoulder and softly asked, "Ya slept alright last night?"

After a while, she said, "Um hum, I slept alright." She paused, then asked, "Where ya went yestiddy wit' a gun?"

He took a deep breath and said, "I went afta Wickliffe."

Her eyes got big and her pulse rate accelerated. "What happen? Did ya shoot him?"

He shook his head. "No, I didn't shoot him. I went ta his house and we had a fight." He stopped.

She guessed he was waiting for her reaction. She wondered why he was studying her. "Well, whatcha waitin' fur? Tell me what happen?"

Again, he was silent. She took his hand and looked at his knuckles. The skin was missing on each one of them. "Aww," she said as concern for him overtook her. "Lord, ham mercy." Tears came into her eyes as she reached forward and touched his face. She turned her head sideways so she could see his appearance well. There was a lump on his forehead, his cheeks and mouth were swollen and crusted with blood. "Ya hurt anywhere else?"

"Ma ribs a little sore," he said. "But, he look worse den me. I promise ya dat much."

"I'm so sorry," she said as she tried to hold back the tears that were just below the surface. "Dat why I didn't wantcha ta know who t'was. But I had ta tell ya, cuz I didn't want ya ta start nothin' wit' the wrong person."

"Do ya feel good nuf ta tell me what happen?" he asked.

She shook her head forcefully. "No, I cain't go back through dat right now. Please don't ax me ta do dat."

"Alright. I understan'. Prayer and time. Dat what Rae and Taunt Julia say. Butcha gotta tell me sometime. I need ta know why a man who been a brother ta me would do sometin' like dat ta ma wife? Ya hear me?"

"Um-hmm. I hear whatcha say. And I'll tell ya what I know. Jus' not right now. Anyhow, I'm not sure I kin help ya, cuz I dunno why ya cousin would do dat ta me. When ya talk ta him, why he say he did it?"

"He say he dunno why." He paused, nodded his head and patted her on her hand. "I don't wanna bother ya. I know ya hurt and all, so I put me two quilts on the floor in the front room fur a few days."

"Alright. Ya sho ya gonna be able ta rest like dat?"

"Yeah, I be fine. Jus' be fur lil while, til ya git better."

∞

An hour after Luke left for work, Feen heard knocking at the front door. She decided to ignore it, but the knocking moved to the back door. A male voice called her name.

"Miss Ford, open up. It's me, Adrian."

She wondered why Adrian was here, but she couldn't ignore his knock. She owed him so much. Maybe he needed help.

"I'm comin'," she said while she crept to the back door. "Ya alright?" she asked.

"Yeah," he said standing with an armload of clothes. She looked at the clothes and it took her a second to realize he was holding Mrs. Frank's clothes from her clothesline. She'd forgotten all about it. "Let me put this in the house. I'll get your basket and pick up the rest of it."

"Okay," she said. Her heart warmed so at the kindness of this young man.

After he'd gotten all the clothes into the house, he said, "I remembered you said Mrs. Frank was coming this evening to pick her clothes up. I can help you do some because my momma showed me how to iron my shirts and pants. But, I can't do dresses and other things."

She stared at him in surprise. The reason she had loyal customers was because she did an outstanding job on her ironing. She was as good or better than any presser shop in town. Looking at Adrian, she did not think he would do the kind of job her customers had come to expect from her. Right then, she didn't have an alternative, but to let him do whatever it was he could do. She figured with his help, maybe she could get it all done by the time Mrs. Frank showed up.

Her whole body hurt when she moved, especially her arm, and the ant bits hurt and itched terribly, but she'd pushed through the pain.

They worked together. She did the things she could do with one hand, such as sprinkling and starching, etc. He made sure everything she needed was in her reach without her moving. He ironed and folded the clothes with her instructions. They weren't ironed as well as she would have done them, but she was grateful they were done. By the time, they'd finished, Feen was weak and he helped her to her bed.

"Oh, ma Lawd," she said, as she moved toward her bedroom.

After she was seated on the side of her bed, he asked, "What time is she coming? Because I can come back to give it to her, if you don't want to face her."

"'Bout four clock. But, Laura will be here by then."

"It's no trouble for me to come back by."

"It be fine. I'll tell Laura not ta take no mo' clothes from her. She kin tell Miz Frank I'm sick and cain't work fur 'bout a week."

"You think you'll be ready to wash on a rubbing board in a week?"

"Yeah, sir. I do. People do what they gotta do. If they git somebody else ta wash they clothes, they might not come back ta me. I cain't have dat." She paused a moment and surveyed the young man in front of her. "Ya know Miz Azalea done a good job withcha. You a fine boy. Ya know, I dunno no men dat know how ta wash and iron. They tink dat woman work."

Adrian shook his head in agreement. "I know you're right. I used to tell my momma that same thing when she was teaching me how to do it. She said she wanted me to know how to take care of myself. Not to depend on somebody to take care of me."

"Hmm," said Feen, "Ya momma a smart lady. Make plenty sense." She paused and smiled at him. "Wonder why mo people don't tink like dat. Tank ya, cuz ya didn't have ta help me today. Miz Frank want her clothes and I need the money. If ya come by tomorra, I kin pay ya afta she pay me."

He kneeled in front of her and took her hand and looked her squarely in the face. "No, ma'am. I don't want no pay. I was glad to do it. When I was helping you home yesterday and I said that you can lean on me, I meant it."

A warm feeling moved through her chest. She was surprised by the emotions this young man stirred in her. His hazel eyes were solemn as their gazes held. She knew how she must look to him with her face all battered, but his eyes never wavered.

"Well, ya were a Godsen', I tell ya. A Godsen'."

He smiled, nodded his head and rose to leave. "I'll let you get some rest. I'll go out the back door so you can lock it after I leave," he said as he left.

Feen's body radiated with pain from standing and ironing, and she needed to rest. She rubbed herself down with liniment and took an aspirin. Before she got into the bed, she got on her knees and thanked the Lord Almighty, for her life, her family and for good people like "Miz Azalea's boy, that nice Adrian Fonteneau." Thanks to him, Miz Frank's clothes would be ready for her to pick up.

∞

Feen eyes shot open. She looked to the foot of her bed and saw her baby girl, Laura, looking at her with her eyes and mouth opened. "Mom," she said. "Somebody hurt you. Who hurt you?" Her shocked eyes were glued to Feen's face.

Feen put her arms out to her, but she did not move. Laura seemed locked in place. She looked scared of her. "Come here, ma chere. Don't be scared," Feen said, as gentle as she could. "It alright. It me and I'm alright. Just hurt ma own self washin' yestiddy, s'all."

Now Laura came closer, but still did not embrace her. She continued to stare at her as though she was a stranger, then asked, "Are you sure, Mom, you hurt yourself that bad washing clothes? I've watched you wash clothes and I can't see no way you could hurt yourself like this."

"Well, I did, Baby. Mom gonna hafta ax ya ta do somethings fur her. Ya a big girl now."

"Yes, ma'am. Like what?"

"Well, Miz Frank comin' today ta git her washin'. I need ya ta brung it ta her and git ma pay. Ya know how ta count money. She pay me fifty cents fur two tub a clothes, wash and iron. Ya tink ya kin do dat fur me?"

She nodded her head in agreement, her eyes still big. Now, Feen's eye was not only swollen shut, but the skin area around both eyes were black. Her lips and arms were swollen and were black and blue with large watery blisters on her arms and legs from where the ants had bitten her. It was a scary sight for a seven-year-old to take in. Suddenly, her face clouded over and she began to cry.

"Oh, Mom," she said. Even though it was painful, Feen pulled her into her arms and Laura came into her embrace. She laid her head on her mother's shoulder and said between her tears, "I'm so sorry you hurt yourself. Mom, you have to be more careful."

"I'll be mo careful," Feen assured her.

"I'll help you, Mom. Don't worry. You can rest and get better. I can help you."

"Okay, ma baby. I know ya kin."

When Mrs. Frank came to the door, Laura delivered the clothes to her without any snags. Feen watched her and felt so proud.

For the next week, Feen didn't answer the door to accept laundry. If someone came in the afternoon, when Laura was there, she told them to come back next week, because her mother was sick.

By the third week, Feen's face had healed sufficiently enough to allow her to meet and greet her customers. She put face powder on and that helped. If they suspected anything, they didn't show it in their demeanor or ask any questions, except to say they were glad she was better. She was still sore from the beating. It would take months for her to heal completely in body and much longer in mind.

Luke continued to sleep on quilts on the floor in the front room. Feen knew she needed to invite him back into their bedroom, but she didn't feel ready to do that yet.

~ CHAPTER 10 ~

Luke's day had been long and dirty. He'd helped a white farmer fix fences for his cows. It looked like it would take a week to finish the job. He'd been doing odd jobs for different people, because he'd finished picking cotton from his own field with the help of Mose and his family, and sometimes Feen, if she didn't have any clothes to wash.

After he'd finished working, he'd walked four miles, which gave him a lot of time to think. He thought about Feen. Any man would love to have her on his arm. She usually wore her long black hair pulled back in a bun, except on Sunday, when she'd wear it down on her shoulders. She'd stopped doing that since the attack. Now she'd wash it and brush it back in no kind of style at all. She still had a small waistline even after Laura. Her brown eyes with long, lovely lashes were vacant, like her soul had left her. Her full lips that once was ready to smile on a moment's notice always seemed to be in a turned down position.

He couldn't reach her. She walked around staring into space. If she wasn't in a daze, she was angry. She'd snap at him for any little thing. He tried to be understanding, but he didn't know how much more of this he could take. He missed their closeness.

She still had not talked to him about what had happened that day on Perret's Path. He had to admit it bothered him a lot. He didn't understand why she hadn't confided in him. She didn't seem to realize he needed to know what had happened. She seemed to think it was her personal business and didn't affect anyone but her. But it did. It affected him. It mattered to him.

"Hey, Luke," she said, startling him.

There, by the side of the road was Clarice Lang. She was smiling at him, with her head cocked sideways. Luke knew she'd had a crush on him since she'd been a small child. Because of that, he'd always thought of it as an infatuation she'd grow out of. But here she was, many years later, still at it. She was short, about the height of Feen. She didn't have the head-turning beauty Feen had, but she had an appealing mouth and nice legs.

However, there was something about her personality that was a little unsettling. She seemed to be obsessive with her attraction to him and she only heard what she wanted to hear. He'd tried not to hurt her feelings. He'd told her, repeatedly, he was married and was not interested in a romantic relationship with her.

"Clarice," he answered. "Whatcha doin' out here?"

"Waitin' fur you. I knowed ya gotta come dis way ta git home." She stood with one hand on her hip, still smiling.

"I don't always come dis way ta git home."

"I know dat, Luke," she said. "I wait in case ya come by dis way."

"I see. Well, don't wait on me, Clarice. I done tol' ya, I'm married. Ta ya sista bes' friend."

She waved her hand as if she was batting away a fly. "I don't care 'bout dat. I done tol' ya dat I the one fur you. Feen dunno what she got. I done tol' ya dat, too. Butcha find out soon nuf."

He looked at her with a frown, "Whatcha mean by dat?"

"Jus' what I say." When he didn't answer, she continued. "How Feen feelin' today?"

"She feelin' fine. Whatcha wanna know dat fur?"

She stopped smiling and rotated her head back and forth. "Nothin' special. Jus' wonder, s'all." She smirked.

He shook his head and started walking again. He didn't know what she wanted to say, but he had a bad feeling about it. He heard her still talking to him, but he continued walking on. He wasn't going to spend his time listening to crazy talk. He was tired and hungry.

~ CHAPTER 11 ~

After church one Sunday, two months after the attack, Luke, Feen, and Laura sat around their table, ate Sunday dinner and played a game Laura'd learned at school. The air between Feen and Luke had been warmer than it'd been in a long time. They'd laughed like old times and when Laura got sleepy, she'd gone to bed.

Feen got up from the table and warmed water to wash the dishes. He walked up behind her and placed his hands on her waist. She didn't move. He encircled her waist with his hands and put his head in her hair, and slowly turned her around to face him. Her heart was beating so loud she thought he could hear it. Their eyes met. His head moved toward hers to kiss her, and she wanted him to. She wanted the closeness they'd had before. But when their lips met, the fragrance of his cologne entered her nostrils and her stomach convulsed.

Her mind said, "This is my husband," but her body said, "He smelled like the rapist."

Without being able to control her emotions, her hands went to his chest and pushed him away. She ran to the back door, pushed it open, leaned her head outside and vomited. Closing her eyes, she tried to compose herself before turning around. That's when she saw his face with his mouth and eyes opened in disbelief.

He turned and walked toward the front room.

"Wait, Luke, wait," she said as she ran after him.

"Fur what?" he said coldly. "You threw up, Feen. Do ya know how dat make me feel? I kiss my wife and she puke."

She ran in front of him.

"I'm sorry. I didn't mean…"

"Ya didn't mean what?"

"I couldn't help it. I cain't 'splain. I tink it the cologne I gave ya. It smell like him. I'm sorry."

Her voice was desperate. She needed him to understand. Now the tears were close. Anytime her mind went back to that day, the tears were near.

"Ma cologne?"

"Yeah. Dat's what he had on."

"Ya don't talk ta me, Feen. How am I s'pose ta know if ya don't tell me? I kin give it ta Rae fur Mose. Butcha don't tell me nothin'."

"I know. Ya right. I didn't say it ya fault."

"I didn't know 'bout the cologne. Ya know, we never talk 'bout what happen. I ax ya, but ya don't tell me. Dat's not fair ta me."

Feen didn't answer. She closed her eyes and bowed her head.

"I been waitin' fur ya ta decide when ya wanna tell me 'bout it. Is now the right time?"

She saw she needed to give him an explanation, but she had that memory encased and tucked away and she didn't want to break it open. If she broke it free, she didn't know if she would survive the flood of emotions that would be unleashed. Feelings that were still so fresh and piercing. "No, not today, Luke. Maybe soon. But not today."

He stared at her for a second, then shook his head. "I dunno how much mo a dis I can take," he said looking away from her.

She touched his arm, "It only been two months. I know I'm gittin' better. It gonna be soon. We kin talk soon."

"Whatcha mean, gittin' better?" he asked.

She gazed directly at him, and said, "Luke, I love ya. I dunno what I do without ya."

He took a deep breath and nodded.

That night he moved back into their bedroom. As they lay in bed, he put his hand on her stomach and felt the warmness of her skin through her cotton nightgown.

She didn't smell the cologne anymore because he'd washed it off, but his hand reaching for her sent her spiraling back to that day. Without moving his hand, she closed her eyes and turned her back to him. With her eyes still shut, she felt the bed move as he turned his back to her. She asked the Lord, silently, to please heal her heart so she could love her husband as he deserved.

Luke was sixteen and so was she. They were dressed in work clothes for picking cotton. He had coveralls on and she had on a long dress and a long sleeve man's shirt. They both wore straw hats.

While sitting on the banks of Red River fishing, he leaned over and kissed her. Her body grew warm with pleasure. When they separated, they both laughed and continued to fish. He leaned in again, this time the odor of his cologne floated up to her nose, and she felt a sharp pain in her sinuses. His clothes changed and so did hers. Now she was wearing the blue dress and long sleeve shirt she'd worn on the day of the rape. Luke's sweet face turned into Wickliffe's. He slapped her hard and she threw her fishing pole into the river. Then she was running. They were on Perret's Path when he caught her. She screamed and screamed and screamed.

She awakened screaming.

Luke took her in his arms. "It okay. Jus' a dream, s'all it is. Jus' a bad dream." he said, repeatedly, until she calmed down. "Hadn't had one of dem bad dreams in a while. Whatcha tink made ya have one tonight?"

She said, "I tink the cologne."

"The cologne?" he asked. "But I took it off."

"I know dat, but when I smelt it when ya had it on, it brought it all back, jus' like it was yestiddy."

"Jus' like it was yestiddy? Ya say tonight ya thought it would be over soon. Now ya say it back like it was yestiddy." He released her and moved away.

The shame, the feelings of anger, helplessness and stupidity was sitting right there on her chest. In her mind. In her bed.

She wondered if she would ever be alright again, and she could tell by his reaction, Luke felt the same way.

When she awakened the next morning, she wondered how could she get all feelings and images of that day out of her system. She wanted to be cleansed. The clothes she'd worn that day had been washed by Rae, but she'd been unable to force herself to wear them. She decided she'd burn them.

So, she'd taken them and placed them on her fire pit in the side yard where she washed her clothes. Although her wardrobe was limited, she'd lit a match to them. Her mother's big hat that had protected her many days from the sun, her blue shift dress, Luke's large shirt that she'd worn as an over shirt. All of it burned brightly.

As she watched, she prayed this would help put some of the past two and a half months behind them. She had no idea the impacts from that day was just beginning.

~ CHAPTER 12 ~

Feen was having a hard time completing her first batch of clothes that morning. Usually, she washed a tub, hung them out to dry, starched and ironed another tub while the first load dried. Today, she was exhausted after the first tub of the day. She'd promised to have the clothes ready by the end of the day. She always kept her word. That's one of the reasons she had lots of business. But today she had to rest. She went inside and reclined in her bed. She never did this during the day, but she felt she had to today.

She'd missed her period for the last three months, ever since she'd been attacked and she suspected she was pregnant. Her emotions were mixed. She and Luke had wanted another child, but this child. This child. This child was probably not Luke's. She'd made love to Luke a week before the attack, right after her cycle. The attack had happened in her fertile time. Most likely this child was Wickliffe's. She hadn't told Luke.

Somehow, she'd finished her chores, cooked supper and greeted Laura when she'd come from school.

Mrs. Frank arrived and picked up her weekly package. While chatting with her, Feen noticed a foul odor in the air. She hadn't detected it before Mrs. Frank arrived. If she smelled it, she didn't say anything about it. Feen was relieved when she'd left and proceeded to look for the source. Scanning the porch, she didn't see anything. She looked under the front porch steps and there were the insides of a dead animal crawling with maggots.

Her hand flew to her mouth, "Ugh," she said.

Luke arrived from work as this was happening. "What's wrong?" he asked.

She pointed toward the steps.

"What smellin' like dat?" he asked.

"It sometin' dead under the step."

"Sometin' dead under the step?"

"Yeah. A dead animal with maggots all over it."

"Hmm," he said bending down.

"Gone inside the house," he said. "I'll take care of it."

As she did what she was told, she wondered who could have done that. Maybe a stray dog had left it there. But she hadn't seen any stray dogs hanging around her house lately.

When Luke came into the house, she asked him, "Whatcha tink it was?"

"Innards of squirrel," he said. "How ya tink it got there?"

"I dunno," she said, shaking her head. "I dunno."

"Hmm," he said. "I say a dog. Sometin' had ta bring it there. Not there dis mornin'."

"Who ya tink coulda done dat?" she asked. "Why ya tink somebody do sometin' like dat?" She paused and placed her hand under her cheek. "Somebody mad witcha at work?"

He shook his head, "No. Not dat I know of. How 'bout you? Somebody mad atcha?"

She shook her head, "No. Not a soul. Well, I sho hope dat the end of it. I got a bad feelin' 'bout it, though. Ya b'lieve somebody tryin' ta hex us? Ya know they kin use guts fur hoodoo spells."

He shook his head, "Nope. Dunno nobody wanna do dat ta us."

"I'm gonna ax Teresa 'bout it. Ax her what dat mean."

"Okay. Lemme know if she find out sometin'. I ax aroun' see if any stranger been down dis way. Cain't be nobody we know. Nobody mad with neither one a us, 'cept Cliffie. I don't tink he do dat. He don't believe in hoodoo."

Just the sound of his name sent a jolt to Feen's consciousness. The thought tried to break through to the part of her buried deep within and she wasn't going to let anybody bring that hurt forth.

"I dunno what he do, but I hope it not him." She turned her mind from him. Her thoughts went toward her baby. He should be satisfied with the destruction he'd already caused to her life.

They'd gotten into a routine at bedtime. Once they were in bed, they'd talk for a minute or so. He'd tell her something that had happened during the day. Something funny or something strange. The difference is before, they'd laugh, cuddle and, a lot of the times, make love. Now, the story was shorter, and afterward, they'd each turn their backs and go to sleep.

That night he went to sleep, but she stayed awake. She was afraid to go to sleep. Every time she'd talked about Wickliffe in conversation, she'd dream about him that night. She prayed to God to let it not happen that night, because she had a tub of clothes to do the next day and she needed to get some sleep. Finally, she drifted off.

Just as she'd feared, there he was, slapping her, beating her, and she woke up crying which awakened Luke. He calmed her as he usually did and once she quieted down, he released her, turned his back and went back to sleep.

The next day, while rubbing clothes on the rubbing board, she decided to tell Luke about the baby that night. There wasn't any need to wait. She was sure she was having a baby.

Her pregnancy with Laura had been easy compared to some stories she'd heard from friends and relatives. She'd never had morning sickness and she wasn't having any with this baby, either. With Laura, when it came time to give birth, her water had broken and with very few pains, Laura had been born. She prayed it would be the same this time.

∞

"Luke, I'm in da fam'ly way," she said that night after Laura had gone to bed.

His eyes calmly surveyed her as they moved down to her stomach.

He took a deep breath and exhaled, "Fam'ly way, huh?"

"Yeah, gonna have a baby." Silence. "Go 'head. Ax the question. I know ya want ta ax the question."

He sat down in his chair and closed his eyes. The silence was unbearable.

"Luke," she said. Luke didn't answer. "Luke," she repeated. He did not move or open his eyes. "I dunno who it fur." She threw up her arms. "Might be yourn, I dunno. We be together 'bout a week 'fore it happen. 'Member? It could be yourn. I pray it yourn."

Still silence from Luke. Finally, he opened his eyes and looked at her. "How we s'pose ta git pass dis? How we s'pose ta git back like it was? With a chile remindin' us all the time what happen? Huh? I know it not ya fault. I know dat. But Feen, I want ma wife back."

He stood up and walked closer to her. "Do ya understand what I mean? Ya don't go nowhere no mo. Ya wait til Sadday and send me ta the store fur ya. Ya don't go ta prayer meetin' or quiltin' or church. The only time I can touch ya is when ya hollin' from a bad dream. I dunno what ta do fur ya. Now ya tell me, a baby comin' dat might not be mine."

Feen stood staring at him. She opened her mouth and closed it again. She walked over and sat at the table. "I guess I didn't know I was doin' dat. When ya say it like dat, I guess I'm not doin' good. Not doin' good a t'all." She looked at him. "Don't give up on me, Luke. Dis is so hard."

Luke lowered his head and closed his eyes. She'd always felt secure in their relationship, and for the first time, she realized she might lose him, and she didn't know if she could bear it. "I wantcha ta know dat I love ya, Luke. And I need ya. Laura and me and dis baby need ya."

He took a deep breath, but he still didn't answer.

"I really do hafta do sometin' 'bout dis, don't I?"

"Yeah. Yeah, ya do," he said. "I tink ya need ta talk 'bout it." He paused. "If not me, den somebody. Have ya talk 'bout it ta Teresa or Rae?"

She shook her head. "No, nobody."

Oh, how she missed her Momma. Just to sit and talk to her right now would be so soothing. She had Rae, but Rae was not Momma. Besides, Rae had been dealing with her own problems.

She looked at her husband. She knew she'd been unfair to him. She couldn't help it. She had this burning need to lash out. She worked a lot of her anger out doing her laundry. Hauling water and fire wood, rubbing clothes on a rubbing board, wringing out and hanging up clothes used up a lot of aggression, but it still wasn't enough. Standing for hours, starching and ironing loads of clothes did not help either, because the pain in her back tended to heighten her rage, instead of extinguishing it.

She tried not to take anything out on Laura, and for the most part was successful. Laura was very attentive to her which softened Feen's heart. She'd catch Laura staring at her when she washed.

One day when she left to go to school, she said, "Mom, be careful today while you're washing, so you'd don't hurt yourself anymore."

Feen answered, "I sho will, ma chere." She knew she needed to ease her child's mind. But she didn't know how.

61

~ CHAPTER 13 ~

As Feen got bigger, she wondered if her marriage could survive if this baby was not Luke's.

She continued to take in clothes up until the day she had her baby. Her stomach was so big she couldn't see her feet, so she had to bend far over to rub the clothes on a rubbing board. But the work made her bone tired and she went to bed as soon as she ate supper and did the dishes. She'd go to sleep as soon as her head hit the pillow and did not wake up until morning. No dreams. No nightmares.

The timing was just right. She'd just finished ironing a load of clothes when her water broke. Laura went to get her sister, Rae. Besides being a farm worker, Rae was also a midwife who'd delivered many babies in the area.

By the time, Rae got there, she was ready to deliver.

It was a girl, and Feen named her Charlotte, after her mother. She was a big baby. Feen didn't know her exact weight, because they didn't have a scale, but she knew Charlotte was bigger than Laura had been.

Charlotte was medium brown with a reddish tint to her skin. Laura had been very light complexioned and darkened a little after a while. Her skin was still a light brown but not as light as when she was a baby.

Feen knew that Charlotte's color now was indicative of her darkening later.

Her eyes, Feen thought, looked like her own, but something about the forehead caused her to pause. It reminded her of Wickliffe. She had prayed so for it to be Luke's. Would anyone question whose baby she was?

As Feen lay in her bed, she heard Laura tell Luke about the baby. Her little voice was so excited. Feen lay quietly as Luke walked into the room. She studied him for his reactions. His eyes were big as he approached the bed where the baby lay next to her. He looked at Feen first and said, "Ya alright?"

She nodded. "Yeah. I feel good."

"Tank ya, Jesus," he answered.

He continued to look at her very intently, as if he was waiting for her to tell him whose baby it was. When she didn't say anything, he looked over at the baby who was lying beside her in the bed. He bent down for a better look and Charlotte smiled. He jumped and stood back up.

He looked at Feen and said, "Did ya see dat?"

Laura said, excitedly, "Daddy, Daddy, Charlotte smiled at you."

"A baby don't smile a few hours afta it born. Do it?" Luke asked.

"Well, dat one did," Feen said. "She smile at you."

"She didn't know it was me. Her eyes were closed," he said.

"Well, I dunno, but she didn't smile when me and Laura look at her," Feen said.

"Hmm," he said. "Hmm, ain't dat sometin'? Ya check her out? She got ever'tin' she s'pose ta have? Ten fingers and ten toes?"

"Yea. I check her out. She got ever'tin' she s'pose ta have."

"Good," he said. Feen watched him as he stared at Charlotte. She knew what he was doing. The same thing she had done. He was trying to see if he saw anything like himself. Finally, he said, "I'm gonna wash up. Den we'll eat some mustard greens with cornbread Rae fixed fur supper. Okay?"

"Alright," Feen said.

He walked to the door, then turned around. "I'm glad ya okay. Charlawt is a beautiful lil gull."

"Yea, she is," Feen said.

They had supper, and Laura went to bed.

Luke said, "Kin I hol' her?"

"Sho ya kin hol' her." She knew why he had asked. He wanted to see if he'd have to ask to hold her now they both believed this wasn't his baby.

He reached down and picked her up, ever so gently and enfolded her. He sat on the bed and looked down at her in his arms.

He said, "Charlawt, do ya know who I is?" He paused and nodded his head. "I'm ya daddy, dat's who I is."

Charlotte lay there with her eyes closed. She seemed to be very content lying in her daddy's arms. Feen took a deep breath and exhaled. This man had just taken a giant step in accepting this child as his own. What a prize he was. She realized she needed to let the fury go. Luke was a good man and she missed how they used to be. He was too precious to lose.

~ CHAPTER 14 ~

It was three months later. She'd started washing some of her customer's laundry and singing Amazing Grace when someone touched her on the shoulder. She jumped and screamed.

"Oh, I'm sorry. I didn't mean to scare you. How are you doing, Miss Ford?"

There stood a young, smiling, grown-up looking Adrian Fonteneau in his Army uniform.

Her hand flew to her chest. "Lord, have mercy, Adrian. Ya scared me ta death." She started smiling. "How ya doin'?"

Feen couldn't help noticing he was no longer a tall, lanky teenager. He filled the Army uniform quite nicely. He was a very handsome young man. His hair was in the Army crew cut syle and his hazel eyes still shone brightly.

"Doin' fine, Miss Ford."

"Well, it so good ta see ya."

About that time, Mose, Rae's husband, who appeared to be drunk, stumbled into the yard. Startled, Adrian and Feen turned towards him.

"Feen," he said in a loud and urgent voice, "ya better talk ta Rae. She 'most kilt me dis mornin'," he said.

None of this surprised Feen. Rae had been more frustrated than usual with Mose's drinking, and sometimes their fights had become physical. The odor of the alcohol coming from him was strong, and on a closer look at Mose, besides his coveralls being in disarray, she could see he was hurt. Blood flowed from a cut above his left eye and lips. When he spoke, blood was all over his teeth.

"Ma goodness, Mose, what happen?" she said.

"I jus' tol' ya, she 'most kilt me," he said slurring his speech. "Whatcha gonna do, Feen? I need ta call the law?"

"Well, I don't have no phone, Mose. Maybe ya kin walk down ta the store and Mr. Donay kin let ya use his phone."

"I don't wanna walk ta the store. I wanna know whatcha gonna do 'bout Rae. I'm tied a her hittin' me like dis."

"Mose, I'm sorry ya hurt, but dat's 'tween you and Rae. I kin put sometin' on ya lip and eye if ya want me to."

He looked at Adrian, "See Adrian I cain't git no help wit' dis crazy woman."

Adrian didn't answer, but Feen's eyes opened wide. She got into the defensive mode. "Alright now, Mose, dat's ma sista."

He looked from Adrian to her, shook his head and staggered away. They both watched him stumble in the opposite direction of where he lived.

"I hope he git where he wanna go alright."

Adrian nodded his head. "Yeah, I'm sure he will. This ain't the first time he been staggering down the road. He's still drinking too much I see."

"Not all the time. But, yeah, he still drinkin'." She turned her attention back to him and smiled. "Ya on leave?"

"Yes, ma'am, and I wanted to see if you were okay. My momma told me you had a baby."

A frown came to Feen's face. "Ya momma tol' ya dat?" She hesitated for a second, then went on. "How dat come up?" It wasn't

Azalea Fonteneau's way to be in other folk's business, but Feen wondered if maybe something had reached her ears and she was checking with Adrian to see if he knew anything.

"How did that come up? I asked her how you were doing, and she said you had a baby." His eyes penetrated her.

She nodded her head. "If ya wond'rin' who she fur," she said, meeting his eyes. "She not fur Luke." It felt good to get it out. To talk with someone who knew all about it. Someone she didn't have to pretend with.

He nodded his head. "Mm-hmm. How's the baby? Is she alright, otherwise?"

She smiled. "Yeah, she fine. Her name is Charlawt, afta Mom. Do ya wanna see her? She three months old now," she said.

"Uh-huh. Yeah, I'd love to see her."

When they walked into the living room, Laura was sitting on the floor with Charlotte, who was laying on her stomach. She raised her head up when she heard Feen's voice.

"Hi, Adrian," said Laura, smiling.

Feen said, "Mr. Adrian, Laura."

"No, no. Adrian's fine," he said, patted her on the head and gave her a big smile. "Hey, Laura."

"Jus' tryna teach her good manners, ya know."

"Yeah, I know, but Adrian's fine with me."

Feen picked up Charlotte as Adrian anxiously waited. She turned the baby, so he could have a good look at her. When Charlotte's rich dark chocolate face turned toward him, he broke into a big grin, and Charlotte smiled right back at him.

"Wow," he said. "She's gorgeous. And that smile."

"Ya know, she must got a second sense 'bout who stood up fur her, cuz she done the same to Luke when she was jus' a few hours old. Now she never seent ya before and she jus' smilin' atcha."

"She doesn't smile at you?"

"Oh yeah, she smile at all us. Me, Laura and Luke. But, she don't smile at nobody else yet, less they tickle her or sometin'."

"Well, she knows good people when she sees dem," he said, lightly.

"Yea, she do," she said. "Ya stayin' fur supper?"

"Well, I hadn't planned to. This is short notice. You didn't know I was coming."

"Stay. Ya welcome ta what we got. It ain't much. Beans, rice wit' some fat back."

"Sounds good to me. I miss these good country meals."

He held Charlotte and talked with Laura while Feen finished her wash. After a while, Charlotte lay her head against his chest and went to sleep. After placing her in her bed, he went back outside and helped Feen hang her clothes out to dry. She loved the way he just jumped in and helped.

Luke was surprised, but pleased to see Adrian when he got home. They went for a walk while Feen finished cooking.

Following Luke's questioning about Army life and whether he liked it, Adrian asked, "So, Luke, how are things really going?"

"Fine. I already tol' ya, ever'tin' good, didn't I?"

Adrian stopped walking. "Man, you know you can trust me. I was wondering how you were handling Charlotte being Wickliffe's daughter."

Luke's head spun toward Adrian. "How ya know?"

Adrian stared at him.

"How ya know?" he repeated. "Feen tol' ya. She tol' ya, but the two a us never discuss it. Can ya believe dat?" He stopped walking, put his hands in his pockets and looked up into the sky. "She tol' ya, but she never tol' me. I know it, and she know I know it, but not one time did she tell me Charlawt is not ma baby." His gaze came down from the trees to Adrian's face and was silent for a second. "She ma wife's daughter. So, dat make her mine." He took a deep breath and nodded his head. "There's sometin' 'bout takin' care of a baby, holing dem, feedin' em, caring 'bout dem when theys sick dat make ya cherish dem. Man, I love dat lil gull. She ma lil gull, same as Laura."

"I understand whatcha mean. She is a pretty baby. Miss Ford will come around and talk to you about it as soon as she's able. But I'm happy little Charlotte's got a father."

Luke nodded his head. "Yep, Charlawt got a father."

They turned and walked back toward the house in silence for a while.

"Okay, I'm gonna be here for the next thirty days, so you want ta go fishing?"

"Yes, indeed. Man, I plan ta go fishin' dis weekend."

They talked on about hunting and fishing. By the time, they returned to the house, supper was ready. Adrian watched how everyone was at supper. Luke held Charlotte when she cried and was gentle with her. Nothing about his demeanor betrayed he didn't think this was his child. He'd said she was, and after seeing them together, Adrian believed she was.

During his month's visit, Adrian visited them often. He'd come by and help Feen with her laundry, and he'd fish with Luke. If fish were caught, Feen would fry them over a fire outside, and they'd laugh and talk as late as they could and still wake up in time for work the next day. Unless the next day was a Saturday and then they'd chat way into the wee hours of the morning. With Adrian being there, it took the stress out of their conversation. They didn't have to try and solve their problems.

By the end of the month, Feen had asked Adrian to stop calling her Miss Ford and just call her Feen. And so, he did. It made him feel important to them and like he'd made a difference in their lives.

~ CHAPTER 15 ~

Charlotte was four months old. Luke came home early and said he would keep the kids so she could go to the weekly prayer meeting. She wanted to go, but she didn't want to answer any awkward questions about why she hadn't been.

She didn't believe she was mentally healed, because it didn't take much to irritate her. There were times when although she didn't speak in a negative way, in her mind, she'd be saying some very inappropriate things. Some mean thoughts. So, she knew she wasn't healed. Nor had she cleansed her soul with forgiveness. She wanted to be healed, and felt she needed to go to prayer meeting.

All that went to prayer meeting went prepared to prayer and talk. While they're praying, they'd get a lot of their trials and tribulations out. Their prayers are laden with their sufferings, such as dealing with boll weevils eating their crops, sickness ravishing the bodies and minds of their families, not enough food to eat, not enough money to pay bills and heartaches of different kinds, including adultery.

It was a time of baring their souls, and the unwritten code was whatever's said at prayer meetings is supposed to stay at prayer meetings. It didn't always stay there, though, but that didn't seem to matter. Because it was kind of like they didn't have an alternative. They needed relief from their problems and prayer was the primary way to do that. Prayer in communion with others is a powerful thing. The other women would say Amen and give other encouraging words. It was a very supportive environment, because they'd all been in the same or similar situations and if they hadn't, they knew their time was coming. She hadn't been lately, because she just couldn't bear anybody knowing about her violation. It was just too shameful.

Teresa always told her about it, hoping she'd come. Whose house it was going to be at. What day and time. That night, it was at Teresa's home and Feen had decided to go.

When she walked into the small living room, all the ladies were sitting in a circle. The Prayer Circle. There were nine women that night. Their heads turned toward the door and their eyes widened as she walked in. They were surprised to see her. One by one, they exchanged hugs and greetings.

"Sista Feen, it's good ta see ya. Glad ya could make it," said Teresa.

"Well, Luke at home ta babysit, so I decided ta come. Glad ta see y'all, too," she answered.

The ladies were in dresses they usually wore around the house if they're expecting company. Not the coveralls or clothes they worked in the fields with nor the dress clothes they wore to church. The home was small, like Feen's, furnished with straight back chairs and two rocking chairs. Some sat on a cot pushed to the side of one wall, because this front room was also the place where Teresa's son slept. The room was dimly lit with candles to save on electricity. The kitchen area was dark. They'd turn on the lights when the refreshments were served.

"Well, I think everyone here," said Teresa. "*Swing low, sweet chariot,*" she began to sing in a strong alto voice and everyone joined in. "*Comin' fur ta carry me home. Swing low, sweet chariot. Comin' fur ta carry me home.*" They sang all the verses.

Rae got on her knees and began to pray. "Lawd, please take the pain from ma mother-in-law's body. Help her ta grow strong again."

Everyone else either continued to hum the song or said "Amen" while she prayed. "Lawd, help ma husband. He a good man. He jus' cain't seem ta fin' his way, Lawd. Help him ta lose his taste fur whiskey so he can be a better father and provider fur his fam'ly." Her prayer continued about his inability to find and keep work. When she'd finished, another lady got on her knees and prayed.

After the prayer, Teresa's voice arose again to begin the next song and everyone joined in. Drops of rain began to fall upon the tin roof of the house.

"Come by here, my Lord. Come by here. Come by here, my Lord. Come by here. Come by here, my Lord. Come by here. Oh, Lord, Come by here.

Teresa got on her knees. The drizzling rain turned to a rainstorm as she continued to pray. She thanked God for her home, food and clothing. She prayed for the health of her family and for everyone present's family. She prayed for hard times to end and for this Depression to cease. She took it to a problem she'd been having with her husband. Her voice sang her prayer, as was the tradition in the Negro Baptist Church. "Lawd, help me ta understan' Emile. I know he a good man. But, he jus' won' leave dis woman alone. Dis woman, Lawd, is takin' food outta ma chirren mouth. She takin' clothes off they back." She stopped and started again. "Oh Lawd. Oh Lawd. Lawd, in time like these, we cain't make it like dat. Lawd, make him understan' what he doin' ta his fam'ly. Please Lawd, please move the stumblin' block. Please Lawd, please move the stumblin' block. Please Lawd, please move the stumblin' block."

Her face was directed toward heaven with her eyes closed, her hands together and her voice high and filled with emotion as she repeated the phrase again and again. She was now crying the words. Feen and Rae went to her, one on each side. They were fanning and rubbing her back, while some of the other ladies shouted Amen and others were humming the song, Come by Here. The sound of the pelting rain on the tin roof served as background. They were oblivious to the storm outside.

She'd brought them all into her trance as she continued to pray, "Please Lawd, please move the stumblin' block."

A bolt of lightning flashed through the window and thunder clapped so loudly and emphatically the house shook, making them all jump and come out of the spell they were in. It illuminated a large area surrounding the house as if someone had taken a gigantic flashlight and shone it upon this house from the sky.

A scream came from the dark kitchen. Everyone stood up and dashed toward the sound. There were slices of cake on saucers on the kitchen table against the wall and a pot of coffee on the stove. The ladies were to have refreshments after the prayer meeting was over. This was all forgotten as they sought to find out why Louisiana, Teresa's daughter, had screamed. She stood by a window in the small kitchen and continued to yell as she pointed to an area in the backyard.

"Daddy," she screamed as she pointed outside.

"What?" said Teresa, as she looked out through the window into the darkness. "What 'bout Emile?"

"I saw him, Momma. When the lightning flashed, it hit him. He's in the yard."

Louisiana opened the back door and a slicker coat hung on a nail on the back porch. She put it on and hurried down the steps. Her mother followed her outside into the pouring rain. Feen and a few of the ladies also went to see what she was talking about. If Emile were hurt, they'd help him. They came upon him lying on the wet ground in the darkened yard. Teresa fell on her knees beside him and called his name.

"Emile? Emile, it's Teresa. What's wrong? What's wrong, Emile?" She kept asking. Her voice was getting frantic.

"Momma, I saw him fall. He was coming through the pasture and the lightning struck him," she said ending in tears. "I saw it and he fell."

"Lawd, ham mercy," said Teresa. "We gotta git him in the house out the rain. Maybe he just fainted. C'mon y'all, help me move him."

Feen and the women situated themselves around him as the rain continued to come down. Two women grabbed each leg and put their arms behind his hips and lower back and Teresa and Louisiana held his arms, head and upper back. He was still very heavy and it was an arduous trek to the house in the rain. Their clothes were also heavy on them, because they were thoroughly soaked. Once inside, they struggled to get him through the small kitchen and into the bedroom, where they laid him on the floor.

"Let's git all these wet clothes off him," Teresa said. The other women went back into the kitchen and front room to give them privacy. Feen, Rae and one of the ladies named Albertine, stayed to help Teresa minister to her husband. Once they'd removed the wet clothing and put a dry set of underwear on him, Teresa bathed his face with a warm damp towel, elevated his feet and put a warm blanket on him. His eyes were closed and his breathing was very slight.

She called the ladies back into the room. "We need ta pray. He still alive," she said.

They sang three verses of *Come by Here.*

His head fell to the side. She rechecked him. She could see no movement in his chest and felt no air coming from his nose. She felt for a pulse in his arms and neck. Nothing. Nothing anywhere.

Louisiana screamed again. "Daddy. Daddy."

Feen was amazed at how calm and in control Teresa was. She didn't break down or go into hysterics. She hugged her children and asked her sister, Clarice, to go get the undertaker.

"C'mon Sistas," Teresa said. "Let's pray fur ma husband soul."

They prayed for Emile again, this time for him to make it into heaven. The rain eased and the ladies left. The ones who'd been outside were still soaking wet. Feen told Albertine, who had to pass right by her house to stop and tell Luke what'd happened. She'd decided to stay awhile with her friend until the undertaker came.

Clarice said, "Albertine's wet. She needs ta go home and change. I'll tell him on my way ta the undertaker."

"Well, ok. Thank ya, Clarice," Feen said. She changed into one of Teresa's old dresses. Now Teresa seemed to be in a daze. She stood by the bed and stared at Emile. Feen went over and put her hand on her shoulder. Teresa jumped as if she'd just realized Feen was still there. Her eyes regarded Feen for a moment, and said, "You know, ya don't hafta stay. I'll be alright. My kids are here."

"I know I don't hafta. I wanna. Dis a shock. Ya don't 'spect ta lose ya husband dis way." She realized she'd probably said it wrong. It sounded like she'd expected to lose him another way. The thought she couldn't get out of her mind was the prayer Teresa was saying when he'd gotten electrocuted. She'd been praying about her husband's cheating ways and the very moment she was asking God to remove the stumbling block, he'd been struck by lightning. Could it be her prayer was answered? Had God removed the stumbling block? Had Emile been the stumbling block to Teresa's happiness?

Feen didn't believe God worked that way. One thing she did know was Teresa's mother was a hoodoo root doctor and the whole family practiced the vocation. All of them disapproved of how he treated Teresa and could have taken it on themselves to hex him.

Teresa picked up Emile's wet pants and went through the pockets. She found the billfold, but there was no money in it. In his front pockets, he had some loose change. She went through his shirt and jacket pockets, also, and found nothing.

Her eyes met Feen's, "He got paid today, but he ain't got nothin' in his pocket." Her voice was not angry, just matter-of-fact. "Whatcha tink 'bout dat?"

Feen didn't answer.

She took his pocket watch out of his pants pocket and laid it on their dresser. She closed her eyes and aimed her face toward the heavens.

"Lawd, I need ya ta help me. Please, Lawd, help me ta survive."

Still no tears. She thought Teresa's demeanor was strange. She'd tried to save him, but her quiet acceptance of his death and finding no trace of the money he should have had seemed odd to Feen.

Once the undertaker came, he discussed the cost with Teresa. She was still staring in that way Feen could not understand. A plain pine box was the least expensive and he agreed to take Emile's pocket watch as a down payment. The rest in installments.

Teresa gave him Emile's church suit to be buried in. As they wrapped Emile's body to take him away, she walked up to the bed. The two men stopped to let her look at him. She tilted her head to one side and then to the other as she looked at him, as though she was trying to figure something out. She slapped him hard. The sound echoed through the room.

"Ahh," everyone said in shocked tones.

"I jus' wanted ta see if maybe I could wake him up. I had ta try it."

The undertaker nodded his head. He'd probably seen worse. They finished wrapping him and took him away.

With the business behind them, Teresa looked exhausted, so Feen said her goodbyes and left for home.

∞

A little before that, Luke heard footsteps on the porch. Feen was over at the prayer meeting and he figured she should've been home by now. He thought she'd been held up by the rain, so maybe it was her on the porch.

When he opened the door, Clarice stood there, with her arms crossed. She had a way of looking up at him with her head aimed down that both irritated him, but also intrigued him. She seductively batted her eyes.

"Clarice," he said, surprised. "Whatcha doin' here?"

She walked into the house passed him. "There was some trouble at the house and Feen wanted me ta come tell ya 'bout it."

He closed the door and turned to her. "What trouble?" His mind had gone to Wickliffe. He listened as Clarice told him about Emile.

His eyes and mouth opened wide. "Holy Jesus," he said. "Man, I'm so sorry. Emile was a good man. Didn't agree wit' some stuff he done, mind ya, but if ya work wit' him, he was a man another man could depend on." He shook his head in disbelief. "Where Feen?" he asked.

"She wit' Teresa, waitin' fur the undertaker. I told her I come by and tell ya." She circled the room and swished her hips, looking back at him in that underhanded way.

"Well, ya tol' me. Now ya kin leave," he said.

"Why? Feen not gonna be here fur a long time." She paused. "We kin have ourself a good time by den."

His brow knotted up, and he whispered, "My chirren here. Now git outta here."

"Why ya act like dat? You need ta be nice ta me if ya don't want nothin' ta happen ta ya chirren."

"Whatcha mean?" he asked, his voice stern.

"Whatcha tink I mean?" she asked, still smiling.

"Gull, ya better git outta ma house, fore I do somtin' ya not gonna like."

She shook her head. "Ya jus' dunno what ya missin'…"

He cut her off and firmly said, "I already tol' ya, ma chirren in the house. Git otta here."

Her smile left her face. She walked up to him, put her hand to his face, and he slapped it away. They stared at each other.

"Ya jus' don't understan'. One day ya will," she said.

They glowered at each other for another second. She turned, walked to the door and left.

∞

On the way home, Feen thought about the evening. She'd come to the prayer meeting speculating if she would pray to God to give her the ability to forgive her attacker and share her truth with this group of women, making it possible the whole community might know about it. She'd contemplated if she'd feel peace, just by releasing this secret.

She hadn't gotten that chance. Instead, poor Teresa had tried to unburden herself by praying about the trouble she'd been having with her husband.

Sadness for Emile losing his life and empathy for Teresa lay heavy on her chest. She pledged to be there for her. How to decrease her own rage would have to be figured out some other time.

She didn't know she had chosen the perfect way to help herself get over her own fury. That would be by helping others.

~ CHAPTER 16 ~

The scene of Teresa praying with all the ladies singing, kept playing over and over in Feen's mind as she and Luke walked to the church for Emile's funeral. The lightning, the rain, the death and the quietness after the storm. Teresa's quietness. Then the slap.

Feen had starched and ironed her one good Sunday dress and pressed Luke's blue suit, and together, they'd walked to the church realizing how fleeting life could be.

When they turned down the church road, they saw the large white wooden structure with a tall steeple. It was larger than or as large as any colored church in town.

On the right side of the church was a huge platform, about six feet high and about six feet wide, that held a large bell. Attached to the bell was a long rope that reached the ground. This rope was used by different men who came early and rung it to signal the beginning of service. The church was an integral part of the community and was used as a meeting place for various things. The bell alerted folks about meetings, fires, and other emergencies. The deep vibrating sound could be heard for miles around.

As they entered the churchyard, they'd come across friends and relatives they hadn't seen in a while. One thing about funerals in a small town, they could become reunions. Sometimes people traveled long distances. But with the Depression like it was, there weren't many from out-of-town. The road in front of the church was lined with two older model cars, a few horses and buggies, and a lot of old wagons. People attending had come by various means, including walking, like they had.

Before entering the sanctuary, they stopped and talked with some friends on the outside.

A long black shiny Chrysler coupe pulled up in front of the church. Everyone's mouth dropped open. They'd all heard the story of the prayer meeting and what Teresa had been praying about before the lightning struck. Here was the source of Teresa's pain, in living color. Miss Bernice Johnson, the Jezebel. Her brother, who'd driven her there, came around the car and helped her out of it.

She was brown-skinned, middle-aged, and slightly plump with shoulder length hair that looked freshly straightened and curled. She'd worn a fashionable black dress, which came to mid-calf, adorned with a cameo brooch surrounded by rhinestones on her right shoulder, nylon stockings, black shiny, high heeled shoes and a black hat with a black veil attached that came down over her well made-up face. In her black-gloved hand, she carried a bouquet of a dozen red roses.

Feen's temple throbbed. The nerve of that woman to come to Emile's funeral dressed like that when his family hadn't had enough money to bury him or to buy new clothes for the service. His son had worn coveralls, because his Sunday suit was too small. Feen had washed, starched and ironed them for him.

Clarice had been standing by the door and saw Bernice drive up. She turned and rushed inside. Feen imagined she had gone to warn Teresa's mother, Clout, and she was correct.

Clout was not her legal name, but Feen didn't remember what her real name was. Everyone called her Clout. She was a large woman, tall and big. She walked with a cane because she had trouble with her legs. When she spoke, most people paid attention, not only because of her size, but because she was the neighborhood root doctor. People came to her for medicine for everyday illnesses, and she dealt in hexes. Mostly remedies of protection if someone thought they'd been hexed. She knew people were afraid of her and seemed to enjoy that fact. She was not afraid to use her power or be physical if it came down to that.

Even though the pain in her legs slowed her down, she'd made it to the door of the church before Bernice could enter.

No one spoke. Everyone's attention was on them. They were ready for the show.

Bernice walked up to the door, leaving the scent of her jasmine perfume where she passed and nodding her head in greetings to different people outside. Nobody answered. They were not going to get on Clout's wrong side.

"How do, Clout?" she said.

Clout didn't answer. She just glared at her.

After a second or two, she said, "I just came by to pay my respects. Emile was a friend of mine."

Clout took a giant breath. "It take all ma willpower not ta knock ya out wit' ma cane. If I weren't standin' in the house a the Lawd, ya be out cold right now."

Bernice stared her straight in the eyes, "Look Clout, Emile was a friend of mine. I'm just here to pay my respects, that's all," she said, this time more forcefully.

"Bernice, ya betta turn yo hoeing behind 'round and git back in dat car. Ya tink ya gonna walk in here, dress all fine, when my chile cain't buy herself or her chirren nothin' fur the funeral? Ya tink ya gonna parade yaself in here when dat fool give ya his paycheck ever' week? If ya tink dat, den ya dunno me, t'all."

Bernice's mouth flew open. "Who told you that? I ain't been with Emile, not like that. I ain't took no money from him. We were jus' friends."

"Married men don't have friends like you. Now turn ya lying behind 'round and git in ya car and go home. If ya know what good fur ya."

Bernice continued to stand there and they stared at each other for a while. Everyone was in alert mode. They knew Clout's temperament and was waiting for her to attack Bernice at any time.

Clout said with an even and deliberate tone, "Lemme give ya sometin' ta tink 'bout. Emile was at yo house on the night he died, right?" She didn't wait for an answer. "He musta left early, cuz I kin tell ya if he woulda been at ya house when the lightnin' started, dat lightnin' woulda come ta ya house. It wouldn't a been in dat pasture. Dat lightnin' was s'posed ta git both y'all, not jus' him. Now, ya were spared cuz he left early. Dunno why. Guess he musta been hungry. Had ta come home ta eat. So, be glad dat the Lawd spared ya. Ya were lucky dat time. Ya might not be dat lucky the next time."

She paused and moved her cane around and Bernice's eyes followed it as it moved in a circle.

"You and ya flowers, betta git in dat car and gone back ta where ya came from. I'm gonna knock dat hat off ya head wit' dis cane and I'll put them roses in a place ya wouldn't like." She nodded toward Bernice's brother. "Ya brotha cain't help ya. I'll hurt him. Git outta here, I say. Not gonna tell ya agin." Their eyes were locked.

Bernice let out a breath. "Fine," she said, turned around and walked back to her car.

The crowd was quiet. It was if everyone was frozen until she left. When Feen's eyes left Bernice's car driving away, they returned to Clout, who satisfied she'd handled the problem, had turned to go back into the church.

Behind her was Clarice, still facing the churchyard and her eyes were glued to Luke. Feen's face twisted into a scowl when she noticed. She looked up at Luke and saw he was looking down at her and not at Clarice.

"What she lookin' atcha fur?" Feen asked.

"I dunno. Dat girl always lookin' at me," he said. He thought for a second. "Feen, do ya tink all dat is true?"

"All of what is true?"

"All dat stuff Clout was sayin'. Dat she mighta hex Emile. Dat she can control the lightnin'?"

Feen shook her head, "I tol' ya how t'was dat night. I cain't explain it. Now, I don't tink she kin control the lightnin', only Gawd kin do dat, but sometin' strange happen dat night. Hearin' her 'count of it sho make me tink."

Luke nodded his head. "Yeah, sho do make ya tink." It gave him an uneasy feeling when he thought about Clarice.

When Feen turned from Luke, Clarice was still gazing at him. Feen's stare must have penetrated her senses because her eyes slide to down to Feen. Their eyes locked for a second, she turned and walked back into the church. Feen's eyes dimmed further in puzzlement. She questioned what that was all about. She made a mental note to ask Teresa about it later. They walked in the church, seated themselves, the service began, and it was forgotten. She would think of this incident and understand it's meaning many years later.

~ CHAPTER 17 ~

Back from the funeral, Luke changed into his work clothes to go check his fishing nets he'd put in the river the night before. They hadn't had any meat in a week. He'd told Feen he'd be back in a little while and she'd nodded her head.

On his walk to the river, his mind went over the events of the last few days. Emile had been a childhood friend, as well as, a fellow church member and hunting buddy. It was hard to imagine he was gone, and from lightning, something so bizarre. The incident at church with Clout had, also, shook him up a little. She'd implied she'd had powers strong enough to control lightning and Clarice looking at him with that knowing look of hers. He'd never believed in hoodoo, but could it be true?

Emile's rowboat was usually at the landing. He'd been using it since his boat's bottom had given out, while Emile had been digging ditches on a road crew. He'd planned to use it today and tell Teresa about it later, but it wasn't there. So, he decided to go home, disappointed.

With his head down, he started walking, feeling hopeless.

"How do, Luke?" she said.

He recognized the voice before he looked up. It was Clarice. When their eyes met, she smiled.

"Whatcha doin' out here?" he asked.

"Lookin' fur ya."

"Lookin' fur me?"

"Yeah, fur you. I know ya would go somewhere when ya got home from the funeral. Times being hard, I figure ya gonna go ta the river ta check ya nets or go ta the woods and hunt."

That surprised him. It must've shown on his face, because she smiled even broader. "Didn't tink I know ya dat well, huh?"

"Have ya been watchin' me? But you cain't be watchin' me? We don't live dat close together."

"I tol' ya. I got ways a knowin' what go on witcha. Ya need ta pay 'tention ta dat. I done tol' ya."

"Yeah, I know ya done tol' me. I done tol' ya I got a wife."

"Ya didn't wanna marry her. I was there, 'member? I was there wit' Teresa in Ole Lady Charlawt's room when she dyin'. She ax ya ta marry her old maid daughter, Feen. I saw ya face when she done it. Ya didn't wanna do it. I saw it. Ever'body saw it, cuz Reverend Barron start tellin' her Feen would be fine. She ain't gotta trouble herself 'bout it. She could go on and take her rest. 'Member dat?"

"Yeah, I 'member," he was more surprised by the minute. Of all the times, she'd cornered him to try and persuade him she was the one for him, she'd never talked about that day when Feen's mother had died. He hadn't known he looked as scared as he was, and that everyone else in the room had known it. But Miss Charlotte had persisted. She waved the Reverend out the way and reached for Luke again. "Luke, she gonna make ya a good wife. She give up so much ta take care me and her sistas. I wanna know she be took care of when I'm gone. I know ya love her. I see it in ya face when y'all together." She'd gotten out of breath and had to stop talking.

85

The silence in the room had been deafening. Finally, Luke said, "Yes ma'am. I'm gonna marry her, if she have me."

The ole lady's body had relaxed. "Good, I'm a leave y'all the house cuz ya both work for it, and the farmland be split 'tween Feen and Rae. Tanks ta Feen quittin' school and goin' ta work, the others got education and they kin make it on they own." Feen and Luke had been surprised and grateful. She'd died thirty minutes later.

They'd married two weeks later, not only because he'd promised he would, but because Feen's mother had been right. He did love her and she'd been a good wife. He'd never been sorry he'd married her. In fact, whenever he looked at her, he felt blessed. She'd been devoted to him, Laura and now Charlotte.

But Clarice was also right. He hadn't wanted to marry her at the time. If her momma hadn't asked him, he don't think he'd have ever married her. It hadn't been anything against her. He hadn't wanted the hard life he'd known a black man would have living in Louisiana. He'd wanted to go up north to Chicago or New York or even Oklahoma and work in a factory or go into business for himself. He'd heard stories about opportunities for colored people up north. He knew Charlotte would not want that. She loved Louisiana and being near her people.

"Yeah, I 'member," he repeated. "I 'member all dat, but I don't 'member ya being there."

"Well, I was there. Teresa come ta help Feen and ma momma sent me wit' her. Miss Charlawt sent fur ya and when ya walk in the room, I knew ya gonna be ma husband. Ya stood so good looking, straight and tall in ya work clothes, fresh air in a place a sickness and death. Den dat ole lady made ya promise ta marry Feen."

While she was talking, Luke was assessing her, probably for the first time. She had a very slim build, with a color a shade darker than Feen. She was still dressed in her church clothes, a simple white blouse and black skirt. Her long hair she usually wore in braids during the week, had been straightened with a hot comb and hung loosely a little down her back. He realized she was no longer a little girl, but a woman who had made no secret of her desire for him. Besides having big eyes, she had very full lips. When she smiled, she looked pretty, not beautiful, like Feen, but pretty, none the less. He'd always looked upon her as a nuisance. But she'd paid attention to him in ways Feen no longer did.

It'd been over a year since they'd lain together as man and wife. He'd buried his needs to understand her pain. With this young girl in pursuit of him, he wondered how long he could do that.

"Well, I need ta make it on home," he said. "By the way, whatcha mean the other day when ya say if I don't pay 'tention ta ya, ya gonna hurt ma chirren? Whatcha mean by dat?"

She didn't answer for a while. "Didn't mean nothin' by it. Jus' sometin' ta say. Jus' tryna make ya talk ta me, s'all." She shook her head with a solemn expression on her face and said, "I would never hurt ya chirren or anybody else, fur dat matter?"

"Dat's strange ta say tryna git me ta talk ta ya. Dat's a guarantee way ta git me not ta talk ta ya. Don't ever threaten ma fam'ly."

"I know. I shouldn't a say dat."

"Like I say, I guess I better be gittin' on home." He turned and she touched his arm.

"I saw dem together dat day," she said.

"Ya saw who together what day?" he asked.

"I saw Wickliffe and Feen walkin' and they turn down Perrett's Path."

His heart almost leaped out of his chest. His face turned red. "Whatcha say?"

"I say I saw dem walkin' and talkin' and laughin'. Den they took the shortcut toward the back a y'all's house."

"What else did ya see?" he asked.

"Well, I followed ta where I could see dem in the pasture and I saw him kiss her."

"Ya saw him kiss her?" Luke's eyes got big and his head started to hurt.

"Yeah, I saw him kiss her and she kiss him back and then I left cuz I didn't wanna be a peepin' Tom."

He just stood there for a while. He was speechless. There had been a witness all along. This is what he'd wanted. A witness. But this was a witness with secret motives. He wasn't sure he could trust what she'd said. He thought some of it was true, but some of it may not be. Like Feen kissing him back and her leaving so she did not see the beating Feen had sustained.

She walked up close to him and put her hands on his chest. He looked down at her. Her eyes were half closed and her full lips were slightly open. His breath caught in his throat and his body surged with desire. She raised herself on her toes and kissed him lightly on the lips, and he jumped back. It had been a long time since a woman had kissed him. The softness of her lips had awakened something in him he'd had to hide. She walked up to him again, put her hands on his chest, and looked up at him with the same expression on her face. His heart beat wildly, and he could not help himself. His head came down and he kissed her. His arms enfolded her and her body melted into his as he kissed her again, this time, deeply.

He savored the taste of her before his senses returned. He released her and shook his head. "Don't ya know betta than comin' up ta a man in the woods. Start kissin' dem. Dat's how people git hurt. Don't ya know dat?"

She beamed. "Not worried," she said.

"Dis cain't happen no mo, ya understan'."

She continued to smile, but did not answer, and started down the road, looked back and said, "C'mon. Let's go home."

He said, "No, go 'head. We not gonna walk together. Ya gone on 'head."

He watched her swish her hips as she walked away and desire coursed through his body. He guessed all that talk about him not wanting to marry Feen and Feen kissing Wickliffe before he raped her had unnerved him to the point of him succumbing to temptation. He felt certain Feen had been violated. What he'd questioned was whether she had encouraged him in any way, so that he may have misunderstood. Now Clarice had said she had. He needed to talk about it with her, but so far, she'd refused to talk about it with him.

When he got home, Feen was in the backyard making her lye soap that she did four times a year. She had a frown on her face and he assumed she was still upset about Emile.

"I know ya still worried 'bout Teresa. She a strong woman. She be fine. She got her whole fam'ly ta help her."

She closed her eyes and nodded her head. "Yeah, I know she be alright. I found dis in front the step." She handed to Luke a small homemade doll made of burlap with no face and a large stick pin stuck through where the heart should be. Feen's eyes were big and fixed on Luke.

"Whatcha tink it mean and why ya tink it at our back step?" she said.

He knew she was frightened. For a fleeting moment, Clarice crossed his mind, along with guilt because of the kisses. But he dismissed it. He didn't think she was the kind of person who would do something like this.

"I dunno what this mean. Could be someone tryna scare us. Did ya talk ta Teresa 'bout the guts under our step?"

"Yeah, I did. She say it prob'ly drug there by a stray dog. I was glad she didn't tink t'was somebody tryna hex us. But now I dunno."

"Don't go gittin' upset. Ax Teresa agin, what dis might mean?"

"I'm a go by tomorra. I'll ax her 'bout it den."

He decided this wasn't the right time to ask her about what Clarice had told him. He'd have to wait. But for the sake of their marriage, they'd need to talk about it soon.

~ CHAPTER 18 ~

A lot of people were around Teresa's small house when Feen arrived the next day. Louisiana lay covered on the cot in the front room. Feen's heart went out to her knowing she'd be reliving the moment she'd seen her daddy struck by lightning for a long time. Her eyes were closed and she didn't move, but Feen knew she couldn't be sleeping, because there was too much noise going on all around her. She patted her on the back and made her way through the kitchen to Teresa's room.

Teresa sat in a rocking chair gazing straight ahead. She was humming *Come by Here*. Clout, Teresa's mom, was sitting on the bed, eating.

"How do, Taunt Clout?" Feen said. Clout wasn't her aunt, but it was an old tradition that older people be referred to as aunt or uncle, as a sign of respect. It probably was a carryover from slavery, when the White people called the old Colored People or Negroes, Auntie and Uncle rather than Mister or Missus.

"Doing fine, Feen," she said. "Ya gonna be here fur a bit?" Clout asked.

"Yes, ma'am, I plan ta stay all the evenin'."

"Good," she said. "I'ma gone home. Be back tonight. Oblige ya came ta see 'bout Teresa. Reach me ma cane."

Feen retrieved her cane and handed it to her. "Well, Taunt Clout, we done been through a lot together, Me and Teresa."

She nodded. "My legs hurt me sometin' awful. But praise the Lawd, I'm here." Feen watched as Clout slowly made it to the door. She turned and told Teresa, "Gonna be back tonight if the Lawd spare." She continued out the door.

Teresa continued to rock. "Teresa, how ya really doin'?"

"How ya tink?"

"I dunno. Dat's why I'm axing."

"Well, I got cotton in the field ta pick, and I got chirren ta feed, and I got water ta haul, and I got a funeral ta pay fur, and I had a husband runnin' 'round on me who got struck by lightnin' in my backyard, and ma daughter saw it. How ya tink I feel?"

"Let it out. Let it out. I haven't seen ya cry one time since dis happen."

"Oh, I cry. Not fur him, though. Fur ma chirren. They love they daddy. And fur me, cuz even though he was givin' all the work money ta Bernice, jus' leavin' us wit' the pickin' cotton money, I could hope someday he'd a come ta his sense. Now. Well. Now. It over. No redeemin' hisself." She turned her head toward Feen and said, "Ya tink where he at, he sorry fur the way he treated me and his chirren. Huh? You tink he sorry?"

"I dunno, Teresa. I tink at the judgment if they dunno what they done wrong they will sho fin' out. St. Peter got the book wit all he done wrong and then he gotta answer fur it."

Teresa nodded her head, "You right. He gotta 'splain what he done. He gotta 'splain it ta St. Peter."

"I b'lieve so. I do."

"Feen, ma chile saw it happen. Lord, I wish it woulda been me, stead a her. She cain't sleep at night. She wake up hollin'."

"I'm sorry, Teresa. I know what she goin' through."

"Ya do?" asked Teresa. "Ya done woke up cryin'?"

Without thinking, Feen answered, "Yeah. Yeah, I have."

"Since when? Ya never tol' me 'bout dat."

Realizing she'd said too much, she waved her hand like it was nothing.

"It happen a long time ago."

"Feen, I know ya all ya life. I was there when ya momma die, but ya handle ever'tin' pretty good. Least I thought ya did. But lately, ya stop doin' ever'tin". Dis the first prayer meetin' ya been ta in a year or so. Now ya tell me ya know 'bout hollin' in ya sleep? What happen ta ya? Tell me, what happen?"

"Teresa, I come ta help you. I'm fine. There is one thing ya kin help me wit', though. "Member when I ax ya 'bout the dead animal under ma step, ya say it a ole stray dog done drug it there. Well, yestiddy, I found a rag doll wit' a pin stuck through it in my backyard."

Teresa's head straightened and her eyes broadened. She looked Feen directly in her eyes. With a frown on her face, she asked, "Have ya made anybody mad lately?"

Feen shook her head, "No."

"Ya sho?"

"Yeah, I'm sho."

She was quiet for a second.

"I don't wanna scare ya, but look like somebody wanna hex you or somebody in ya fam'ly."

Her face was somber as she looked at Feen, waiting for a response.

"I ain't done nothin' ta nobody, Teresa. I'm telling ya the truf." Shaking her head. "I don't understan' why somebody would wanna hurt me or ma fam'ly."

Teresa got up and went to a table drawer and pulled out a very small sack, big enough to put rings or a cameo necklace in. It already had items in it, like a dried chicken hoof. Teresa got a pair of scissors and cut a small piece of Feen's hair and nipped the end of one of her fingernails and put them into the sack, also. She laid it in Feen's hand, and with her hand also on the sack, she prayed. "Father God, please protect Feen and her whole fam'ly. Don't let nothin' harm dem. In Jesus Name. Amen." She continued, "Cut a snip a Luke and Laura and Charlawt hair and put it inside the bag and den put in ya bosom. Wear it all the time. Never take it off, 'cept ta wash up. Pray over dis mojo bag often. Understan'?"

"Tank ya so much, Teresa. Dis serious, ain't it?"

"Dunno," she said. "Depend on if they know what they doin'. If they mean ta hurtcha or if they jus' tryna scare ya." She stopped a second. Her brows gathered together in thought. "If it sometin' they got from a root doctor, den it dangerous." Feen knew she was thinking of Clout. Feen, also, knew Teresa would never accuse her mother of doing anything wicked. "If not, maybe it ain't. Either way, don't take no chance."

"I won't," Feen said. "Ya tink Taunt Clout got sometin' ta do with it?"

She hunched her shoulders. "Don't tink so. I know she wouldn't do it if she know it fur you. Ma momma love ya momma, and she love you too, and would never do nothin' ta hurt ya. Ma momma is not the only root doctor or the only one deal in hoodoo round here. I dunno who behind it, so jus' be careful."

Clarice appeared at the door with two plates of food. "Plenty food out here," she said. "I brought y'all some." She handed one plate to Teresa and was about to give the other one to Feen when Louisiana appeared.

"You took the last piece of brisket. I don't know the last time I had brisket and I sure wanted some," she said.

"Well, dis plate fur Feen," Clarice said.

The disappointment on Louisiana's face was so intense that Feen said, "Let her have it. I'll get sometin' else."

"No," Clarice snapped and everyone looked at her surprised. "I fix it fur Feen," she said in a now calm voice. Feen smiled and touched Clarice's arm.

"Tank ya very much," she said. "But I can get 'nother one. Let her have dis one." She took the plate from Clarice and handed it to Louisiana, who grinned from year to year. Feen felt good about letting her have it, after all she'd been through. Clarice's face got a strange, almost frightened look as she turned around and went back into the kitchen.

The next day, she heard Louisiana had fallen ill later that night. She'd vomited so much they'd had to take her to the doctor. He thought it was food poisoning. The strange thing was no one else had gotten sick and they'd all had the same food.

Feen was thankful because that plate had been intended for her and if she would've eaten it, she would've been the one sick as a dog for days with two small children and work to do. She just didn't have time for troubles like that.

~ CHAPTER 19 ~

Luke was coming down the River Road from checking his nets and he half expected to see Clarice waiting for him. But she wasn't. He had a feeling he could not explain. Was it disappointment she wasn't waiting for him. Waiting to kiss him. Waiting to roll her eyes at him in that underhanded way. He shook his head trying to get those kisses out of his mind. He thought about what she had said about Feen kissing Wickliffe and encouraging him. He would talk to Feen when he got home.

He'd clean the fish first and then play with Charlotte. She was a sweet baby and when he played with her, she'd grin at him and he'd feel like he could solve all the problems of the world.

When he did get home, Feen was taking clothes down from the line. He watched her for a moment, then unpacked his fish and got his tools to clean them. She heard him and turned around.

"How many ya got?" she said, excited to have fish for supper.

"I brought ten home. I left some in the water, cuz I'm not gonna have a chance ta go sell dem today."

"We can give five ta Rae and have the rest for supper tonight and tomorra night," Feen said.

"Um-hmm. Dat sound good."

She came over and sat by him and watched him clean the fish. There was an awkward silence. After a while, she went inside to work on her ironing.

When he'd finished, he came inside and decided to talk about what Clarice had told him.

"Feen," he said.

"Umm?" she asked.

"Since ya stop havin' bad dreams, do ya tink nuf time done pass fur me ta ax ya sometin'? Kin ya tell me what happen dat day?"

She looked up from her ironing and moved her eyes around as if she were trying to decide if she wanted to talk to him or not.

"I dunno what ya want me ta tell ya. Ya saw how I look, ma face, arms, ever'tin.' Ya know what happen."

"I mean were y'all walkin' and talkin'? Did he, maybe, tink ya wanna do sometin' else?"

"We was walkin' and talkin'. I dunno what he thought. I was tryna get home to start supper."

"Somebody tol' me they saw y'all in the field. He kiss ya and ya kiss him back."

"What?"

"Yeah. Dat what they say."

"Well, dat's not true. Who say dat? Dat's not true. He kiss me and I spit in his face and he hit me and then..." Her voice got shaky.

He walked over where she was and drew her to him. "I b'lieve ya," he said.

He put his arms around her and she wept into his shoulder. He whispered in her ear, "It alright, Feen. I b'lieve ya."

He enjoyed holding her in his arms. As she wept, he massaged her back. When she quieted down, she raised her head and their eyes met. He bent down to kiss her gently. She didn't pull away.

He whispered in her ear, "Feen, I need ya, Baby." She didn't answer, but she didn't move away. Taking that as an encouraging signal, he led her into their bedroom, pulled her into his arms and kissed her again. Her lips were soft, her kiss was sweet and his heart skipped a beat. When his lips released hers, her eyes were large and the hope he'd felt began to dwindle. With his arms still around her waist, he could feel a slight tremor beneath her skin. He did not want this. He did not want a woman who, literally, shook out of fear or vomited when he touched her. He needed to know she wanted him like he wanted her. His hands fell to hers and for a while, they stood holding hands and staring into each other's face. Her eyes widened even farther when he released her hands and walked away.

~ CHAPTER 20 ~

One morning, when Charlotte was six months old, Feen was working in her garden, while her clothes dried on the line. Someone called her name. She turned and it was Julia, Wickliffe's mother.

"Oh," she said.

Julia said, "I know what my son did to you and I came to apologize. No woman should ever be treated that way."

Feen didn't want to talk or think about it. Why is she here? Why is she bringing all that pain back?

"Alright," she said.

"I know you don't want to hear this, but he's sorry. He's very sorry for what he did to you. He and I pray together every night. We read the Bible together every night. He's a changed man."

Feen didn't care whether he felt bad. He should feel bad. She didn't care if he prayed, read the Bible or changed. She didn't want him in her atmosphere. That's all. She didn't want to deal with him in any form or fashion.

"I'm glad he sorry and I'm glad he pray," she said out loud.

"I heard you had a baby?" Julia asked.

Feen's back stiffened up. "Yeah, I had a lil gull. Why?"

"Because I wanted to know if it's my granddaughter," she said honestly.

Feen closed her eyes and moaned, "Ahh." This was one of the things she had feared. She looked down and back at her. "I dunno. Not sho. Ya know I got a husband."

"Can I see her?" she asked.

"I dunno. I dunno. Why?"

"Because I would like to see a child that might be my grandchild."

"S'pose she not ya granchile. She ma daughter and I don't want him ta have nothin' ta do wit' her."

"That's fine. I'm not asking for him to see her. I want to see her."

Feen stopped again. Julia had always been kind to her. She didn't have any valid reason to not let her see Charlotte. She knew that, but she didn't want them in her life. Seeing Julia reminded her of Wickliffe. Her sanity was hanging by a thread as it was.

"Please, Feen. Let me see her."

"Okay. Jus' dis one time. Ya cain't be comin' over here ta see her. Ya cain't. If ya tink ya cain't see her jus' one time and no mo, den don't see her. Besides, I really don't b'lieve she ya granchile."

"I'll accept that for now. I'm not going to say I won't ask you again."

"Okay," said Feen. They walked to the back door. "Shh. She was sleepin' 'fore I came outside."

Julia walked into the bedroom where Charlotte lay in her crib. Her breath caught in her throat.

"Aww, what a beautiful child," she said. Her gaze made a complete inventory of her features.

"Dat's nuf," Feen whispered. "Ya gonna wake her up and I still have a lotta work ta do outside."

"Okay. Just one more moment. What's her name?"

"Charlawt."

Julia nodded. "After your mother."

When they were back outside, she looked at Feen, "You know that child is not Luke's."

"Jus' cuz she dark complected don't mean nothin'. I have dark grandparents, and one of ma sistas dark as she is. So, I dunno."

"How does Luke treat her?" she asked.

"He treat her fine. He love her and she love him."

"I'm not judging you. I know he hurt you. But, don't punish little Charlotte and me. Your mother's dead and so's Luke's. Don't you want her to have a grandmother?"

"I done tol' ya. I dunno."

"Well, thank you for letting me see her. By the way, he's leaving town for a while. He's gonna look for work up north. Things are bad everywhere, but he heard of a place up north where he might be able to find work."

She didn't want to show the joy she felt at hearing this. After all, this was Julia's son. But Feen's heart started to hope again. She could begin going places again. She wouldn't be afraid she'd run into him.

"Really?" she asked.

"Yes, really. I hope it's not permanent. But at least for a year or maybe more."

"Tank ya fur lettin' me know."

Watching her walk away, Feen prayed to the Lord and asked him for forgiveness. She knew Charlotte was not Luke's. No amount of wishing, hoping and praying could change that. Sooner or later, she'd have to admit that fact to all concerned. Right now, she wasn't ready to do that.

But the good news was she could go to church again and other places in town and not worry about seeing him there.

~ CHAPTER 21 ~

April 1937

When Charlotte was two years old, she loved to play with her cousin, Toyotae, who was seven years old and Rae's youngest child, while his family worked in the cotton fields. Feen babysat him if she was at home all day doing laundry. When she couldn't keep him, he'd spend the day in the field, on the turn row, with Rae checking on him every chance she got.

The weather was sunny and cool. She'd only had one load of clothes to launder, so she'd decided to make soap. Toyotae played in the yard, while she boiled the hardwood ashes in a big pot over her fire pit and skimmed the liquid lye from the top. She heard two-year-old Charlotte cry when she awakened from her nap, hurried into the house and called Toyotae to come, also. Which he did.

While getting Charlotte settled down, she heard Rae enter. "Hey Feen," she said.

"Hey Rae. Me and Toyotae in ma bedroom wit' Charlawt."

"Whatcha doin' leavin' lye out there like dat," said Rae. "Don't ya know a animal like a dog or worse yet a hungry chile passin' by might tink dat's milk and drink it."

"I's only gone a minute. Charlawt cried and I came ta see 'bout her. Mos' chirren round here know 'bout makin' lye soap, and it sho don't smell like milk."

"Dat's true, but jus' the same, don't leave dat out there like dat."

Feen wasn't in the mood for any of her lectures, so she said, "Alright. How's Mose?"

Rae looked at Toyotae and motioned for Feen to follow her into the kitchen.

"Useless. Sometime I feel like I'm in dis by maself."

Feen nodded her head. "Ya know he pass by here jus' 'bout ever' Friday night and he be so drunk, he kin hardly walk. He come tell me ya done hit him and he want me to call the law. I gotta say ta him every time I ain't got no phone."

She chuckled. "What he say when ya tell him dat?"

"Nothin'. Jus' stagger on 'way."

"I'm sorry he botherin' ya, Feen. But he right, we fight 'mos' ever' Friday night. He come in drunk and I cain't take it. I hit him. I know it's wrong. But I cain't help maself."

She walked closer to Rae and put a hand on her shoulder. "Ya kin help yaself. Ya gotta help yaself. Dat ain't right, Rae. Ya know dat ain't right."

Their eyes held. "It used ta be diff'rent. 'Member, Feen."

"Yeah, I 'member. He was twenty-four years old and you were almost thirteen. Mom didn't want him to come 'round the house. She said he was too old fur ya. Course, lots of gulls married men way older than dem. But, Mom didn't want him no wheres 'round ya."

"Yeah, she sho didn't, but I use to sneak off and meet him. He was different from the boys ma age. I thought they ack silly, ya know. Hittin' on ya, pullin' ya hair, den takin' off runnin'." She nodded her and smiled. "He was so manly and a gent'man. He'd bring me lil presents, a bracelet one time, candy 'nother time, even pick some wildflowers fur me." Her face took on a pleasant expression. "He'd say nice ting ta me. We'd go walking and he'd kiss me and I like it and I love him a lot." She stopped a took a deep breath. "Den one day, he take me out ta the woods," she looked down, embarrassed, and took another deep breath, "and den I gits pregnant." Her eyes looked away from Feen. "Mom was so mad, but he marry me and I thought the sun rose and set in him. We had chirren, den he change. He start gittin' drunk. I gotta make sho tings git done so's ma fam'ly kin eat. Pastor say a man s'pose to lead the fam'ly. He ain't leadin' the fam'ly."

"I know it hard. But Rae, stop hittin' him. Dat don't help. It might make it worse."

She nodded. "I know ya right. I gotta stop. I jus' git so mad, cuz it ain't s'pose ta be like dis. He promise dat lil twelve-year-old gull the world, not a world of me cleanin' up afta him when he drunk."

"Does he ever hit ya back? He kinda skinny, but he strong. I done see him carry big load a stuff."

Rae cocked her head to the side. "Mos' time he too drunk ta hit me back. One time he do, I smack him agin real good."

"Aww Rae, fur real?"

"Um-hmm. Ma chirren were hollin' and cryin' and one time they pull me off him."

"Ya know I'd be mad if he were hittin' you like dat. Ya know dat, right?"

Rae nodded.

Well, jus' cuz he a man don't mean ya kin hit him."

She looked at her hands. "I know."

"I wish I knew what ta tell ya. I'm a pray fur bof y'all. Because whatcha doing is dangerous. One a these days dat man gonna blow up and somebody gonna git hurt real bad or kilt."

Rae nodded her head and looked pass Feen into the bedroom. "Much prayer is needed. Toy, c'mon. Time ta go home."

He ran out the other room to leave with his mom.

Rae walked out into the yard, returned and poked her head in through the door and said, "Feen, come out here and git dat lye. Too many po chirren die from lye poisoning fur ya to leave dat stuff out here like dat."

"Gone home, Rae. I tol' ya, I's comin' right back and I is."

~ CHAPTER 22 ~

Two months later, while Feen combed Charlotte's hair as they sat on the porch, she saw a familiar sight, a rag doll with a pin stuck in it. They'd turn up at least once a month in the front or backyard, and she'd burn them. Dead animal guts had also appeared twice, and she'd bury them.

Her mojo bag was always in her bosom like Teresa had told her. She'd always pray with her mojo bag after one of the occurrences. That's what she did this time.

That same day Mrs. Frank came by to pick up her laundry.

"Feen, I have an offer for you," she said.

"An offer?"

"Yeah. Why don't you come and work for me? No more washing clothes outside. I have a washing machine. You'd still have to hang them out to dry, though."

"Ya got a washin' machine, Miz Frank?" Feen asked.

"Sure do. But I love the way you iron, so I drive all the way out here for you to starch and iron my clothes."

"Hmm," she said as she looked toward the pasture in thought. "What else I gotta do?"

"Cook. Clean. Ya know, all the things a housemaid does."

"How much?"

They discussed a weekly rate, that was generous as maid's wages go.

"Yes. Sooo, whatcha say?" asked Mrs. Frank.

"Lemme tink 'bout it, cuz town is a long way and I ain't got a car. We got a horse, but sometime ma husband use it. And he gittin' ole anyway. Don't think the pave road good fur his hoof."

"Well, I can come and get you, which mean I'd pay ya a little less. Now since the Depression is easing up some, there are a lotta ladies with maids. So, maybe you could catch a ride."

"Umm. Okay. I tink 'bout it and let ya know."

She talked it over with Luke that night who left the decision up to her. Mrs. Frank had been her favorite customer. Always gave her a little something extra when she paid her. However, she hadn't been a maid since before her mother got sick. She liked the independence of being her own boss and being at home when Laura came home. But, the income was not stable and the work was hard, especially, in the winter time. So, the next week, she accepted. She found a way to get to town every day, and she'd bring Charlotte until other arrangements could be made. She'd still take in laundry on Saturday for a while until she was confident the arrangement would work out.

When Feen arrived at the Franks for the first time, she was awed by how large everything was. The yard, the house, the rooms. Mrs. Frank's pride was evident as she showed her around. She'd hired a New Orleans decorator, and the furnishings were as grand as Feen had ever seen. Feen had worked in nice large homes before, so she was not easily impressed, but this place impressed her.

When they reached a small bedroom off the kitchen, she said, "This is your room."

"Ma room?" said Feen. "I'm not livin' in or stayin' overnight."

"I know, but you need a room to keep Charlotte when you bring her."

Mrs. Frank was a slim, attractive, well-dressed woman, a few years older than Feen, with short brown hair that was always coiffed, who'd been Homecoming queen. She always spoke in a calm tone. She expected things to be done a certain way and would bring it to Feen's attention if it was not to her liking. Feen would try to rectify whatever the problems were immediately. So, they got along fine.

Mrs. Frank's husband was hardly ever home. They'd been high school sweethearts, and he'd been her escort when she was Homecoming queen. Now he was a respected physician with a large clientele. He was a slim, average looking man of medium height with thinning blond hair. When he was there, he was very respectful if he and Feen happened to meet in the house. He just wasn't there often and when he was, he was in his study. They had three children, one teenager and two preteens. If Mrs. Frank left instructions for them through Feen, they obeyed her without question.

With a good paying steady job, Feen's future was looking up. She had no idea, this was the calm before the storm.

~ CHAPTER 23 ~

Luke took the opportunity to go fishing because it was sundown and the air had cooled off from a blistering hot day. There Clarice sat on the riverbank fishing. He'd known he should leave when he saw her, because the kiss she'd given him two years ago had stayed at the back of his mind. She hadn't sought him out and they hadn't been alone since.

When she saw him, she looked as if she'd been waiting for him. She put her pole down, rose and approached him. In his mind, it appeared she was walking in slow motion. His heart raced for he knew he was entering dangerous territory. The top three buttons on her shirt were opened and revealed small perky breasts. He resisted the urge to touch them. She stood in front of him, looked up at him, stood on her tip toes and kissed him. His mind was telling him to leave, but he seemed unable to move.

Taking him by the hand, she pulled him to a cool grassy spot under a tree and he followed as if he had no mind of his own. She smiled and laid back on the ground. The invitation was more than he could handle. He kneeled beside her and kissed her. She started to say something, and he put his finger over her lips to stop her. Their eyes held and she kissed his finger. He kissed her again, and he heard birds in the trees overhead, and he stopped.

Feen appeared in his mind, and he removed himself from above her and lay on his back looking up into the tree. The birds had reminded him of the doves and doves always reminded him of Feen.

"What's wrong," she said.

"Ya know what's wrong. I'm married. Ya know dat."

She rolled toward him and lay on her side. She leaned in and gently kissed him on his cheek. When he didn't object, she leaned further and kissed him on his lips, and a groan of surrender flowed from him as his arms surrounded her and he rolled back on top of her.

When their bodies joined together for the first time, she'd moaned, "At last."

The fact he meant so much to her pleased and excited him. Afterward, he felt guilty, but he knew this would not be the last time.

∞

One day, Feen walked into the master bedroom to pick up clothes to wash and found Mrs. Frank crying.

"Miz Frank, what wrong?"

"Nothing," she said, as she dried her eyes and continued to put on makeup.

Feen's eyes fell on one of the doctor's shirts that was laying on the bed apart from the other clothes. There was a bright, red lipstick spot on the collar of one of the shirts, and Mrs. Frank wore pink.

She saw Feen looking at the lipstick stain.

"You been here for a while. What do you think 'bout the doctor?" she asked.

"What do I tink 'bout the doctor?" Feen thought for a second. "Well, I tink he a fine gentleman. Yeah. I do."

"What makes you think that?"

Again, she paused. "Well, I never hear him say nothin' mean ta nobody," she said, nodding her head.

"Yeah. That's true. But that's because you don't hear him say nothing at all," she said, waiting for Feen's answer to that one.

Feen chuckled. "Well, I guess ya right 'bout dat. But least he don't have a mean spirit. Dat mean a lot. Mean he don't hurt cha."

"Feen, that means he doesn't hit me. It doesn't mean he doesn't hurt me. He hurts me plenty without laying a hand on me."

Feen put two and two together about the lipstick. She didn't answer.

"Feen, how would you feel if you found out Luke was cheating on you? What would you do?"

A hard thump occurred in her chest. Just thinking about it caused her pain. "I'd feel awful bad 'bout it, Miz Frank. I jus' dunno what I'd do."

"Would you leave him?"

"Leave him?" Feen stood up straight. "I dunno. I cain't see dat happenin'. Luke so sweet to me and Laura and Charlawt. I cain't see him not bein' there wit' us."

"Hmm," said Mrs. Frank. "Dr. Frank is kind, too. That is when he chooses to grace me with his presence. I'm pretty sure there's a woman."

"Oh, Miz Frank, I'm so sorry."

She wanted to ask her what was she going to do, but she didn't want to overstep her bounds. She'd listened to whatever Mrs. Frank wanted to tell her and answered any question she was asked, but it would have been improper for her to go further into the discussion on her own.

Mrs. Frank nodded her head and left the room. Feen went on with her work, but that conversation had bothered her all day. Although her demeanor didn't change, Feen could see that Mrs. Frank was different. Her shoulders were a little rounder. She'd caught her sitting on the porch gazing into space several times, and she didn't eat lunch that day. With all her beautiful clothes, jewelry, big house and respected standing in the community, she was a woman in pain. A woman afraid of losing her husband.

She thought about losing Luke. Like Mrs. Frank didn't want to lose Dr. Frank, she didn't want to lose Luke. She had allowed a great divide to grow between them and hadn't worked to close it up. The last time he'd tried to make love to her was two years ago when Charlotte was six months old. He'd walked away and hadn't approached her in that way since.

She had to admit she'd been grateful to him for leaving her alone and not forcing her to deal with being intimate. They'd been cordial to each other and co-parented well together, but they were just roommates. How could she keep her husband when she feared a man's touch? Mrs. Frank's marriage problems magnified the problems in her own marriage and it bothered her all day.

Was the mojo bag still protecting her family or were the rag dolls tearing it apart?

~ CHAPTER 24 ~

It was Saturday and Feen didn't take any clothes from customers to launder so she'd be fresh that night. She took Laura and Charlotte over to Rae's so she could be alone with Luke. She wanted her marriage back, the way it was before Charlotte was conceived.

She washed and ironed her Sunday dress, washed and hot combed her hair and cooked some smothered chicken with rice. She put wildflowers in her room and in water to sprinkle on herself. All of this was done without talking to Luke. The plan was to surprise him. She'd taken a bath and waited. She'd never worried about when he came in, because she was busy doing something all the time. Whenever he'd come in was fine. She'd serve him supper and boil some water for him to clean up. Now she wasn't doing anything, except waiting for him to come home and the hours seemed to drag by. She wondered, where could he be?

A little frightened by the fact he'd not come home, she got on her knees and prayed. "Lord, don't let it be too late."

∞

Luke lay in bed. A pang of guilt struck near his heart as he watched Clarice cook in her small kitchen. They'd been meeting on a regular basis for a month, ever since that day by the river.

He'd worked today for a farmer who needed chicken coops built for his pullets. Afterward, he'd come to Clarice's. He didn't think Feen would even notice he hadn't gone home. She, usually, did laundry for her customers and the family on Saturday, and didn't seem to be aware of whether he was there or not.

Once Clarice had started the affair with Luke, she'd become very industrious. She'd gotten a job working in a kitchen in a white restaurant in Marksville and had moved out of Teresa's house. While working at the restaurant, she'd met some white owners of a large hunting cabin in the woods by the river. For being the caretaker of the large cabin, she'd been permitted to live rent-free, in a small cabin behind the large cabin. The white owners were seldom there, and it had been their hideaway.

As he continued to watch her cook, he knew it was time for him to go home, but she'd insisted on preparing him a meal.

"Supper ready," she said. "Is sometin' I learnt at the restaurant wit' shrimp. I just add some of ma mama's seasonin'," she said as she pointed to a row of jars filled with ground herbs displayed on a shelf above the stove. "Jus nuf ta add a lil special flavor."

When she said "her mama's seasoning," it gave Luke a jolt, because the memory of what Clout had said at Emile's funeral entered his mind. He wasn't sure he wanted to eat anything she'd had anything to with. Looking at Clarice, who looked adorable dressed in her slip and the anxious to please expression on her face, he quickly dismissed the thought there could be anything harmful in the herbs she'd used to season the food, whether they'd come from Clout or not.

"It sho smell good," he said. "Ya spoilin' me wit' all dis good cookin'."

He sat at the table and she rubbed his shoulders. Bending over to build a chicken coop had tied up his muscles. "Ooh, dat feel good," he said. The food tasted heavenly on his tongue.

"Dis is some good stuff."

"Anytin' fur ma man," she said.

After taking his last bite, he said, "I gotta go."

"No, ya don't," she said in a sugary voice.

"Baby, ya done wore me out," he laughed. "I gotta go home and res'."

"Plenty mo where dat came from," she said.

"Baby, I gotta go."

"When ya gonna leave dat witch, anyway," she said, her voice growing more irritated.

"Hey," he shouted, abruptly getting up. "Don't talk 'bout her like dat. Ya hear me. Dat's ma wife. Don't ya ever talk 'bout her."

She knew she had pushed him too far. She backed off for the time being.

∞

He walked in his front room at nine o'clock that night and heard soft music playing, which was unusual. He'd expected everyone to be in bed asleep, including Feen. When he walked into the kitchen, he saw her. She was sitting at the table in her Sunday dress. He was baffled and his pulse increased.

"Feen, whatcha doin' up? I didn't 'spect ya up."

"I is waitin' fur ya. I is waitin' fur ma husband," she said in a tone he hadn't heard in a long time.

He was at a loss for words. He hadn't thought of an excuse, because he didn't usually have to give one. She's usually so tired and pre-occupied she wouldn't even know whether he's late or not.

"Feen, ya look real nice. Why ya dress up?"

"I want a night fur us. I brought the chirren ta Rae's so it'd be jus' us."

"Dat sound good, but I know ya tied afta washin' today."

"No, I ain't do none a dat today. I didn't wanna be tied tonight."

He knew he was in a bad situation. It appeared Feen had planned a romantic evening for them. His problem was he'd just been with Clarice late afternoon and evening. There's no way he was going to make love to his wife after just being with someone else. What was he going to do?

"Feen, ya know I went build a chicken coop dis mornin'. Den I went huntin', but didn't see nothin'. I wish you'd a tol' me whatcha plan was, cuz I woulda come home right afta the chicken coop. Now, I'm beat."

"I understan' ya tied," she said, trying to hide her disappointment. "But I know ya mus' be hungry. I fixed ya some smother chicken."

He could tell she was disheartened.

"I dunno if I can eat. Ya ever hear people say, 'too tied ta eat.' Well, dat's me right now."

She stood looking at him with her face long.

"I'll try," he said.

The walk home had moved some of the food from his previous meal down, but he was stuffed after a few bites. He managed to eat most of it and complimented her on how good it tasted.

Once in bed, she crawled over, laid her head on his chest and asked, "Where ya went huntin'?"

He didn't answer. He hadn't prepared a story to tell. He closed his eyes and pretended he was asleep, and soon he was.

~ CHAPTER 25 ~

June 1945

By the time Charlotte was ten years old, Feen's mental health had improved, tremendously, since the attack in 1934. Prayer and time had worked wonders. No longer was she always on the verge of tears when she thought about her attack. Her family life was good, not like it was before, but good. They were not intimate, but he was always kind and thoughtful to her. She thought all couples settle down after a while and are more peaceful with each other than passionate.

Since Wickliffe left, she'd become active in the church again and served on the usher board and clean-up committee, where Julia was the chairman. The cleanup committee cleaned up the church once a month. Most of the time, she'd take Charlotte with her and Julia's face would light up. Charlotte looked forward to seeing her because she'd always have tea cakes or cookies "just for her."

Feen would say, "Say tank ya ta the nice lady."

Julia would smile at Charlotte and say, "Don't worry about saying thank you, Charlotte. The pleasure is all mine."

She'd look at Feen and shake her head. She was a "nice lady" alright, she was her grandmother. She wondered if Feen would ever stop playing this game. Charlotte was missing out on a relationship with her grandparents, uncles, aunts, and cousins.

Feen stood steadfast in presenting Charlotte as Luke's child. Therefore, Julia came up with the idea to tell Charlotte she was her great aunt. Which is what she would be if she were truly Luke's daughter. She would take whatever she could to be a part of Charlotte's life. Feen relented and told Charlotte to call her, Taunt Julia, and even allowed her to spend time at Julia's home.

From time to time, she'd mention Wickliffe to Feen and tell her how he was doing. It didn't bother her to hear his name anymore. She was very thankful he'd left town which stimulated her to heal. Julia always told her how sorry Wickliffe was and how he'd repented. He'd met a girl and gotten married, and gone to seminary school. He'd graduated at the top of his class and was now a preacher. His mother had gone to his graduation and visited him and his family often. She'd said they were doing well. All of this was fine with Feen, long as she didn't have to see him.

~ CHAPTER 26 ~

July 1945

Feen was sitting on the porch mending one of Luke's shirts when Wickliffe drove up in a black shiny horse-drawn buggy. This was the first time she'd seen him since that day, eleven years before.

Now thirty-nine years old, he was dressed in a suit and tie and his hair was pepper gray. His nose had a slight knot and crook right below the bridge. She felt a nudge of satisfaction thinking that must be the place where Luke had broken his nose. Other than that, the years had been kind to him.

"How are you, Feen?" he said.

She didn't answer. Her breath had become shallow and she was finding it hard to breathe. In front of her stood the monster who had changed her life. He'd damaged her and almost destroyed her marriage. Both Laura and Charlotte walked onto the porch. As his eyes took them both in, she fought to stay calm in front of them.

"Laura," he said. "You don't remember me, but I'm your cousin. Cousin Wickliffe. I knew you when you were a little bitty girl."

Laura gave him a big smile. She said, "Hi Cousin Wickliffe. I think I remember you."

"How old are you now?" he asked.

"Seventeen," she answered. "I graduate from high school next year."

"Seventeen, my goodness, and almost out of school. Seems like just the other day," he said. His eyes drifted toward Charlotte and Feen's heartbeat accelerated.

"You must be Charlotte," he said. "My momma talks about you all the time. You're every bit as pretty as she said." She gave him a big smile. "Look what I have for y'all," he said as he leaned in the buggy and pulled out two wrapped gifts. Both girls were ecstatic as they took the packages wrapped in shimmering paper with ribbons and bows.

"Can we open them?"

"Yes, you can. They're yours. That is if your momma says so," he said.

They both looked at their mother, who sat stone-faced and who hadn't uttered a word.

"Take dem in the house and open dem," she said with a cold voice, not smiling. Both girls noticed her demeanor and did not move. She nodded toward the door and repeated, "Take dem in the house and open dem."

They looked at each other, shrugged their shoulders and went into the house.

Walking closer to the porch, he said, "I don't mean you any harm. I'm not staying."

"Why ya come here?" she said. "God bless me when ya left. If ya gotta come see ya momma, fine. Do dat. But don't come here."

He paused, "My mom told me she told you how sorry I am for what I did that day, but I wanted to tell you myself." He paused and when she didn't answer, he continued. "I have no excuse. I pray for you and your family every day. I would like to ask for your forgiveness. If you can't, I understand. But I need to ask for it."

As she sat on the porch, listening to him, she studied him carefully. He seemed sincere. She'd thought about this day many times. What she would do if she ever laid eyes on him again. The things she would say. The items she would hit him with. How the hatred for this man had at one time consumed her. But she hadn't thought about it for a long time now. Through much prayer, she'd learned forgiveness was good for the soul. It didn't mean she had to be friends with him, she would just no longer allow herself to cry over what he'd done to her. She wasn't going to waste time even thinking about him.

It had been difficult when he pulled up. That old anger had reared its head. But as she got control of her emotions, her breathing had returned to normal.

She shook her head up and down.

"Yeah, I furgive ya. I heard ya say ya were sorry dat day. Afta ya done beat me so bad I couldn't see."

His eyes opened wide and his head turned slightly showing his surprise.

"Yeah, I heard ya. When I lay there too hurt ta move, ya tink I care if ya sorry? Dat's s'pose ta make ever'thin' alright? I don't tink so." She got up and walked off the porch into the yard and faced him. "So, ya want me ta furgive ya. Now, dat don't mean I wantcha 'round here bringin' ma chirren no present. Dat's sho not true. I don't wanna see ya agin in dis life. But fur as furgivin' ya, I furgive ya long time ago."

He pursed his lips together, nodded his head and said, "Thank you."

"Oh, it weren't fur you. I furgive ya cuz it good fur me."

"I understand. I understand perfectly, and I thank you, anyway." He continued to nod his head. His voice cracked slightly as he said, "I know I don't deserve it, but thank you. One day I'm gonna do something that will make you know how sorry I am."

She felt like an observer in this scene. She saw his emotion and felt his sincerity, but none of it had any effect on her.

The girls came back outside with shawls on. They both gushed, "Thank you, Cousin Wickliffe. We love them."

He smiled, "Y'all welcome, Girls! My wife picked them out. They're not as pretty as the two of you, though." He looked at Feen, then back at the girls and said, "I have to go. Church service tonight and I'm preaching. I hope to see y'all there."

Laura said with a big grin, "Yeah, we're going. We always go to church. Almost every time it opens."

Feen said, "No, we not goin'."

"What?" both girls said.

"We not goin'," she said emphatically.

"But Mom," said Charlotte. "Toy's ringing the bell tonight and he needs me to help pull the rope."

An adult man had to put all his weight on the rope to ring the big bell at church. Accordingly, when Toyotae rung the bell, which he loved to do, he'd get somebody to help him. Charlotte loved to help him do that.

"He gonna have ta git somebody else ta help him tonight, cuz we ain't goin', and I don't want ta hear nothin' else 'bout it."

Disappointed, they'd gone back into the house.

She'd forgiven him, but she wasn't ready to sit in church and listen to him preach. She watched him ride away. She wondered what he meant when he said he'd do something that would make her know he was sorry. She didn't wonder about it long, though. It would be four years before she saw him again.

~ CHAPTER 27 ~

Before Feen started working for Mrs. Frank, her work was at home, so when Adrian came for his yearly leave, he'd spend days at a time with her. He'd help her with her laundry, play with the kids, eat meals with her and the whole family. The last few times he'd been home, she hadn't been able to do that. She missed those days of idle conversation.

She'd never taken a weekday off from Mrs. Frank, except half days on holidays, so that year, she felt fine asking for a day off during one of the weeks Adrian was home on leave.

The knock on the door told her he'd arrived. Luke was baling hay for a farmer and Laura and Charlotte were at school. She smoothed her hair back as she answered the door.

"C'mon in here. Want some breakfast?" she said with a big grin on her face. Her eyes took in his tanned, muscular arms, blue jeans and a plaid shirt. He'd grown so much since that day on Perret's Path.

"Sho do," he said. He had packages in his hand and Feen eyed them. He sat them on the floor in the front room and followed her into the kitchen.

They talked as they sat and ate cornbread and milk. She could hardly believe he was there and kept looking up at him, smiling.

"So, ya been cross the water?" she asked.

"Yeah, I been cross the water," he answered. "Brought y'all some souvenirs back. Just something to give y'all a feel for where I been."

"Oh," she said. "Dat's what in dem packages on the flo?"

"Yeah, I hope you like them." He paused.

She followed him back to the front room where he opened his bags. He gave her two pillows the size of a chair seat with beautiful pillow covers made with glossy ivory fabric. Each pillow had frilly borders made of golden threads twisted like a rope. A world globe and the Eiffel tower, along with the word Paris were printed on one of the pillow covers and Big Ben and the word London were written on the other. Her eyes opened wide as she took one in her hands and let her fingers feel the silkiness of it.

"Aww, tank ya, Adrian. I like it a lot. I'm gonna sit dem right here on dis lil what not table. Cuz they too pretty ta sit on."

"Well, I bought them so you could use them as chair cushions on these hard-back chairs."

"Yeah, I know. But they jus' so pretty. I don't wanna dirty dem up. Maybe I do it sometime. But fur right now, they gonna stay where I can jus' look at dem."

The smile on her face spoke volumes about her satisfaction with the presents. It gave him pleasure to see her excited.

They resumed their conversation at the kitchen table over coffee and he told her where he'd been since the last time she'd seen him. Her hand flew to her mouth in embarrassment when he talked about the red-light district in Paris. They laughed at her naïveté. He told her about the food and how the people dressed.

Soon it was lunchtime and she fixed some soup as they continued to talk.

Adrian said, "Luke is a hardworking man."

"Yea, he is," said Feen. "I worry 'bout him. But that the kinda man he is."

"When I get married, I want it to be just like y'all marriage."

"Ya mean, agin?"

"Yeah, when I get married, again."

"Oh, ya do?"

"Yea. Why are you surprised by that?"

"Well, we have our up and down." She paused.

A scowl came to Adrian's face. "Y'all alright?" he asked. "Something going on now?"

She shook her head. "No. We jus' like anybody been married a long time. He don't pay a lotta 'tention ta me, not like he use ta."

"Have ya talked to him about it?"

"No, I tink it jus' dat we been married close ta seventeen years now. It jus' quiet down."

She and Luke were kind to each other, but he hadn't touched her sexually in years and she didn't know how to rectify that. She'd tried to be sexy, but he was always working or always tired. He only saw her as the mother of his children.

"Oh, I see. Do you want me to talk with him?"

"Oh nah," she said. "Don't do dat. Ever'tin' all right."

She tapped him on his arm and said, "Nuf 'bout me, tell me 'bout London."

Footsteps could be heard on the back steps signaling the arrival of Laura and Charlotte. Both ran to Adrian with big grins on their faces. He rose to his feet and hugged each one enthusiastically, while Feen looked on smiling.

"Y'all must've had a good day in school."

"Just glad to see you, that's all," said Charlotte still standing on one side of him with her arm around his waist.

"Well, I can tell you one thing," he said smiling down at her. "You are getting bigger and prettier every time I see you. I'll hafta fight the boys off you pretty soon."

Charlotte grinned with pleasure.

He smiled at Laura and winked, "Same to you, Pretty Girl. Since you're almost through school, I really need to look out for you." There was a young man on Laura's mind, but she just smiled.

He gave them their gifts, a silver bracelet with their respective names engraved on them. They both beamed with pleasure. He sat on the floor and talked with them about school and other things that were happening in their lives, while Feen cooked supper.

Luke came home and noticed Adrian sitting on the floor with the girls. His eyes went to her cooking in the kitchen.

"Well, well, well. Dis sho look homelike. If I didn't know better, I might say ya the husband and I'm the comp'ny."

Adrian jumped up laughing, walked over and shook hands.

"Hey Man. Just spending time with the girls. You know how I look forward to it. Y'all my family, Man."

Luke shook his hand smiling. "Yeah, I know. Feel the same way. Ya been a real friend ta us."

His eyes moved to Feen. She looked so happy and relaxed. Her hair was shiny and pulled back, and the belt on her dress accentuated her waistline. Over the years her waist had broadened only a little, and her butt and her hips had rounded out quite nicely. He was glad to see her happy. He didn't make her face shine and her eyes light up that way anymore, and it saddened him to realize that.

"Wanna go hunting this weekend," Adrian asked.

"Sho nuf. Why not? I got a few things I can teach ya."

"Okay. Good. We'll see who teaches who," he said.

As they sat around the supper table, Luke noticed how Feen kept looking at Adrian with a smile and hanging on his every word. He enjoyed Adrian too, but he was sure not as much as she did. He didn't quite know how he felt about that. When Adrian was a boy that was one thing, but now he was a full-grown man. He felt sure they'd never betray him, but their eyes seemed as though they couldn't get enough of looking at each other, and a disheartening feeling entered his chest.

126

~ CHAPTER 28 ~

Laura finished school, fell in love with and married a young, handsome Texan named Rick, who was visiting family in Marksville. They moved to his hometown, Port Arthur, Texas, and soon after, their first child, Lonnie, was born.

Charlotte did well in school. She was mature for her age, because she'd spent a lot of time with companions who were older than her. Although, she'd had friends her own age at school, her mother, father, Taunt Julia, Laura and Toyotae all spent countless hours with her and she'd soaked in a lot of their wisdom.

Luke continued to live the double life. He was a provider, comforter and guide to his wife and Charlotte. As far as the community was concerned, there was no better husband than Lucien Ford. At the same time, he continued to have a passionate affair with Clarice Lange.

The relationship with Clarice was a roller coaster one. Sometimes, he'd break up with her because his conscience would get the better of him. Other times, they'd break up because of her jealousy and possessiveness. But no matter what the reason, they'd always seem to reunite. He didn't love her the same way he loved Feen, but there was a lustful pull to her that kept him coming back. Each time they'd separated; however, it'd left an additional dent in the armor of their relationship, and with so many dents, Luke had reached a point of ending it for good.

He didn't know how they'd kept it a secret in a small town like Marksville, but they had. In the beginning, he'd worried Clarice would let it drop somewhere on purpose. But Clarice didn't want her sister, Teresa, to know. There were only two people Clarice seemed to fear, that was Teresa and her momma.

When he arrived at Clarice's one-room cabin, the number three tub was in the center of the room filled with warm bath water ready for him. The robe she'd made for him lay on the bed. He'd stopped in, but hadn't intended to stay long. However, the bath was so inviting, he'd yielded. Afterward, he didn't feel as tired. She enticed him to stay longer by offering to massage his neck and back. As her hands passed over muscles, the tension eased and he went to sleep. He woke up with a start.

"Why'd you let me go ta sleep. I tol' ya I gotta git home," he said, getting up.

"Baby, you tied. Ya need ta sleep."

"But I tol' ya I gotta go."

"Ta dat old ugly witch," she said.

Sometimes, when she said disparaging things about Feen, it only amused him. Other times it infuriated him. This time it amused him, because he knew she knew Feen wasn't an ugly witch.

That angered her more. "Ya don't appreciate me. Don't nobody love ya like I do."

He removed the robe and got back into his dirty clothes.

"She always walkin' 'round smilin' at men. I know ya don't b'lieve me, but it's true. She ain't no good, Luke."

He stopped and looked at her sitting in the middle of her bed. What he saw was a spiteful woman, with her mouth all twisted in a sneer. Occasionally, when she'd get angry, he'd think about all the weird things that happened around his house and wondered if she might have something to do with it. He always talked himself out of it. He reasoned that since she loved him, she'd never do anything to harm him or his family.

"Look, I don't tink we need ta see each other no more. Dis here ain't good fur neither one a us."

Her eyes widened and her hands balled up into fists. "Don't say dat, Luke. I ain't got no one else. You know dat. Don't say dat."

"I been tellin' ya fur years now dat I'm not gonna leave ma wife."

"Dat right, Luke. Fur years. Yet ya keep comin'. Ya keep lovin' on me. She cain't satisfy ya like me. Dat's why ya keep comin'."

"Well, I tell ya one thing, she don't nag me like ya do," he said.

She jumped out of bed and ran to him, and with her arms around his neck said in a whisper, "She don't love ya like I do, either."

That play usually worked on him, because he knew when she said something like that, she would try her best to prove it to him. But not this time. It was time to go home and he was going.

∞

When he walked into his house, it smelled of meat cooking, seasonings and coffee brewing. Feen was dressed in a white V neck top and straight blue skirt that hugged her hips. Mrs. Frank had redone her wardrobe and had given Feen some of her old clothes. This was one of the outfits. No longer working on Saturdays made her feel more in the mood for talking when Luke was home. Lately, they'd been doing just that, talking and laughing together. The sight of him when he walked in made her smile and he was glad he'd come home.

"Nothin' in the nets today?" she asked.

"No, ma nets busted. Could ya make me some new ones when ya got time? I was fishin' with a pole and didn't catch nothin'."

"Well, I'm glad ya home early Yea, I'll make ya some new ones."

Their eyes met and held for a moment. The center of his eyes seemed to expand, and she knew he appreciated the care she'd taken to dress today. It reminded her of those rainy days many years ago.

He turned and walked over to Charlotte who was reading a book. "How ma big girl doin'?"

"Fine, Daddy. Next time you go fishing with a pole, I wanna go."

"Okay, Baby Girl, ya got it," he answered without hesitating.

After supper and after Charlotte went to her room, they went to theirs. She lay in bed and watched him undress. His hair was straight and now showing a little gray around his temples. His once light complexioned skin had darkened to a reddish brown after years in the sun. The line at the bottom of his neck exposed the difference in color.

Her eyes scanned his massive chest. The size of it had surprised her the first time she'd seen it many years ago, and as she gazed upon it, she remembered how much she loved to encircle her arms around it and lay her head upon it.

He looked at her when he sensed her eyes probing him. Again, that look came on his face, the look of appreciation.

As he pulled the covers back and got in beside her, he said, "Ya look mighty good tonight."

"Tank ya," she said. "Ya look mighty good, too." She touched his face.

"Luke, we live a long-time jus sharin' space. Hardly talkin'. Jus' working hard. Never taking time ta be husband and wife. Tryna keep clothes on these chirren back and food in they bellies. I know I turn 'way from ya dat day lon' time ago, but I always love ya. I never stop lovin' ya."

He exhaled. "I gotta say I didn't know ya love me. Ya turn away from me and ya never turnt back 'round. So many time ya right there by me and I kin smell ya, but I cain't touch ya. Sometime, I dunno how I made it."

A pang of guilt touched him, because he did know how he'd made it. Clarice. That's how he'd made it, but he couldn't tell her that.

She rested on her left side facing him. With her right hand, she ran her index finger down his chest. "Sometime, I feel like ya don't love me no mo," she whispered.

He looked up from her finger and looked back at her. "Why? I always take care of ya."

"True, but ya never say ya do. Ya git in the bed and turn over and go ta sleep. Jus' like I'm not here."

"I guess we talk, but not 'bout dis. I thought ya didn't want me and ya thought I didn't want you."

He turned on his side and touched her cheek. A tear ran down her face, and a wave of compassion overcame him.

"I never stop lovin' ya," he said. "I jus' givin' ya time ta heal and one day lead ta the next and one week lead ta the next and one year lead ta the next," he said. "Ya know how long it been?"

"Close ta 'leven years. How could we let dat happen?"

"Afta what happen, it look like ya don't want dat from me. Ya want comfort from me and I give ya dat. My job is ta take care a ya and tryna give ya whatcha want."

"I want chu." she whispered.

He leaned over and kissed her on the cheek he'd just wiped the tear from. She slowly leaned forward and kissed him gently on the lips. They stared at each other and his pulse raced. He was still very much attracted to her, but he did not want to be rejected again, and his guilt about his affair lay heavy between them. She moved closer to him until her breasts were against his chest and he leaned down and took one of her breasts into his mouth. She moaned as she hugged his head. Releasing her breast, he kissed her on the mouth. His arms encircled her and her body moved even closer until their bodies melded together. The kiss was long and sweet.

"It's been so long," she whispered.

His breathing became ragged as she planted soft kisses on his chest. Her hands traveled his body, over his strong muscles built from years of hard work. Her hands roamed as though she was a blind person trying to find her way. The feel of him gave her so much pleasure, and she moaned.

He whispered, "Oh Feen."

Her head rose from his chest and their eyes met. She kissed him deeply on the lips. He pulled her to him as they continued to kiss and explore each other's body. There was no hesitancy tonight as they wrestled with the tide of emotion overcoming them.

As they made passionate love, she found herself repeatedly saying, "Oh, Luke." It was like they had done when they were first married. She kept trying to get closer to him and she couldn't get close enough.

The pressure inside of her built until she was filled with sensations and she squealed one last time, "Oh Luke." She heard his ragged moan. He kissed her on the forehead and moved back to the bed beside her.

As the tide of emotion subsided, she closed her eyes and lay with her head on his shoulder, and whispered, "I miss ya so much. Ya my dove."

He squeezed her tightly, but didn't reply. With the mention of a dove, his guilt returned. He'd been drawn to them both in different ways.

Clarice needed him so much. He was an obsession with her, which in a way was frightening, yet alluring. She'd been young, adoring and she'd had no one. She'd had a son when she was a teenager, but he'd been raised by an aunt, and didn't even call her Mom. He could fool himself into thinking he was helping her, by being there for her. Now he admitted to himself he'd been selfish.

With Feen, it was the opposite. It was he who needed her. Even though she'd just said she loved him and had been so ardent making love to him, he didn't believe she needed him. She had gone through that terrible ordeal with Wickliffe and never let him help her with that.

She'd never even talked to him about it. She'd found her way back to peace on her own.

He whispered in her hair, "I love you so much, Feen. Despite how I acted, I never stop lovin' ya." And he meant it with all his heart.

She turned her face up to him and gazed into his eyes, and said, "I still got dove eyes fur ya."

For the second time that night, she'd brought up their pledge to each other and his heart jumped into his throat. The guilt he'd felt earlier that had subsided now returned. He hadn't kept his vows to her. He hadn't had dove's eyes only for her. He kissed her on her forehead and squeezed her tightly, silently, vowing to set things straight.

The magic of that night stayed with her for days afterward. Every time she looked at him, she smiled. If he was looking her way, he smiled back. She felt reborn. When they were in each other's vicinity, they'd touch. At night, they were like newlyweds who'd discovered how fortunate they were to have each other.

Two months later, Feen found out she was pregnant. Somehow, she'd known she would be. Anything that exceptional would have to end in something extraordinary.

When she'd told Luke, at first, his face was somber and he'd gotten a faraway look in his eyes.

"Maybe, we git a boy dis time," she said.

His eyes were thoughtful as they met hers.

"Dis will be our last chance. Ya wanna boy, don'tcha," she said.

He nodded his head. "A boy would be nice, but I love ma gulls. So, a gull would be fine, too. Ya feel good 'bout havin' 'nother baby now?"

"Ever'tin gonna be alright, I tink. But, it gonna be ma last one, cuz by the time it come, I'll be forty-two. Are you alright wit 'nother baby?"

He'd nodded, pulled her into his arms and said, "Um-hmm. I'm glad we havin' a baby." He closed his eyes and held her.

~ CHAPTER 29 ~

Feen had just gotten home from work when she answered a knock at her door. It was a drunk Mose.

"Mose, whatcha doin' drunk? I still ain't got no phone."

"Feen, It's 'bout Toy. He been poison."

"What? How ya know?"

"Been ta the doctor and he look down his throat and dat's what he say. He say lye poisonin'."

"What?" Feen repeated.

She couldn't believe it. She knew lots of poor rural kids got poisoned with lye, because the commercial kind used to make soap was usually kept in the kitchen and the white crystals looked like sugar. When it was stirred in water to make a cleanser for floors, it could look like milk.

But Toyotae was seventeen. He knew about lye. She and Rae made their own and their children had all been educated on the dangers of lye. Therefore, she didn't understand how this could've happened.

She wanted to go to Rae's, but she didn't want to bring Charlotte. She was so close to Toy, she'd find it overwhelming.

"Mose, tell Rae I'm comin'. Charlawt," she said. "I'm going down ta ya Taunt Rae's house. When ya daddy git home, tell him where I'm at."

"Can I go?" asked Charlotte coming into the front room. She looked at the door at Mose's retreating figure.

"No, not dis time. I need ya ta stay here ta let ya daddy know where I'm at."

Charlotte's face clouded up.

"I want to go, Mom. Toy didn't feel good yesterday. He's had a sore throat for a week."

Even though Toy was five years older than her, they'd always talked about everything. He gave good advice.

"Not dis time. Ya stay here."

Charlotte nodded and Feen left for Rae's house.

∞

Luke found himself in a shaky position. He sat on Clarice's bed as she raged on and on. She'd learned from Teresa that Feen was pregnant.

"How can she be pregnant? Huh? How can she be pregnant, Luke? Who it fur? Ya don't touch her. Ya been touchin' her, Luke? Dat's why ya ain't been comin' round here? Huh? Answer me?"

He wanted to answer her, to give her solace, but he couldn't and be truthful. He knew she wouldn't like what he had to say. Everything she thought was true. He'd been sleeping with his wife and enjoying it, immensely. The reason he'd not been around was because he didn't know how to tell her it was over between them. He'd always known he'd never leave Feen and now he knew he no longer wanted to be unfaithful to her.

Self-reproach had been a constant companion. When he was with Feen, he'd been guilt-ridden about being with Clarice. Now being with Clarice, he still felt guilt-ridden about being with Clarice. Looking at her raging about the room, he recognized he had virtually used her for eleven years, taken those years from her. When their affair had begun, she was young, pretty with big brown eyes and a pouty mouth. It wouldn't have been difficult for her to find herself a husband. Now she was older. While her skin was smooth, it didn't have the gleam of youth, her mouth was turned down at the corners, and her eyes no longer had that mischievous sparkle. Instead, they were bitter and blazed with jealousy.

Coming back to the present, she continued to scream accusations at him. He got up to go to the door. Suddenly, her whole persona changed.

"No. No. No. Please, don't leave, Luke," she said in a breathless pleading voice. She ran to him, catching his hand. "I'm not mad. Really, I'm not. I'm jus' surprise. Don't go. C'mon ta bed. Ya ain't been here in a long time. I miss ya so much. Please, c'mon ta bed."

Luke put his hand in front of his face as she tip-toed to kiss him. He had come by today to end their affair, not really knowing how he'd do it and had found her in a tizzy over Feen being pregnant. He didn't have the words to explain it to her in a humane way, so he'd decided to leave, think it over and come back another day.

"Calm down, Clarice. It alright. Gotta go take care a sometin'. Be back soon and we kin talk."

"Ya be back today?" she asked.

"No. Not today," he said.

"When, den?" she asked.

"Not sho."

"Ooh," she cried. "Ya cain't go now. We need ta talk."

After going back and forth several times, she accepted his assertion that he'd be back, and when he'd come back, they'd have a long talk.

∞

Feen walked into Rae's house and found her other nieces and nephews frightened. Their eyes were wide and their face unsmiling. Toy was laying on a cot in the front room with his eyes closed. Rae turned terrified eyes to her.

"My Gawd Rae," said Feen.

"I dunno what ta do. The doctor say lye poisoning. At first, I thought he mighta got it from ya house cuz of dat time long time ago when I fussed atcha fur leavin' it out. But he tell me, no. He don't 'member drinkin' nothin' like lye. Doctor say somebody maybe put sometin' in his food. But I say, who would do sometin' like dat."

Feen shook her head. "Yeah, who would do sometin' like dat. When would they do it?"

Rae caught Feen's arm and pulled her outside on the porch.

"Dunno. Cain't figure it out. The only time he eat sometin' dat I don't cook is at yo house or at church the other day at the supper."

"Ya, but nobody else sick at ma house, so it cain't be from ma house."

"Yeah, I know dat, and it cain't be from the church, cuz nobody else got sick," she said, shaking her head. "I dunno where he coulda got it from. But I tell ya, the med'cine high. I could only git a lil bit. Took all the money I had. If dat don't work, I dunno what to do."

"I kin ax Luke, but I know we ain't got no extra money."

"Okay," she said.

"How he doin'?"

"He cain't eat nothin' or drink nothin'. He cain't git nothin' down his throat."

Feen's hand flew up to her mouth. "Po baby. Lawd, ham mercy. Let's pray."

They stood on the porch holding hands and fervently praying for Toyotae. "We need a miracle, Lawd," prayed Rae. "ta save ma boy."

When Luke got home, she told him what had happened to Toyotae, and they needed money to buy med'cine. They agreed to pinch in what they could, but it wasn't enough.

The next day at work, she told Mrs. Frank about the situation and she suggested Feen talk to Dr. Frank. Up until then, Dr. Frank and Feen hadn't had any long conversations. It was on a need to know basis between them, so she was a little uncomfortable discussing a private matter with him. But she took Mrs. Frank's advice and waited for an opportunity to talk to him. He happened to come home for lunch that day, and Feen seized the opportunity.

After she placed his soup and ham sandwich on the table in front of him, she said, "Dr. Frank?"

"Yes, Feen?"

"Kin I ax ya advice 'bout sometin'?"

"Depends on what kind of advice you need."

She went on to explain about her nephew. As she talked, it was evident how important this was to her and the deep connection she had with him. From the expression on the doctor's face, she could see he was listening to her and taking her concerns seriously.

He was silent for a second. "You know, a lot of poor kids die from lye poisoning."

"Yeah, I know."

"Look, tell your sister to bring him in tomorrow. I'll give him some medicine and she doesn't have to worry about paying me."

"Oh no, Doctor. I didn't mean dat. I'll pay ya. Ya kin take it out ma pay. I jus' be so tankful if he can git some med'cine."

"I understand. We're not gonna keep half your pay, though. Just bring me some fresh vegetables every now and then."

"Oh Doctor. Tank ya, sir. Tank ya very much. I'll tell ma sista ta bring Toyotae in ta see ya tomorra."

"One more thing," he said. "I don't want to get your hopes up. There are a lot of complications to the throat with lye poisoning. The medicine doesn't work all the time, because it treats the symptoms mostly."

Feen looked at him with her eyes wide, but did not answer.

"I just wanted you to know, I'll do the best I can. But my best may not be good enough," he said still holding her gaze.

She nodded. "I understan'."

As she walked out the kitchen, she turned and looked back at the doctor whose attention was now on eating his lunch. She shook her head in disbelief. She wouldn't have ever expected that from him. You just can never tell about people. About which ones will come through for you when you need them.

Rae brought Toy in to see Dr. Frank who verified the other doctor's diagnosis. He said that it was a severe case. The scarring in his throat was tremendous and he didn't know if the medicine would work. But he would give it to him, along with some pain medication.

They returned home and with the medicine and constant care from Rae, Feen and his siblings, Toyotae got better. They watched over him and made sure he ate very soft foods and drunk a little at a time. He started feeling better.

He didn't go to school, because they didn't want him to exert himself too much by walking that far. He wanted to go ring the bell at church, but Rae told him not to. Pulling such a large bell was strenuous and might be too much on his injured body, even if Charlotte helped him. Thus, he sat on his porch, read, fixed light meals for the family and walked over to Feen's house to socialize with Charlotte. When he didn't come over to visit her, Charlotte would walk over to call on him.

This went on until the fourth month after the diagnosis, then his throat closed again. Something he ate was too rough causing his throat to bleed and inflammation to set in. Dr. Frank made several house calls, but he didn't get better, because no food could get down his throat. It was hard for everyone to see him suffer. Rae was angry all the time and Mose was drunk.

Everyone in the family was there the night he passed on. They'd felt the time was nigh. Feen approached Rae and put her arm around her.

"Lawd, help him," Rae said.

Rae burst into tears and Feen took her in her arms.

"I see him wit'rin' away. But I don't want him ta die. Is dat selfish a me?" she asked.

She rubbed and patted her on the back as she cried. "No, dat's not selfish. Ya love ya boy and ya want him here witcha, s'all. I don't wanna see him go neither, Rae."

They released each other. Rae kneeled by his bed, held his hand, caressed his face, rubbed his forehead, and kissed him on the temple.

"Rest now, ma sweet boy." She turned her face up to heaven. "Lawd, heal him, but if you cain't, den usher him into the pearly gates. Watch over him. No mo suff'ring fur ma boy."

There wasn't a dry eye in the room. He passed away, peacefully, thirty minutes later. The world lost a sweet, gentle soul. No one really knew how and why it had happened.

They held a private service, because Rae could not stand to be around people, other than her family. She had a hard time being civil. She didn't want to hear condolences or anything like that. She had lost her baby boy and she'd watched him suffer. His siblings and Charlotte cried so much at the funeral, the preacher had to cut his sermon short.

When they closed the wooden box, Rae screamed, "Why? Lawd, we don't even know what happened ta him."

Feen held her sister tightly, but she did not answer her, because she had the same questions. Why? How?

~ CHAPTER 30 ~

Feen worked at Dr. Frank's up to her eighth month. It had been two months since Toy had died and she didn't know if she should ask Rae to be her midwife or if she should find somebody else, because Rae was in a deep depression.

She walked over to Rae's house and asked, "Rae, do ya want me ta git somebody else ta help me when the baby come?"

"Whatcha do dat fur?"

"Because I know ya grieving and I don't want ya ta take on nothin' ya not ready fur."

"Feen, I'm not doin' it fur nobody else, dat's true. But ya ma sista, and ya been there fur me and I'm gonna be there fur you, when dis precious soul come in ya life," she said as she patted Feen on the stomach.

"Tank ya Rae. Mean a lot ta me."

∞

Because of her age, Dr. Frank had cautioned her about the danger associated with have a baby at forty-two. She'd taken every precaution that she could. She had faith everything was going to be alright. Luke was home when she went into labor. The delivery went smoothly, just as she'd hoped it would.

Luke tiptoed in the room. He was anxious to see the new addition. When he picked her up, she squirmed, but went right back to sleep. He looked down on her and marveled at how splendid she was. "'We got 'nother pretty lil gull.'"

"Are ya disappointed it not a boy?"

"No way. I'm crazy 'bout her already."

"What we gonna call her?" he asked.

"Angela, we kin call her Angie, as a nickname. I 'member the night we made her. She a angel God sent down here ta bind us back together."

He nodded his head, still looking down at her. "Yeah, she is. She sho a lil angel. She look jus' like Laura."

"Yea, she do," said Feen.

Rae stood by with a smile on her face and said, "The Lawd took one sweet soul from dis fam'ly and he sent us 'nother one. I tink Angel is a good name to call her."

From then on that's what Rae called her. Angel. Everyone else called her Angie or Angela, but Rae called her Angel.

∞

When Angie was about two months, Luke found a package on the porch wrapped up in bright shiny paper. The package was addressed to Angie. He thought about who could afford to send Angie a gift and took it inside to Feen. She looked at it and smiled.

"Ya bought a present fur Angie?" she said.

"No," he said. "I found it on the porch."

Her mouth opened wide and eyebrows moved up in surprise. Her heartbeat quickened.

"Take it outside," she said in a panicked voice.

"Okay. How come?" he asked.

"Cuz a lot a ugly stuff been poppin' up in the yard. I don' trust no package dat jus' show up on the porch."

She followed him to the backyard where he opened the package. Inside was a dead kitten.

Feen screamed. "Lawdy, ham mercy. I gotta talk ta Teresa. She need ta put a spell on the one doin' dis."

Luke didn't answer. He was looking at the writing on the box. He knew Clarice's writing. Two of the letters in Angie's name looked like Clarice's A and G. He'd known she was a possibility, but had deluded himself. He couldn't deceive himself anymore. It all added up. It had to be her.

He tore off a small portion of the shiny paper, the part with Angie's name on it and placed it in his pocket.

~ CHAPTER 31 ~

After work the next day, Feen walked to Teresa's house. The dolls and the dead animals had all the signs of somebody using hoodoo. She was tired of being scared. Someone hated her family and she didn't know why. With Angie in a blanket, she made her way to Teresa's house. When Teresa opened the door, she bolted inside.

"Teresa, I need ya help."

She explained about the things happening at her house, including the present addressed to Angie with a dead kitten in it. When she got to the dead kitten, Teresa's eyes opened wide. The same way she'd done when Feen had told her about the rag dolls with pins stuck through them.

"Feen, have ya been praying ever'night, like I tol' ya?"

"Yeah, I have."

"Have ya kept the mojo bag witchcha all the time?"

"Yeah, I have. When the old one fell ta pieces, I cut a piece of grass sack and made me 'nother one and put the stuff in it," she said.

Teresa nodded her head. "Good. Den ya protected. Nothin' gonna happen ta ya or ya fam'ly. Ya safe."

"Do ya know if someone might a ax ya momma ta put a spell on me?" she asked.

144

Teresa frowned, "Ya ax me dat before, when Charlawt was a baby, Feen and I tol' ya ma momma wouldn't do nothin' ta ya. She like ya."

Feen wandered if she had crossed the line.

"Yes, I did ax ya dat many years ago, probably twelve or thirteen years ago. I don't know what else ta do. I jus' wonder if someone had a complaint wit' me and mighta ax her 'bout puttin' a hex on me." Feen looked at her with pleading eyes. "All dis mess gotta stop. It gotta stop."

"There are tings ma momma wouldn't do, 'less it was a threat ta our fam'ly. Ya not a threat, ya ma best friend. Ma momma know dat and she love ya and she love ya momma when she was alive. She would never do nothin' ta hurt ya."

Feen acknowledged that by shaking her head. "I know ya right. I always like Taunt Clout and felt like she like me. So, I b'lieve ya." She paused a moment, then said in a stressed voice, "I dunno what ta do. I cain't let nothin' happen ta me or ma chirren."

"I dunno 'bout the other root doctors round here. I thought 'bout ma sista, Clarice, cuz she used ta watch ma momma a lot, but I don't think she would do nothin' ta hurt ya, either. She wouldn't do sometin' like dat fur no reason."

"No. Ya sista wouldn't do dat. Well, can ya put a hex on the one dat doin' dis ta me?"

"Whatcha mean?"

"Do a spell dat make dem sick or sometin' dat would stop dem from comin' round ma house. Make dem break a leg or sometin'. I don't care, but they need ta stop hurtin' animals and stop scarin' me. They need ta feel what I'm feelin'," she said.

"Uh uh, no," she said, emphatically. "I don't do dat. I tol' ya. I only do things ta help people. I don't hurt nobody. If ya sick and ya need some med'cine, I can help ya with dat. Listen ta me, Feen. Prayers and the mojo bag will protect ya."

Feen started to cry. She had reached her limit. If Teresa didn't help, she had no recourse. A feeling of total helplessness engulfed her.

"Well, I 'member one time, ya didn't help somebody," she said.

A frown came across Teresa's face. "When was dat, Feen?"

"The night Emile died. Ya pray fur God ta move the stumblin' block and it was moved. And Emile died."

Teresa's head jerked back, her eyes and mouth opened wide. She stared at Feen, stood up and walked to a window.

"I cain't b'lieve ya say dat. I did no such tin'," she said. "No such tin. Ya tink I pray fur Emile ta die? No matter what he done ta me, I would never pray fur him ta die. Dat was ma husband, ma chirren father. I couldn't live wit' myself if I done dat. Dat why I didn't cry much. I know God know what bes'. Emile ain't done right by me. Runnin' round here fornicatin' wit dat woman and drinkin' and not takin' care a his fam'ly."

She walked back to Feen and pointed her finger at her.

"Gawd was in the lightnin'." She looked passed Feen toward the kitchen. "Dat's what ya been thinkin' all these years? Afta all these years, ya dunno me. Of all the people. I thought ya know me better'n dat."

Feen didn't know what to say. She felt bad. She hadn't wanted to hurt Teresa, but she could see she had. She hadn't known what else to do. Angie, who'd been asleep in her arms, begin to squirm.

"I'm sorry, Teresa. I dunno what I was thinkin'. Jus' beside myself worryin'. S'all. I know ya don't hurt nobody. I just assume ya might know how ta fix it."

She could have told her that her mother had insinuated there was something supernatural involved in Emile's death, and that she was responsible for it. That she'd guided the lightning to Emile, and had scared everybody, including Luke, who didn't believe in hoodoo, half to death. But, she decided to leave it alone and not upset her any more than she already was.

"Gimme dat baby," she said with her arms extended. "Let me hol' her." Feen handed Angie to her and she looked at Angie and cooed for a minute, then back at Feen. "Ya gotta b'lieve. When ya pray, ya gotta b'lieve. Ya gotta b'lieve dat ever'tin' gonna be alright."

She paused. "Ya hear what I say. It's not gonna work if ya don't b'lieve. Ya gotta b'lieve. Ya got the power ta keep ya family safe, if ya b'lieve," she said. "Keep ya mojo bag close ta ya, keep on prayin' and keep on b'lievin'."

~ CHAPTER 32 ~

A rice farmer named Nichols asked for workers and Luke jumped at the chance to make some money. He'd worked two weeks for him. The first week, he'd gotten cash money, but the second week, he'd gotten a twenty-pound sack of rice. He'd worked hard all week and felt like going straight home, but, he'd promised Clarice he'd go by before going home.

"Hey Luke," she said, as he entered the cabin.

"He said. "Come sit down by me. I need ta talk ta ya 'bout sometin'."

She walked over to the bed, sat, crossed her legs and looked at him with a small smile on her lips. He pulled the scrape of shiny paper from his pants pocket. She saw the paper, sat up straight for a second, then relaxed and returned to her former posture.

"Ya know what this is, don't ya?" he asked.

"No," she said. "I don't."

"Yeah, ya do. I saw ya face when I pulled it from ma pocket. Where did ya git the cat?"

"I'm telling ya, I dunno whatcha talkin' 'bout."

He got up to leave. She jumped in front of him.

"Where ya goin'?"

"I want some answers. I want the truth. If ya don't tell me the truth, I'm goin' home."

She closed her eyes tight, and shook her head.

"Whatcha wanna know?"

"Why in the world would ya send a dead cat ta ma house?"

"I didn't mean no harm. I jus' wanted ta scare her."

"It don't make sense. Scaring her is not gonna make me leave her and it's not gonna make her leave me. You the one dat been leavin' rag dolls with a stick pin through the heart, too? Is dat s'pose ta scare her, too?"

She started to cry, "Yes."

"Look, I tink we need ta end dis. Ya need ta fin' yaself a single man. I cain't leave ma wife, even if I wanna. And git it straight, I don't wanna."

She'd been whimpering with her hands over her mouth. Now she broke into a wail. "Ya cain't leave me, Luke. Ya jus' cain't. Afta all these years? I know ya love me. Ya wouldn't have come here all these years if you didn't love me."

"I do care 'bout ya, Clarice. And it's not fair ta ya not ta have a husband. I'm cheatin' ya outta ya life. If ya goin' round puttin' dead cats in boxes and wrappin' it with pretty paper and puttin' it on somebody porch, don't matter who t'is, sometin' wrong wit' dat. Us being together jus' not right. And I needs ta let ya find a life."

"I don't have a life without ya, Luke. Don't ya know dat?"

"Stop tellin' yaself dat. Ya have a momma, a sista, whole lot of aunts, uncles and cousins. Ya kin cook good. Ya kin sew. Ya pretty. Ya kin have a life without me, Clarice."

"Luke, ya cain't be the man ya wanna be wit' Feen." She shook her head. "All I done fur ya, and ya treat me like dis."

"Stop it, Clarice," he said in a loud voice.

"'Member how we used ta lay across the bed and talk. Ya told me how ya wanna leave Marksville. How ya tied a workin' ya hand ta the bone with crops dat depend on the weather. Ya gotta work ya own field, and afta ya done pick all the cotton outta ya field, ya gotta find work in some white man field. Then someone else's rice field, or potato field, or handyman the rest a the time. Always searchin' fur the next piece of hard work somewhere. Always tryna beat hard time."

"Course, I 'member dat. What dat gotta do wit' dis?"

"I 'member ya tellin' me the main reason ya didn't want ta marry Feen, cuz she wouldn't leave Marksville. Luke, I'll go witcha. We can leave from here. Ya kin have a diff'ent life wit' me," she pleaded. "Luke, you kin have a life like ya want wit' me."

"I ain't gonna leave ma wife and chirren. I know it'll be hard at first. But I know ya kin do it. Ya got fam'ly ta help ya. Dis the las' time I'm comin' here. Ya gotta leave ma fam'ly be. Let us be."

He walked over and sat on the bed beside her and touched her on the shoulder. "Dis not jus' fur me and ma fam'ly, it fur you, too," he said. "Dis is what best fur ya. Ya kin git yaself a single man, a man who kin marry ya and have a fam'ly."

She shook her head and said, "No. No." She decided to try a different approach. "Luke, lay down wit' me one las' time," she said in a seductive voice. "Gimme sometin' ta 'member ya by."

She was attempting to be seductive, but all he saw was that dead kitten in a box. He didn't tell her that. They'd been together too long for him to hurt her if he didn't have to. But it was hard for him to look at her without anger and disgust. He'd started for the door when she ran into the kitchen and grabbed a knife.

"Luke?" she hollered.

He turned and saw the knife she held in the air aimed at her own body. "Clarice. Clarice, don't," he said.

"If ya leave me, I'll kill maself," she said. "Ya dunno all I done ta keep ya here wit' me."

Luke wasn't sure what she meant by that, but at the time he was concentrating on the knife in her hand.

"Be careful wit' dat knife. I don't wantcha ta hurt yaself," he said.

"I got no life unless ya wit' me. None."

He walked toward her with his hands up. Her eyes were wild and her hands trembled. For the first time since he'd known her, he was afraid. She'd shown herself to be unpredictable and could hurt herself, him or his family. It would have been easy for him to let her kill herself right there. But he would not have been able to live with himself, afterward. He had, after all, used her to salve his own ego for years.

"Okay, Clarice," he said. "Don't send nothin' else ta ma house. No ragdolls, dead animal, presents, nothin'. I come by two days from now and we'll talk 'bout what we can do. Okay?"

She still had a wild look in her eyes and held the knife in the air. "Dis ain't the las' time you gonna come here?" she asked.

"No," he said. "Dis not the las' time I come. I gotta work the next two days, but I'll be by afta dat. Now put the knife down."

He could tell she wasn't sure if she believed him. But she gradually put the knife down.

He said, "I gotta go now, but I'll be back like I say."

"Okay," she said. "Kiss me goodbye." Her eyes were questioning. She was testing him.

"Come here," he said, making sure she was not close to the knife. She walked over to him, and he kissed her on the lips long enough to satisfy her doubts about him coming back.

Once outside, he took a deep breath and walked by the tree where he had left the bag of rice and walked home. He contemplated what he was going to do. He was tired of living this double life, and he wanted his family safe from Clarice. He had no idea how he was going to accomplish that in two days. But he had to solve this problem once and for all.

~ CHAPTER 33 ~

In the rice field the next day, Mr. Nichols came by and told him the owner of Donay's store wanted to see him after work. Donay's store was where he'd been extended credit and who he paid once he got paid from work.

When Luke went by the store, he'd found out Mr. Nichols' check hadn't been good. Donay told Luke he would have to pay the money back or else go to jail. Luke explained he'd put in a week's work for that check and it wasn't his fault if it was not good. Donay said he didn't care whose check it was. He'd gotten the check from him and it was up to him to get the money from Mr. Nichols. But he needed his money back the next day, or else he would have to send the sheriff for him.

When he'd spoken to Mr. Nichols the next day, he'd hemmed and hawed and finally told him he didn't have the money right then. He could pay Luke in rice if he wanted that. Rice would have been fine any other time, but this time he needed the money.

The weight of the world was on Luke's shoulders as he made it home. A colored man giving a bad check to a business was a serious offense in Marksville. It was punishable by imprisonment. A colored man had gotten two years in Angola State Prison for writing bad checks.

How could he support his family in prison? Then, there was this problem with Clarice. How could he break up with her and keep his family safe from her hexes?

He remembered the things Clout had said at Emile's funeral. He didn't know if her family had the power she'd talked about that day, but if they had, he didn't want to take a chance. When he got close to home, his spirits fell, because he saw Adrian Fonteneau's father's car in front of his house. He enjoyed Adrian's company, but this really was a bad time for him to pay a visit. As he neared the house, he heard music playing from the radio. He looked through a window and Adrian, Feen and Charlotte were sitting in the front room listening to music. The scene seemed so serene, he hated to break it up.

"Hey Man," Luke said as he came through the kitchen.

Adrian jumped up and shook hands with him. "Hey Man, I heard you been putting in long hours in the rice field."

Luke nodded his head. "Yeah, I have."

Feen went to the kitchen and fixed Luke a plate. As Luke sat down to eat, Adrian said, "Look Man, I have a month off. I'm not sure if I'm staying in Marksville the whole time, though. But I'll be here at least a week, so whatever you need help with, I'll be glad to help you."

"Sure Man, okay," he said.

"I know you're tired and want to go to bed, so we can talk later." Luke jumped up to walk him out. Adrian said, "Eat your supper, Man. I can find my way to the door."

After Adrian left, Feen sat at the table with him, while he ate. She could tell something was bothering him. He explained the problem at the store. He wanted her to know, in case Donay brought it up next time she was in the store.

Thoughtfully, she said, "Ya mean he won't wait 'til ya can git the money. Maybe I can sell some eggs and do some laundry on Sadday agin 'til we raise the money."

"No, he want his money now," he said. He reached over, took one of her hands in his, brought it to his lips and kissed it. "These here hands don't need ta be in no hot water wit' no lye soap. Ya did it fur years and I was glad when ya stop. Don't start it up no more."

She smiled at him. "Alright, I won't. We figure sometin' else out."

Later, in bed, he thought about what Clarice had said about leaving town and starting over somewhere. Somewhere without cotton fields, rice fields and potato patches. The life he'd dreamed about, long ago.

He asked her, "Do ya ever tink 'bout leavin' dis place, Marksville, I mean?"

"No, not really. Dis ma home? Why ya axin'."

"Well, dat would be one way we could handle Donay and the problem with' the dolls and dead animals. Jus' pack up and leave."

She laughed, softly. "How we gonna do dat, Luke? Dis our home. Ma sister here. Ma church here. What we gonna do with the chickens, the cow, the horse, all our stuff and the land my momma left us?"

"Those jus' tins, Feen. Don't you ever git tied comin' from work when the crop's ready and goin' in the field 'til night? There gotta be sometin' better. Maybe, we could find dat up north."

"Ooh, dat sound so scary," she said. "Startin' out where we dunno nobody. I 'member ya talkin' like dis when we first got married. I thought ya furgot 'bout dat. We got chirren now."

"Yeah, we do," he said. Seeing he was getting nowhere, he decided to change the subject. "Whatcha talk 'bout wit' Adrian?"

"We talk 'bout how Charlawt doin' in school. Talk 'bout Laura's chirren. Dis time he was in Germany and he talk 'bout dat."

"So, he got a gull friend?"

"Yeah, he got one," she said. "But, ya kin ax him yaself tomorra."

"Um hmm," said Luke.

As he lay there, he wasn't sure what he'd ask Adrian tomorrow. A plan was forming in his head. They both went to sleep. He woke up early and watched her as she slept. He touched her face, reached for her

154

and pulled her to him. Without opening her eyes, she wrapped her arms around his neck and her legs around his body. He made love to her and tried to memorize every inch of her.

"What got inta ya dis fine mornin'? Ya know I gotta go ta work," she said while getting up. "Might as well git up now. By the time I git back ta sleep, it be time ta git up."

While she washed up to go to work and tended to the children, he went into the kitchen and made himself some coffee. He sat and watched her finish getting dressed. She looked at him, tilted her head to the side with a perplexed expression on her face. He got up and looked in on Charlotte and Angie, who were already dressed.

"Hey, Charlawt," he said. "Ya have a good day, ya hear?"

"Yes, Daddy." He walked over to her and hugged her tight.

"Ya take care of yaself," he said.

He walked to the door with her and watched her as she ran to meet her schoolmates to walk to school.

Feen sat on the porch to wait for her ride to work. He took Angie out of her arms, kissed her on the cheek and laid her in a chair. He pulled Feen to him and squeezed her tightly and said, "I love ya very much. Always."

She pulled away from him and looked him in his face, "Ya in a strange way dis mornin'. Stop worryin'. We'll work out sometin'. I know Donay all ma life. He not gonna put ya in jail."

His eyebrows shot up. "Ya may be right. I jus' felt like holding you. S'all. Sorry."

"Don't be sorry," she said. "I like it. Jus' not like ya ta be like dis in the mornin'."

He looked away.

"Ya still worried 'bout Mr. Nichols money? Don't worry 'bout it. We gonna figure sometin' out."

He nodded his head, still not meeting her eyes.

"Ya gonna go see him today. Are ya workin' there today?"

"Not sho. I gotta tink 'bout sometin' I need ta do," he said with his brow coming together.

"Okay," she said, "Love ya."

"Love ya, too."

After her ride came, and she'd gotten in the car, he stood in the middle of the road and watched it until it was out of sight. He went inside and packed. He didn't have much. His Sunday suit. Two pairs of coveralls. His Sunday shoes, underwear, socks, handkerchief and toiletries. He sat and wrote a note:

Dear Josephine,

I got to go. Mr. Nical owe me one week pay. Git it from him. He say he kin pay with rice. That's good. Mr. Donay not gonna put you in the pen like he would me. I be back. Don't no when. Don't worry bout me. I took care of the thing with the doll and the dead cat. That person not gonna bother yall no mo. Tell Laura Charlotte Angie I love them. I will be back, soons I git thing set up good. You my dove.

Luke

He walked outside and around to his backyard. He went to the barn and rubbed Star on the nose and patted Sophie on her back. She was an old girl now but had provided a lot of calves and milk. He looked at the chicken coop he'd built years ago. A leg on it was leaning and he hadn't had a chance to fix it. He sighed thinking it wouldn't get fixed now, at least not by him. He looked at the garden and pictured Feen planting her tomatoes and harvesting her okra from the vines. He wondered if he was making the right decision. His chest was hurting and he didn't want to leave his home and family.

He looked at the gray unpainted house they'd planned to fix up after her mother died. All he had a chance to do was replace rotten boards whenever one occurred. It'd been more critical to rebuild the barn almost entirely to keep the animals out of the rain, which they'd done. He'd planted a lot of himself here. A lot of his sweat had been poured into the grounds of this place and the fields by his house and across the road.

It was too much to bear.

He looked up to the heavens and said, "I don't see any other way." He was not a man who cried. In fact, he hadn't cried since he was a child when his mother died. His whole being seemed like it was being squeezed so he could not breathe. When he exhaled, tears flowed from his eyes and he bowed his head and wept.

Finally, he turned and walked out of the yard, down the road on the way to the river.

He'd left his wife and children. He wasn't sure he could ever make peace with that. But, this way, he would not go to jail and Clarice could not hurt Feen and his children. He could see she was on edge and when a person is on edge, they'll do anything. It was partly his fault and he felt responsible. He'd made love to her and used her for many years. Without meaning to, he'd lead her to believe they'd have a future together. Now, he was paying the price for his sin.

When he reached the cabin, Clarice was not there. She was at work. So, he slept. He had not slept well the night before and he needed his rest. He would be doing a lot of walking the next week.

She was surprised, but glad to see him when she came in. He told her he was going to New Orleans. It should take him about two months to get settled. Then he'd send for her. It was happening, he was leaving Feen and they could start their life together. She jumped up and down with glee. She ran and jump into his arms. Tears ran down her face.

"Tank ya, Luke," she said repeatedly. She buried her head in his chest.

He hugged her and said soothing words to her to calm her down.

When she got in the bed that night, she reached for him, but he pulled away.

"Not tonight," he said. "I gotta save my strength fur tomorra. I got a long way ta walk." He turned his back to her.

Feen had been home for a while now, and he sensed her pain when she'd read the note. He wished he could erase her hurt. He was so sad and lonely, he wanted to cry again. Somehow, one day he'd make it back to her, and he hoped she'd understand and forgive him. Until then, this was his life.

~ CHAPTER 34 ~

Coming in from work, Feen went directly to her bedroom and placed Angie in the bureau drawer that had been prepared as a bassinet.

She noticed the note on her bed. It was in Luke's handwriting, and she wondered what he'd be writing a note about. With a scowl on her face, she picked it up and read it. It didn't make sense. She reread it again and again. Staring at the note, her mouth flew open, her fingers involuntarily opened and it dropped from her hands.

She stood shaking her head from side to side in disbelief. Walking slowly to the mirror, she saw her reflection staring back at her. Putting her shaking hand to her face, she couldn't believe this was her face, because she didn't feel it. This must be a dream. The shaky feeling continued and the reality was overwhelming. She needed some release or else bits of her would fly all over the room as she exploded. She opened her mouth and a loud guttural sound came out. It went on and on until she was out of breath and had to take a huge gulping sound that a drowning person makes when they've been revived. Her legs were too weak to hold her up and she fell to her knees still screaming.

"Oh Gawd," she screamed. "Oh Gawd. No, not Luke."

With her throat became sore and her body was exhausted, she crawled back to the bed, pulled herself up on it, laid on her back and stared at the ceiling.

Charlotte came home from school and walked directly to the stove. Her mother usually had a snack there for her to eat before supper. When she found nothing, she walked into her mother's bedroom and found her in what looked like a trance.

"Mom, Mom, What's wrong?" Charlotte said.

Hearing her daughter's voice served to jolt her back to reality, and she tried to pull herself together. She didn't want to scare her. She couldn't explain to her what she didn't understand herself yet. Surely, Luke was playing a joke on her. Surely, he would step out from somewhere and tell her this was a joke. A man doesn't walk out on his wife and kids. Certainly, not a man like Luke. A man who'd always honored his obligations. Besides, they'd been very loving lately. If he'd written this note two or three years ago, she might have understood it better. Not now. Not when they were so happy.

"Nothin', Charlawt. I guess I had a hard day today, S'all." Until she could understand this herself, she wasn't going to tell Charlotte anything.

She fixed supper and she kept watching the door. But no one came in. She kept her spirits up because no matter how she felt, she still had to be a mother and take care of these precious gifts the Lord had given her. She thought about their conversation in the bed the night before when he was asking her questions about leaving town. At the time, she'd no idea he was serious. She would've answered differently or explained her point of view more clearly if she'd known he was serious. This also explained his behavior that morning. What she'd thought was so sweet was him saying goodbye.

In his note, he'd said he would be back. She'd hold onto his promise.

A knock at the door. Adrian. She'd forgotten all about Adrian. Charlotte ran to the door.

"Adrian, Mom's upset about something."

"Oh?" he said. She heard him walk into the kitchen, and she rushed out of her bedroom.

In a bright voice, she said. "I ain't fix nothin', but I got some leftover soup and I kin cut up some tomatoes and cucumbers from ma garden fur a salad."

"Yes, indeed. Sounds good to me. Char said you were upset. What's wrong?"

She shook her head. "I'm alright," she said as she looked at him and tilted her head toward Charlotte. He got the message. They'd talk later.

After supper and after Charlotte was in bed, Adrian asked, "Okay, now you can tell me what's wrong and where's Luke? I came by here and went to the rice field he'd been working at, and he wasn't either place."

Feen couldn't hold it any longer. She started to cry. She walked to her bedroom and got the note.

Adrian read silently. His face and eyes telegraphed his horror and surprise.

"Is this a joke?" Adrian said. "Y'all trying to play a trick on me or something?"

"If it be a joke, I ain't in on it," she said.

He just shook his head back and forth for a minute. "I don't believe this," he said.

"Me neither. I jus' don't b'lieve it," she said.

"Have y'all been havin' problems?" he asked.

She told him about the problem at the store. That was the only problem she knew about.

"What's he talking about when he said for you not to worry about the dolls and the dead cat?"

"I been gittin' rag dolls with a needle stuck in dem reg'lar fur years. The other day, we got a dead cat wrapped up like a present fur Angie. I dunno where they come from, but he say he fix dat. I dunno how, 'less he fin' out who it is and maybe they don't live 'round here, so he gotta go there ta stop dem."

"Umm. Interesting," he said. "I remember one time you told me something about yall marriage slowing down or something. Did something else happen?"

"Yeah, I 'member talkin' 'bout it. But, No. We so close now, cain't git a pin 'tween us. I love him, Adrian, and I know he love me" she said looking down. "It make no sense ta me. No sense at'all. We always face our problem together. I don't understand why he leave me with two chirren ta raise by maself."

Adrian said, "Well, I don't know what's going on, but he says he'll be back. I believe him. I want you to know I'll help any way I can. I'm in the Army, so I don't make much money, but if you get in a fix, let me know, and I'll do what I can."

Feen looked at him with wonder and gratitude. "I cain't do dat. Don't worry, we'll make out."

"Listen to me. I mean what I say. Write to me, call me. Do whatever you got to do to let me know if you need something. Like I told you a long time ago, you can lean on me. I meant it then, and I mean it now." He put his arms around her and stroked her back until the tears subsided.

"Tank ya, Adrian." She nodded her head. "I sho 'member when ya say dat. On dat awful day. And here ya are agin today. Ya seem ta show up when I need ya."

Their eyes locked as their hands clenched together.

After he left, she crawled in her bed and drew up into a fetal position and cried. She wanted to scream, but she couldn't. She had sleeping children in the house. Tomorrow, she'd have to put on a brave face and continue, but tonight, all the hurt and disappointment caused many tears to flow. She could not envision a life without Luke. She cried her heart out and prayed for him to come back. He had to come back.

∞

During the next weeks, Adrian helped Feen retrieve the rice for the week's pay Luke was owed. She told everyone at church she was selling rice at a lower price than the store and several people bought some, and she paid Donay a large part of what was owed and agreed to pay him small amounts, weekly, when she got paid from her job. He was fully paid in two months.

~ CHAPTER 35 ~

Life without Luke was hard. In the beginning, it was like he was just away at work and he'd be back home at supper or when she was in bed. But as the weeks and months went by, it slowly sunk in that he was gone and she didn't know when he'd be back. She maintained the animals and worked. Mose, Rae and their children helped with the planting and harvesting of her share of the inherited land.

One of the hardest parts had been explaining it to Charlotte. Charlotte, who loved and adored him so.

"What?" she said with her eyes big.

"Ya daddy gone fur a while. He gonna be back, though."

"He's gone? But he never told me he was going anywhere. And he never said bye. He wouldn't leave and not say bye."

"Well, he did dis time."

"Momma," she said as tears flowed down her face.

Feen took her in her arms and powerful body wrenching tears poured from them both. Finally, Feen knew if they were going to survive this, she'd have to set a good example for Charlotte on how to handle a devastating disappointment like this.

She pulled herself together, pushed Charlotte away from her and looked in her eyes and said, "We gonna be fine 'til he come back. He want us ta keep ever'tin' goin' 'til he come back."

She brought her back into the folds of her arms and held her. Thankfully, Angie was a baby and she didn't have to explain to her.

All their friends, family and the community had such high regard for Luke. They couldn't quite understand what had happened. She told them he had business to "tend" and he'd be back. She didn't offer any further explanation.

In the beginning, they'd asked about him, would he be back for a certain event, but as time passed, everyone stopped asking. The neighborhood was alive with speculation for a while, but things settled down. Like any small town, different stories popped up about where he was or what had happened to him, but when new things popped up, they pushed this situation to the back burner. Any rumor that showed Luke in an unfavorable light never reached Feen's ear. No one wanted to hurt her any more than she was already.

∞

She was in her barn, feeding the animals when Rae walked swiftly toward her. She'd come to tell her their pastor had been found dead that morning. This man had been their pastor all Feen's life. He'd christened, baptized and married her. He'd been her spiritual father.

Life seemed to be continually changing for Feen in significant ways. Almost too much to handle. Toyotae, Luke, now the pastor. This wouldn't be so hard if Luke were here.

The whole congregation took it hard. He'd been a popular pastor. They covered the pulpit and his chair with sheets dyed black.

Visiting preachers came for six months to preach Sunday service before an official search was launched for a new pastor. Feen was not concerned about it and paid little attention to it. She was consumed with

Luke and how she'd survive, financially and emotionally, until he returned.

∞

One Sunday, about a month into the search for a new pastor, she sat in a church meeting thinking about if she should get rid of Sophie and Star when she was jerked back to reality. The secretary was reading letters sent by preachers who were interested in becoming their pastor. Her eyes opened wide, and her heart jumped in her throat because Wickliffe's name was called. This couldn't be happening. As she looked around the church taking notice of how other people were considering this, hers and Julia's eyes met. Julia's eyes were fixed directly on Feen's face.

She put her head down and closed her eyes. Julia held a lot of power in the church. She was one of the more substantial and more consistent tithers, a Sunday School teacher and an officer in most of the church auxiliaries. If she wanted her son to be the pastor, he probably would be. Feen shook her head, then raised her hand.

"Do you have a question?" asked the secretary, pointing to Feen.

"How many preachers we lookin' at?"

"Well, the committee has narrowed them down to three," she answered.

"When we gonna decide?"

"In two weeks."

Her mind was going in circles. She had two weeks to make sure he was not voted in as pastor, and she had no idea how she'd do it. Julia made a straight line to her after the meeting.

"I need to talk to you," she said.

"Ya don't need ta talk ta me," Feen said. "I already know whatcha gonna say. Ya gonna ax me ta furgive him. I already done dat. Dat don't mean I wanna sit in church and listen ta him on Sunday. Uh uh."

"He's a good pastor and he done changed. He could make this church grow. We lost a lot of members since Rev. Barron got old. He couldn't deliver a sermon like he used to. Now we have a chance to get some power back in the pulpit."

"Power," said Feen. "What 'bout righteousness. I want a save man in the pulpit. I wan' somebody who kin lead the church. How can he lead when he a loss soul hisself?"

"The Bible says to repent and be baptized and you shall be saved. He done that. He knows what he done to you was wrong. He ain't hurt nobody since."

"As far as ya know," Feen said.

"I'm gonna come by your house next Saturday. That will give me a chance to see my little nieces, and we'll talk."

"I done tol' ya. We don't need ta talk. I already know what ya gonna say."

"Let me come, Feen. It can't hurt to talk. I just want to talk."

"Okay. Fur you. But I'm not promisin' ya nothin'."

~ CHAPTER 36 ~

The smell of coffee brewing filled the house. A covered white frosted vanilla cake sat in the middle of the table, with shiny empty china saucers Feen had gotten from Mrs. Frank when she'd bought a new set of china for herself when several of her old set had gotten broken. Coffee cups sat on little saucers, cream was in the cream bowl and sugar was in the sugar bowl. Charlotte and Angie were both neatly dressed as Feen waited on Julia to come for her visit.

Julia arrived in her horse and buggy. Charlotte ran out the house to greet her, hugging her with enthusiasm. Julia reached down and eagerly embraced her back.

"Well, hello Char," she said, laughing.

"Hi, Taunt Julia," she said, giggling.

Feen stood on the porch holding one-year-old Angie. Watching them together gave Feen a twinge of remorse. It was apparent Julia loved Charlotte and Charlotte loved Julia, but they didn't know they were grandmother and granddaughter. At least Charlotte didn't. Was she being fair to them? No, she probably wasn't, but she didn't see any other alternatives.

"C'mon in."

Julia raised up from hugging Charlotte and her eyes met Feen's. "Hi Feen. Thank you for letting me come over."

"You welcome. And ya can come anytime I'm here. Jus' work and chirren keep me so busy nowadays."

Julia's eyebrows went up. She certainly had never been given an open invitation before. Julia doubted if she meant it. She climbed the steps and followed her into the house.

"I have something for you," Julia said as she pointed to Angie, "and one for you," as she pointed to Charlotte. Angie's little fat cheeks widened as she gave her a big smile.

She opened her bag and handed Charlotte a snow globe. The snow globe had a girl and boy dressed in bright colored wintery clothing, sitting on a sled, by a pine tree.

"Aww," said Charlotte with awe in her voice.

"You love to play with it when you come to my house and I wanted you to have it."

She gave Julia another big hug, "Thank you so much, Taunt Julia. I love it."

A red plastic bell rattle came out of the bag for Angie. She shook it and the little sound it made caused her to giggle.

Feen sat Angie down on a blanket on the floor. "Play wit' her, Charlawt. Me and Taunt Julia gotta talk fur a while."

Once situated with their coffee and cake, Feen asked, "Whatcha wanna talk 'bout?"

"I want to talk about getting a pastor for our church. We want someone who knows the Bible and can preach the gospel. That man is Wickliffe. Now, he says he doesn't want to come back if you're not okay with it. Frankly, I feel the same way. I know you've been going through a lot with your poor nephew getting sick and dying and Luke leaving and all."

Feen felt herself getting warm. She didn't want to talk about Luke or Toyotae. "What dat gotta do wit' Wickliffe?"

169

"Didn't mean to upset you. I'm just saying I know you're going through a lot right now. I'm telling you, he'll be good for the church. He's not going to bother you or Charlotte. I promise you that. He's married. Any action he has with her will be the same as any other church child."

Feen said, "Are ya sho?"

"Yeah, I'm sure. I know things are hard for you right now, but if you like I'd like to pitch in and help."

"Help how?"

"Well, I know with Luke gone, you don't have anybody to keep the children if you want to go to prayer meeting or quilting or anything. I know you need a break, sometimes. I've always wanted to be here for you, but you wouldn't let me."

Feen sat quietly as she spoke.

"If Charlotte ever need a dress or anything and you don't have the money, you know you can come to me."

Feen closed her eyes. She understood what she was offering, but she had vowed never to take anything from or be beholding to Wickliffe's people in any way. But with Luke gone, she might have to accept help from them sometimes, at least until Luke came back.

"Let me tink 'bout what ya say," she answered. "I'll let ya know how I feel 'bout him being ma pastor in two days at the next usher board meetin'."

"Alright," said Julia feeling very hopeful.

"Would ya like some mo cake and coffee?"

Julia smiled, "Yes, I would."

"Charlawt," said Feen. "Bring Angie up here and y'all can have a piece of cake."

Feen held Angie and fed her some cake and Charlotte sat next to Julia. They sat around the table and talked. Julia had given Feen a lot to think about. Seeing how much Charlotte enjoyed Julia's company, she really couldn't see how she could deny either one, the chance to spend time with each other.

At the usher board meeting, Feen told Julia she wouldn't fight him becoming pastor, but she expected him to stay clear of her. She, also, said she could see Charlotte and Angie on a regular basis, if she agreed not to tell her about their true relationship.

~ CHAPTER 37 ~

November 1949

Wickliffe was unanimously elected pastor and Julia had been right. Under his leadership and with his fiery sermons, the church had grown to its former prominence and beyond. Churches in town and nearby areas invited him to preach revivals, anniversaries and other special occasions to draw members to their churches. The ever-present building fund was now in full gear to construct a bigger sanctuary. He'd kept his promise to never approach her about anything. If he needed to discuss church affairs with her, he did it through his mother.

She and Julia became very good friends. It's difficult not to like someone who she could see loved her daughter, and Feen could see the affection she had, not only for Charlotte, but for Angie as well. Besides, Feen had been a mama's girl, and she missed her mother, especially when she was having problems. Julia had been an older, wiser ear to talk to, not to solve her problems, but to listen and encourage.

Feen kept the sharecropping agreement Luke had with a white landowner to farm an additional twenty acres of land. Mose, her nieces and nephews helped her. During cotton picking season, she worked in the fields after work and on Saturdays, but Rae's family did the lion's share of the work.

Although they continued living together, Mose and Rae's relationship remained rocky. His drunken binges lessened, but they still happened, and when they happened, they customarily ended in a physical altercation.

One day when Mose was repairing a fence in Feen's yard that had been blown down by a wind storm, she took the opportunity to talk to him about his drinking. She brought him a cool drink of water.

"Tank ya so much, Mose," said Feen. "It means a lot ta me fur ya ta come fix ma fence."

"I don't min' doin' dis fur ya."

"Ya don't seem ta be drinkin' as much as ya use ta."

He nodded his head. "Well, I learnt ta not pay 'tention ta ya sista when she carryin' on 'bout sometin.'"

"Ya don't pay her no 'tention?"

"Dat's right. Why ya surprise?"

"Cuz I 'member a time, when ya paid her plenty 'tention," Feen said, as she chuckled.

"Yeah, I did. She was so lil and pretty."

Silence. Feen said, "She still pretty and she not fat, she big boned and solid."

"Yeah, but she's tall as me and she fuss all the time," he said.

"Well, Mose," Feen said. "Ya mean ya didn't know a twelve-year-old chile might git bigger. Dat she probably would git bigger. Ya mean ya didn't know dat?"

Mose's eyes got big. He could see that he struck a nerve.

"Calm down. I didn't mean no harm. I jus' meant I like small gulls, dat's all."

"Well, you the one snuck her out ta the woods and got her in the fam'ly way. If ya desire was ta have a lil wife, ya shoulda been chasin' afta a twenty-year-old lil lady, den ya woulda know how tall she be. Rae still had some growin' ta do. Ya shoulda knowed dat. So, make peace wit' it."

"I did. But she fusses all the time."

"And as fur as her fussing go, if ya stop gittin' drunk, she'll stop fussing. Ya kin do it. Ya cut down a lot. Ya kin stop altogether if ya set ya mind ta it."

He shook his head in agreement, but she didn't believe he would stop, although she prayed that he would. For everyone's sake.

∞

Several years the crops didn't produce a profit. One year was because of a hurricane, another boll weevils, another not enough fertilizer. To be able to pay for the gas and supplies bought on credit, she ended up selling her inherited land. All except the home site and the barns.

Adrian called and visited on a regular basis. When he'd come, they'd spend hours and hours together talking and laughing. Her spirits would rise as soon as she knew he was either coming or he was already there. At those times, she felt young and carefree. The girls loved it when he came. To them, it seemed like Feen was his queen and the girls were his princesses. Some in the town assumed they might or should be lovers, but they'd both been careful never to cross that boundary. As far as Feen was concerned, she was still married to Luke.

She developed a routine of going to church, taking care of her children and property and going to work. At night, she dreamed of Luke's return.

Because of Julia's influence, when Charlotte graduated from high school, she wanted to go to college and become a teacher. She admired the love and respect the students had for Julia. She hoped to contribute as much. Julia had gone to Leland College, in Baker, Louisiana, to get her teaching degree, and she wanted Charlotte to go there, also. But, Charlotte disappointed her and went in the opposite direction, to

Grambling College in Grambling, Louisiana, because that's where several of her friends went.

It was a financial struggle, but between Julia, Adrian, and Feen, they put enough money together to pay her tuition and transportation. Charlotte worked in the lunchroom for her meals and other miscellaneous expenses.

Angie continued to grow and blossom and Feen had sustained her living arrangements and was able to afford a phone, so that Charlotte could call her from college if she needed to. When she received her degree, she was fortunate enough to get a job in town at Marksville Colored High School.

Feen was an elementary school dropout and here she was with a daughter who'd finished college and was an elementary school teacher.

~ CHAPTER 38 ~

August 1960

Concern for Charlotte was uppermost in Feen's mind when Keykey, a dear childhood friend of Charlotte's died after a long illness with cancer. Feen, now fifty-four years old, was also concerned about Blain, Keykey's husband and Lil Rae, Keykey's young daughter. She identified with him. Her husband hadn't died, but he was gone just the same. She'd had to learn how to survive without him.

About two weeks after the funeral, she rode over in Charlotte's car to Blain's. His eyes opened in surprise when he answered the door. He was puzzled to see her.

"Blain," she said. "I'm not gonna stay. I jus' came by ta drop off some food. Jus' some beans and rice with a lil fat back in it. Should be 'nuf fur today and tomorra. And a sweet tater pie fur dessert."

His face was solemn, but after listening for a minute, he smiled. He didn't know what to say. He'd never had a conversation with her before. He only knew her as an older lady in the church and his wife's best friend's mother.

"Oh," he said, after realizing they both were standing on the porch looking at each other. "Come in. Please. Let me take this out your

176

hand." She handed him the pot and bought the pie inside herself and laid it on the table.

Lil Rae was sitting at the table swinging her legs. "How you do, Miss Feen," she said with her eyes big.

"I'm fine, Baby" said Feen. "Gotcha some fresh food fur supper."

She smiled and looked at her Daddy, "Can I have some pie now, Daddy?"

He looked at Feen. "You think it's alright for her to have some now. Keykey always took care of that." He got a vacant faraway look. "I know she misses her mama, so I guess I've been givin' in."

Feen said, "Sho, ya kin have some now. But, the best time ta have dessert is afta ya eat. But today, ya kin have somma dis pie right now, if ya wanna."

Feen walked around the small kitchen opening drawers until she found a knife. Blain took a seat, seemingly relieved she was handling the situation.

She looked over at him and asked, "Do ya want some, too?"

He nodded his head, "Yes, please." After Feen gave the piece to Lil Rae, she said, "Say tank ya."

"Thank ya, Miss Feen." They both said, which tickled her.

She looked around the kitchen some more until she found something she could transfer her beans and rice into. They both told her how good the pie was.

"Well, do y'all like mustard greens and cornbread," she asked.

"Yeah, we do," Blain said.

"Well, I'll bring y'all some next Sadday."

"Thank you, ma'am. I appreciate it, but you don't need to do that. Me and Lil Rae can make it on our own."

Feen was surprised by his answer. "I never said ya couldn't make it on ya own. Never said dat a'tall. But dat chile need mo than bologna sandwiches."

His eyes opened wide in surprise. Her eyes had taken in the bread and lunch meat slices.

His tone softened. "Didn't mean no harm, ma'am. I just don't want nobody feeling sorry for me."

"I jus' wanna give ya a chance ta git on ya feet. I know it's hard losing the one who took care of ever'tin.' I mean the cookin' and all. So, I will be by next Sadday, if it's alright witcha."

"Yes, ma'am. That'll be fine with me."

He watched her leave. He'd seen her doing things around the church, but he'd had no idea she could take control like that. He looked at her retreating back with new found respect.

Gradually, a routine fell into place. On Saturdays, she'd cook an extra pot of whatever she was having for Blain. Sometimes, she took twelve-year-old Angie with her and sometimes, she didn't. Sometimes, she stayed and talked awhile and sometimes she didn't.

She could see he was depressed, so on the days Angie came, she'd talk to Blain about doing things in a way he didn't miss Keykey so much, while Angie kept Lil Rae entertained. She helped him change his bedroom around and paint the walls a different color, so when he walked into it, it looked like a different place. They all began to look forward to those Saturday visits.

∞

Charlotte hadn't been herself since Keykey passed. One Saturday morning, a little over a year after Keykey died, Adrian paid a visit, and again Feen's world changed. Charlotte had become pregnant by a married man and to save her job and reputation, she and Adrian had gotten married.

This whole thing blindsided Feen. She never saw it coming. Adrian, her rock, her friend now was her son-in-law. He wasn't her best friend anymore. Charlotte was now his best friend. Even though she worried for them, a mother sacrifices for her child and in this Feen took a back

178

seat without complaint, although she was concerned about them hurting each other. If one fell in love with the other and the other did not reciprocate, then the one that loved would be hurt.

Feen buried herself in other activities. The one bright spot she'd always counted on to have an uplifting effect, was no longer going to be there. Even if Adrian and Charlotte's marriage didn't work out, she and Adrian could no longer have the relationship they'd had before. Thus, she buried herself in taking care of Angie and her church work, when she wasn't at work at Dr. Frank's.

On her days off, she concentrated on making life meaningful again for Blain and Lil Rae. It typically was with food. She tried different recipes on them, and she loved to see their faces when she was successful. He had come to depend on it and started giving her money to buy the groceries for his meals.

Blain now called her Feen, instead of Miss Feen. Mostly, she stayed for a visit until early evening. They all sat together, listened to the radio and sometimes he read the Bible to them. It was a lovely tranquil setting, and it was her hideaway.

She felt safe, because even though her husband had been gone for many years, she was still married and he'd never made any advances toward her. Even though she knew he found her attractive, because she'd caught him looking at her in a complimentary way. A few times he voiced those sentiments about something she'd worn. It was done in a respectful manner and helped her self-esteem. She knew that Blain was handsome enough to have his choice of the young women in town.

She was very careful not to illicit gossip by staying too late in the evening, and she only went on Saturdays. As far as she knew, the gossip mongers had not made a point of targeting her, and she meant to keep it that way.

∞

Laura's husband Rick had been very abusive to her, and when she left him, he drove from Port Arthur to pick her up and bring her home. Feen tried to intervene and was shot. She'd been transported to the hospital and had undergone surgery. Everyone had been worried about her, especially, Blain who visited her twice.

Her relationship with Blain came up for discussion one day when she was visiting Charlotte and Adrian. Charlotte wanted her mother to know it was scandalous for her to still be bringing food to Blain, two years after his wife had died. It infuriated Feen, that Charlotte all snug and happy being married to Adrian, would want to deny her the pleasure of companionship. Their relationship was platonic. It wasn't Charlotte's concern. She felt warm and protected with Blain. If he needed her, she would be there for him.

When he decided to go courting, he could do so with her blessings. She didn't have any problems with that.

Then one day out of no where, her dreams came true. Charlotte called and told her she knew where Luke was. At first, she didn't believe it. Could it be? Could fourteen years of suffering be over? No more wondering where he was. She would have someone to talk through problems with. No more loneliness. But there was something in her voice that said everything was not fine and dandy. She calmed herself to listen to the details of this miraculous discovery. Rae thought she'd seen Luke in New Orleans. Charlotte and Adrian had gone immediately and yes, it was true. It was him. Luke was alive and living in New Orleans and he had not been living alone.

~ CHAPTER 39 ~

In New Orleans, Luke was apprehensive when he'd gotten off work from his job as an orderly at Charity Hospital. The last few days had been emotion-filled time for him. First, he'd seen Rae, who'd been at the hospital for a check-up. The very next day, Adrian and Charlotte had shown up. He knew Feen, Laurie and Angie would be next, he just didn't know when. It had been difficult explaining to them why he'd done what he'd done, because he couldn't tell them the truth. Clarice was still very fragile and it's no telling what she'd do.

Sure enough, he heard another familiar voice. Another voice, he hadn't heard in fourteen years, but one that he'd have known anywhere.

"Is it really you, Luke?" she asked.

He turned and looked at her in the light of the sunset. His eyes scanned her face. She was older, but time had treated her well. She was still beautiful and he stopped breathing for a second.

"Feen," he said. "Feen."

"Luke?" she said. "I kin see it you. But I cain't believe it. Not afta all these years. No letter, no call. All dem years I wait fur ya ta come back."

He put his head down. He couldn't look at her in her eyes. "Did Charlawt talk ta ya? Did Charlawt 'splain ta ya?"

"Splain ta me. Splain ta me?" she repeated, loudly and incredulously. "How kin ya 'splain sometin' dat got no way ta 'splain it."

She dashed to him and started beating him in the chest. "How kin ya 'splain it?" she asked, now crying.

He stood there and let her pound on his chest. Even though it hurt him, he believed he deserved it.

Laura walked up behind her and held her. Feen's head fell and Laura turned her around and continued to hold her. She'd tried to give them some time alone. But she saw her mother's anger was more than she could handle. Laura whispered to her, while Luke stood watching, helpless.

"It's alright, Mom," she said. "We're here to find out what happened. But, no matter what happened, it's alright."

When Feen calmed down, Laura glared at Luke, "Daddy," she said.

His eyes dimmed as he scrutinized her. He wanted to hug her, but was not sure if she wanted him to. Her eyes were big with concern.

"Laura, did I ever tell ya dat ya look like ma mama. You too, Angie. It really show now on bof y'all."

Angie stood wide-eyed and didn't answer. Unlike the rest of them, he was a stranger to her.

Laura nodded her head. "Yeah, Daddy, you used to tell me that all the time, before you left." The last part, "before you left," was emphasized. "Now, Mom tells us that all the time," she answered. "But, Daddy, why?"

"C'mon ta ma house. I'll try ta 'splain ta y'all like I did ta Adrian and Charlawt."

Feen said, "I don't wanna go ta ya house. Why would I wanna go there?" she asked, angrily. "I had ta sell some of the land, else I gonna lose it all. Did ya know dat?" she said.

Luke understood her anger.

"No, I didn't know ya had ta sell it. I'm sorry 'bout dat. I mean the house I'm living at." He paused and said in a pleading voice, "We's out here in the public. Folks gonna be comin' and going ta work. Let's bring our bidness inside. S'all I'm sayin'."

Feen took a deep breath, "Okay," she said. "Alright. Where ya house at?" she asked.

"Y'all follow me," he said.

As he was driving home, he thought about Feen not wanting to go to his house. He wished he had somewhere else to bring them. Last night had been exhausting with Clarice after Charlotte and Adrian left. He knew what kind of night it would be tonight after Feen and the girls left.

When he arrived at his home, Luke looked at his house and tried to look at it through Feen and Laura's eyes. What were they thinking? The house was small with old gray unpainted sides and a rusty tin roof with a porch with loose boards. He entered the house first and called out to Clarice. She didn't answer. He took a breath of relief and hoped she would stay hidden.

The house was dark as usual. Luke lit a candle on a small round table situated on the wall opposite from her sofa. He pointed to the beige, lumpy sofa for Feen and his daughters to sit. He sat in the straight back chair he'd sat in the night before.

Feen looked around the living room, and her eyes fell upon the identical picture of Huey P. Long that hung on the wall, which also hung on the wall at her house. She jumped in surprise and looked at Luke. He saw her reaction and knew she was thinking about when they'd acquired the picture on the wall at her house.

They'd been peering through a storefront window in Marksville, whose owner, Feen and her mother had once worked for. When he'd seen them, he'd brought the painting from the back of his store. He told them that a customer had returned it and it was damaged on two of the corners and had a slight scratch on Huey's face. He said he'd marked it down twice to sell it, but had been unsuccessful. He offered it to them as a wedding gift, and they'd accepted it. It had been their only wedding gift and they'd always said it brought them luck.

When he'd seen a duplicate of the picture in a flea market in the French Quarter, he'd bought it. He couldn't afford it, but he had to get it, and it had been a comfort to him over the years. Clarice didn't mind, because she didn't know the significance it held for him.

As he stood there, looking at Feen remember that time, he felt like telling her the whole truth about why he'd left and not the version he'd told Charlotte and Adrian. But he knew he couldn't do that. Not yet. Not until everything was in place.

"So, why did you leave, Daddy?" asked Laura, bringing them back to the present. He motioned for them to sit.

"Where's Clarice?" Feen asked.

"She's in the back," he said. "Fixin' supper." He hoped Feen didn't want to see her. When she didn't say anything more about it, he looked at Laura and decided to tell her his story.

He repeated the story regarding Mr. Donay and Mr. Nichols.

"I knowed 'bout dat," said Feen. "I paid it off years ago. If ya woulda come home, ya woulda knowed dat. Ya say ya was coming back. Why ya didn't come back?"

"I know he wouldn't a sent you ta jail, but he'd a sent me ta jail."

"No, he wouldn't a sent ya ta jail. He tol' me dat he wouldn't a sent ya ta jail. He was jus' tryna scare ya. Tryna make sho ya pay him his money. S'all."

Luke looked down at his hand. This was not going like it had gone with Charlotte and Adrian. They'd accepted what he'd said, but Feen was asking more questions.

"Tell me why ya didn't come back, Luke?" she asked again. "Tell me 'bout Clarice and the time ya spent being wit' her behind ma back, when I thought I had a good and faithful husband. Tell me 'bout dat?" Her voice was low and deliberate. Her eyes boring into him.

"I never met ta hurt ya. That's why I left."

"I don't wanna hear how ya didn't wanna hurt me, cuz ya did hurt me. Ya hurt me bad. Ya hurt me den, and ya hurt me now," she said. "I don't wanna hear how ya didn't wanna hurt me."

He looked at the floor.

Finally, he said, "Whatcha want me ta say? I'm sorry. Well, I is. I'm sorry 'bout ever'tin.' Ya want me ta say I love Clarice. Yeah, I love her."

He stopped and looked at Feen. He could see the last words had hit her hard. He saw her bite her lips. He knew she was trying to hold back tears.

Finally, she choked out, "And ya were foolin' round with her all the time?"

He closed his eyes. "No, not all the time. Ya know me and you went through a bad patch, Feen. I know it ain't no 'cuse fur what I done. I know it. Jus' sayin' a man need love…"

"Stop it," she said forcefully and jumped up. Laura jumped up, too, shocked by what Luke had said, caught and held her.

"Mom, don't," Laura said. She looked at Luke. "Daddy, how could you? How can you sit here and say these awful, hurtful things?"

"I'm tryna tell y'all I was in a bad way. I lost my way and Clarice found me."

Feen shook her head back and forth in disbelief. Luke knew she wanted to hit him again. He stood and faced her. His heart ached for her and himself.

"Feen, I'm proud of how ya took care a the chirren," he whispered.

"Of course, I did. They ma chirren. Of course, I gonna take care a dem."

"Ya look good," he said.

At this, she burst into tears. He wanted to hold her and ease her pain, but he couldn't, even if she'd let him and he knew she wouldn't let him.

Laura frowned at Luke and said, "Daddy, please," she said, as she patted Feen on the back. "You okay, Mom?"

She nodded.

"Daddy, I don't understand. I'm trying to digest all of this. Although I'm speaking calmly, I want you to know that I'm very angry with you. In fact, furious and disgusted."

"I understan', Laura. I understan' how y'all feel. As soon as I kin, I'ma come down there and we all kin talk 'bout it. Let it cool down lil bit."

She shook her head as if to say no, but said, "Okay, Daddy. I don't see how you think we'll ever understand this. I'm in Marksville for a while. It's a long story. We'll try to catch you up on things after we're able to digest finding you alive and well after years of silence."

He nodded his head. "Laura, Angie, I gotta favor ta ax."

She spun her eyes sideways at him.

"What kind of favor?"

"Lemme hug ya fur a minute," he said.

She looked at him and frowned. She was still holding her mother.

"Okay, for a minute." She unwound from Feen and step cautiously into his arms. He hugged her and laid his head on her head and closed his eyes. He did the same to Angie. Feen looked away.

"I'm sorry dat I hurt y'all, but I had ta leave. It's hard ta 'splain. One day, when we kin sit down and talk calm 'bout it, cuz I wantcha ta know all 'bout it."

"Okay, Daddy," they said.

Feen walked toward the door, turned and looked around his home, then looked back at him hard. She shook her head and walked out the door.

Standing on the porch, he waved to them as they left and took a deep breath before walking back into the house. Clarice stood in the kitchen doorway.

"Well," she said. "Are ya gonna go back home? Are ya gonna go back ta Feen? I heard the excuses ya made why ya left."

He looked at her for a second, and asked, "Whatcha want me ta tell her? Ya want me ta hurt her mo. Don't ya tink I hurt her nuf?"

"I don't wanna listen ta ya tellin' her ya sorry ya left her. I kin tell ya dat much."

"Look, Clarice. I'm tied. I ain't slept good since night 'fore las'. We kin talk 'bout dis tomorra night."

"I want ya ta tell her ya left her cuz ya love me. Like ya tol' Charlawt. Dat ya want ta be wit' me. Dat what I want ta hear ya tell her. I guess it was diff'rent lookin' up in Feen face, huh?"

"Like ya jus' say, Clarice. I tol' Charlawt all 'bout how much I love ya and ya kept me up all night anyway, axing 'bout whether I was gonna leave ya or not. It didn't do no good ta tell her dat. Did it?"

She rubbed her hand on her apron, looked at him and her face softened. "I'm sorry 'bout last night. Real sorry. It jus' upset me. Ya know comin' ta the door and seein' her and Adrian standin' there. I cain't tink 'bout losin' ya, Luke." She walked up close to him and looked up into his face. "I love ya."

He nodded his head, and said. "We kin talk 'bout dis tomorra." Walking into the kitchen, he put water to warm to clean up before bed.

She followed and put her arms around his waist. He removed her hands and lifted his supper from the oven. Quietness remained as she watched him eat and get ready for bed.

"Luke, ya cain't leave me. Not afta all dis time. I gave up a lot fur ya. Even ma peace of mind."

He didn't know what she meant by that. Her peace of mind. She was always saying things like that.

"Clarice, we not gonna do dis agin tonight. Ya hear what I say. I gotta go ta work tomorra. I gotta sleep," he said, as desperation shone through in his voice. "I say we gonna talk tomorra night. I don't wanna hear 'nother word 'bout it."

He got in bed and turned his back. Exhaustion had its way and he went to sleep immediately.

~ CHAPTER 40 ~

It was the Saturday after they had driven to New Orleans to see Luke. Everything had been a blur since they'd returned. She'd scrubbed and mopped everything she could to work out the anger and hurt she'd felt.

She was excited about stopping by Blain's. She needed to see the admiration that always shone in his eyes whenever she entered the room. The things Luke had said to her had wounded her deeply, and her self-worth needed to be massaged. She had two Sunday dresses now and she decided to wear the older one. Looking at herself in the mirror, she changed her mind and thought this was too much for an afternoon visit and took it off. She changed into a work dress, but after assessing herself, again, she wore her Sunday dress after all. She needed to feel good about herself.

She had been able to stay detached before because she'd had her marriage as an armor. After New Orleans, that shield was no longer there. In her mirror, she saw a lonely woman whose husband had left her for another woman. No matter what uplifting things she told herself, she couldn't deny that.

She arrived at his house and when he opened the door, his eyes widened, his mouth opened slightly and cheeks relaxed. The look she'd been longing to see was there. Words were not necessary, but he said them anyway.

"My, you look really nice today." They stood gazing at each other for a second.

"I fix ya some mustard greens with sausage and a loaf of cornbread."

His face widened into a big grin.

"Hmm. Cain't hardly wait," he said.

He opened the door wider, and she walked by him with a consciousness of him she'd never felt before. He followed her and when she turned around, their eyes met again.

"You look beautiful. Ya going somewhere after you leave here?" he asked.

"I ain't got nowhere else ta go today. When I leave, I'm a go work in ma garden. Dis a ole dress. Fixin' ta turn it ta a house dress. So, I thought I'd wear it today. I was hopin' it make me feel better. It been a bad week."

Blain frowned at her. "Bad week? Why?"

Feen realized she had not heard or seen Lil Rae. "Where Lil Rae?"

"You won't believe this, but Keykey's sister, Mary Liza, came and got her for a week. I was surprised. She said she'd been thinking 'bout that for a while and just decided to come git her if it was alright with me. I let her go because she need to know her people. You know, she ain't been around them much since her mama passed. So that's where she is, in Alexandria."

"Wow. So, they decide ta treat Lil Rae like fam'ly. I'm so glad fur her."

"You just said you didn't have nowhere to go. So, c'mon and sit down."

Feen hesitated for a second. The living room was small, and a green sofa took up a whole wall. She sat, adjusting her skirt so that it covered her knees. He smiled at that motion and sat beside her.

"Now," said Blain. "tell me what happened this week."

Just thinking about it brought up the feeling one gets before tears. She closed her eyes and tried to compose herself.

"My husband, Luke, is alive," she said, her voice shaky.

His head jerked back and his eyes opened wide.

"Huh? I hadn't heard that."

She nodded her head, "Yeah, he's alive. We jus' found him. He in Naw Orleen."

"Wow," he said. With a scowl on his forehead, he asked, "What's he doin' in New Orleans. Why hasn't he let you all know where he was?"

Feen explained about Clarice. Blain sat in silence as she talked. When she broke down in tears, he pulled her into his arms. The gesture made the tears flow even more.

He rubbed her back, and said, "Go on. Cry. You need to cry." And she did, sobs that made her entire body shake. He hugged her tightly until she was completely spent.

"Here," he said as he gave her a handkerchief to wipe her eyes with. For a long while, neither one said anything.

She said, "I feel so bad. He left me fur 'nother woman. 'Nother woman. What she got dat I ain't got?"

Even after all the crying she had just done, the tears were still right there below the surface and she cried some more.

"Well, I don't know him. But I know you got everything any man would want or need. Like I said, I don't know why. But I know it wasn't your fault."

"Thank ya. I know what ya sayin' and I use ta b'lieve it too, but now, now I jus' dunno. I jus' dunno."

"Well, you kin believe me. Any man would be a fool not to want you." He put his hand on her arm and she looked at him. At his words and with his eyes, she knew what he was saying to her.

"I better be gittin' home. In case Laura need her car."

"Laura's not going anywhere tonight, you know that."

She sat with her head down looking at her hands. She was aware of a pull in the air that had never been there when she'd visited before. His eyes were smoldering, and her heart was pounding. She wanted to run out of the house, away from his yearning eyes.

"Stay a little while longer and have some of this supper you fixed," he said.

"Well, I don't want ta take up too much a yo time. I done cried on ya shoulder nuf. 'Sides since Lil Rae not here, ya kin go ta the Fourth of July party tonight. Charlawt and Adrian gonna be there."

He shook his head, "I hadn't planned on going. You know without Keykey, it's not the same."

"Yeah, I know," she said. Now it was her turn to console. She looked him in the eyes. "Ya know ya need ta go out and find somebody. Ya a nice-lookin' young man." She emphasized young. "Plenty girls out there lookin' fur somebody like you."

"Are you going?" he asked.

"Oh no, not me. I don't go ta no party like dat. The pastor say they worldly and I tryna stay 'way from sin. 'Sides dat, I always thought I's married, so I couldn't go out wit' a man. Now I find out I'm married by maself." She gave a short laugh.

"You wanna go with me? We kin go together, you know."

She stared at him in surprise. "Ya don't wanna go wit' me. Ya need a young gull."

"Well, like I said, I don't know Luke. But there is nothing wrong with you," he said, looking her in the eyes. "You all dressed all pretty. You'll be the prettiest girl there. And I'd love to take you."

She smiled and touched him on the cheek. Her mind ran to Adrian and Charlotte. They'd be there, and Charlotte would be shocked if she walked into the dance with Blain. Of course, it wasn't any of Charlotte's business. The rest of the town wouldn't think anything about it, at first. They'd think they'd just come together.

He leaned forward quickly before she realized what was happening and their lips touched. His arms drew her to him and he kissed her long and deeply. Her whole body responded. It had been a long time since a man had kissed her. She'd forgotten how it felt, but her body hadn't. She didn't want to release his lips, but her mind told her she had to, so she drew back and looked him in the face.

"Sweet Baby, I'm married," she whispered.

"You just told me you been married by yourself and you don't have nowhere to go tonight."

He kissed her again and this time she did not resist. His eyes told her she was desirable and attractive. His words told her she was worthy of love. He pushed the skirt back she had so carefully covered her knees with and caressed them. As he continued to kiss her, he pushed her back on the sofa. Her arms went up around his neck and her hands caressed his face.

He kissed her earlobe and whispered, "Let me make love to you. You know how I feel 'bout you."

Out of habit, her mind thought of Luke. For the last fourteen years, she'd kept everyone at bay, because she'd thought her husband was coming back.

"No. I cain't," she whispered.

He continued to kiss and caress her. Long sweet kisses that went on and on and she felt like her body would explode. One arm around her shoulder, the other hand kneading her breast when he pulled her tightly to him and he whispered again. Doubts passed through her mind. She was married, but not to him. Her moral conscience was drumming in her head telling her this was a sin. But her body was longing for the comfort his arms could bestow.

This time she whispered, "Okay, sweet Blain."

He stood up and led her into the bedroom that she'd help him paint and redecorate. As he undressed her, she worried about what her older body would look like to him. He kissed her neck and she reclined on the bed.

As his eyes traveled her body, he whispered, "You're as beautiful as I thought you'd be."

He undressed, joined her on the bed and kissed her with a fierce passion that put all fears to rest. Her body responded to him, just as fiercely, as she savored the fact that he wanted her, and found her worthy to love. Afterward, they lay entwined.

"That was wonderful," he said.

"Um-hmm," she said, placing her arm across his chest. Both fully satisfied, they went to sleep. When she awakened, she saw him lying beside her and the realization of what had happened came to mind. Her feelings were mixed. She touched him, then ran her hand across his chest, savoring the feel of him under her fingers. He turned to her and their eyes held. She touched her lips to his and his arms surrounded her and pulled her to him. She leaned forward and kissed him deeply.

"I gotta go," she whispered, moving out of his arms and out of the bed.

"Why? You don't have to go?"

"Yes, I gotta bring Laura her car," she said, softly. She looked down at her hands, "I dunno what happen. I'm not sho I feel right 'bout it."

"Well, I feel right 'bout it. Bring Laura's car home and I'll come pick you up. You can spend the night and I'll run you back home in the morning."

"No, Blain." She shook her head. "We cain't do dis no mo. We not married. In fact, I'm married ta someone else. Dis is wrong and I cain't spend the night here. Whatcha neighbors gonna say? It be all over town."

"I'm not worried about what the neighbors think, but since you are, and I understand that, come back tomorrow and we'll talk some more"

"I'll come back next Sadday …

"Next Saturday," he cut her off, in disbelief.

"Yeah, next Sadday. Dat'll gimme time ta tink. I know dis here ain't right. I'm married."

Now standing over her, he said, "Whatcha talking 'bout you still married to Luke? He's with another woman? Been with another woman for fourteen years. He doesn't deserve you, Feen. It's time for you to move on. He has."

She takes a deep breath. "Yeah, I know ya right. But two wrong don't make a right. Dat what ma mama use ta say." She looked up at him and took his head into her hands. "I enjoyed today. I tink I had furgot how good it feel ta love a man. I tank ya fur dat. But there's a lot wrong wit' dis. Even if I wasn't married to Luke, I'm not married to you, and what we just done should be done between a husband and wife."

"Okay. You said there's a lot wrong with this. What else is wrong?"

"Ya too young fur me."

"Too young? Was I too young an hour ago? Huh?"

She looked at him, but didn't answer.

"Answer me, Feen. Did it feel like I was too young for you?"

"Now ya tink it don't matter, but soon you'll see a gull ya wanna talk ta."

"I'm looking at a girl I wanna talk to right now," he answered.

She smiled, "Sweet Baby." She kissed him lightly on the lips.

He followed her to the door. "If I cain't see you til Saturday, can I call you?"

She nodded. "Um hmm, ya kin call me."

Her emotions were still high as she ran out the house. He was a sweet, handsome man and he'd been a powerful, thoughtful and ardent lover. Still, she did not know whether she would've ever made love to him if Luke hadn't resurfaced with Clarice. Besides that, she did have real reservations concerning his age. Not only because of their compatibility, but the rumor mill would eat her alive.

Was their attraction enough to build a healthy relationship?

~ Chapter 41 ~

A car stopped in front of Feen's house and she heard Charlotte and Laura talking. She was still aglow from last night's visit with Blain, and since Charlotte had voiced her disapproval on more than one occasion, she decided not to tell them what had transpired the night before.

"Not they bidness, no how," she thought.

She heard Laura telling Charlotte she'd found a job in Pineville at the Charity Hospital and a small house to rent. Afterward, Laura got in her car and left.

Charlotte walked into the room Feen shared with Laura, took a seat on the bed, looked at Feen with a somber expression.

"Hi Mom," she said. "Are you feeling better about Daddy?"

"Yeah, I am," she said thinking about last night with Blain. "Feelin' much better."

"Good," she said, "I'm glad."

There was silence as Feen continued to put clothes away. She turned and noticed the expression on Charlotte's face.

"What's wrong wit' ya?" she asked. "Why ya got dat long face?"

Still silence.

"Chawlawt, if ya don't wanna talk ta me, why ya came over here?"

"I found out something last night that I don't understand."

"Whatcha find out?"

"Adrian told me last night, that you were raped, and Daddy is not my father."

Feen's stomach did a somersault. Adrian had asked her for permission to tell Charlotte the horrible story surrounding her birth. He'd said he'd choose a good time to do it. Feen didn't think this was a good time, but Adrian had, evidently, thought so.

"Mom," Charlotte said. "I must've asked you a hundred times why I looked different and you always made me feel as though I was crazy for asking. Why did you do that?"

"I don't know. Probably, to stop ya from axing 'bout it. How was I 'spose ta tell ya dat, Charlawt? Dat I was raped. Dat Luke not ya daddy. Tink 'bout it."

"I have been thinking about it and I can't understand it. Maybe, when I was little, but I've been of age for a long time. You could've told me."

"I trust Adrian judgment, but I don't tink dis a good time fur ya ta find out 'bout dis. Ya jus' found ya daddy."

"He thought since I was handling that, might as well clear the air about some other things that I needed to know. And this was definitely something I needed to know."

Now it was Feen's time to be quiet. She'd known this day might come one day and here it was.

"You knew I had so many questions about how I fit in this family and you could have cleared it up a long time ago," she said.

"Furgive me, Charlawt. I didn't know what else ta do."

"I know if there wasn't so much going on right now, I'd be madder than I am right now. There's only room for so much rage, you know, because I'm so mad at Daddy. It's hard to be mad at you, because I sympathize with you regarding being raped. I can't imagine what you went through being assaulted."

"Yeah, dat was hard, but I don't want ya ta worry 'bout me. I leaned hard on the Lawd in ma time of trouble, and I come a long way. Right now, ya still gittin' over what ya Daddy done ta us. We bof tryna git over dat."

She paused. "Charlawt, I'm so sorry ya hurt, cuz I didn't know what ta do. Luke 'cept ya as his own and love ya like his own. Ya say he not ya real father, well I disagree wit' dat. He was a real father ta ya, 'fore he left. Much father ta ya as he was ta Laura. Dat's why I guess I wanted ta b'lieve it don't matter. I did the best I knew how."

Charlotte said, "I'm still trying to understand why you didn't tell me once I got older."

"Like I say, didn't see no reason ta."

"Adrian didn't tell me who my father is. He said he would if I asked him."

Feen started moving around. She was getting a little apprehensive. She hoped that Charlotte wasn't about to open that can of worms.

"Don't worry, Mom," Charlotte said. "You look like you got nervous. I'm not going to ask you about that right now. But, as soon as I feel like I can handle something else, then I'll want to know the whole story."

Feen didn't understand why Charlotte needed to know such a gruesome thing. She wanted to shield her from such an inhumane debasement. She'd never shared it with anyone, not even her husband. Adrian had seen her lying on the ground, but he hadn't see the attack. Rae had cleaned her wounds, but never asked any questions, and she'd never offered any details.

"I'll do what I kin when the time come," she said.

∞

A week later, Adrian told Charlotte the pastor wanted to see her. This was unusual, because although she'd been active in church all her life, the pastor never talked with her privately. There'd always been an intermediary of some sort. He'd had one-on-one discussions with friends of hers, but never with her. Occasions where she'd be in line to shake his hand, for instance, after a rousing sermon, he'd hurriedly shake her hand without making any eye contact. She'd always wondered about that.

She walked in and he was sitting at his desk writing. It was a large office, with wood paneling, a large mahogany desk, bookshelf, one large cotton stuffed chair, and one straight-backed chair. He was dressed in a black suit, white shirt and black tie as he always was.

"You wanted to see me?" she said.

"Yes, Charlotte," he said. "Have a seat."

When she was seated, he said, "If you don't mind, I'd like to read scripture to you. It's Isaiah 1:18. 'Come now, and let us reason together,' says the Lord, 'Though your sins are like scarlet, they shall be as white as snow; though they are red like crimson, they shall be as wool.'"

She wondered if he'd heard something bad about her and had called her in to reprimand her. Surely, he wouldn't go through Adrian to do that.

After he'd finished reading the scripture, she said, "Beautiful scripture, Pastor. What does it have to do with me?"

"I just wanted to make sure you knew that all have sinned and fallen short of the glory of God. We all need second chances, sometimes."

"Yes, I know we do and I really try to live by that," she said. There was silence as they studied each other.

He took a deep breath and said, "I did an awful thing when I was young. I pray for forgiveness every night. I know that the Lord wants me to pastor. I know I've done a good job since I've been here. Haven't I?"

"Yes, you have, Pastor. You're doing really good with the growth in membership."

"Yes, I have. I've brought quite a few folks to God."

"Yes, you have, Pastor."

Silence.

"And I visit the sick, counsel people with marriage and other kinds of problems.

"Yes, you do."

They fell silent, again.

Finally, Charlotte said, "Is there something specific you wanted to talk to me about? Because Adrian didn't say. Just that you wanted to talk to me."

"I'm going to tell you something, but you have to stay and listen to everything I say. You can't run out before I get a chance to explain."

Charlotte started to feel afraid.

"What in the world are you talking about?" she asked.

"One day a long time ago, I did an unforgivable thing that I need to ask your forgiveness for." He leaned forward his eyes held hers. "I raped your mother, Charlotte." Pause. "And I'm your father."

Her eyes dimmed as she tried to process what he'd just said. This was Pastor and he was her father's cousin. Even though, this did not make sense in her mind, little connections were being made. This explained why her mother had always been standoffish with him, and why he'd regularly kept her at a distance. Now, it made sense why her Taunt Julia used to squeeze her so, tightly.

Finally, she said, "So, it was you."

He put his head down and nodded.

Charlotte retorted, angrily, "You come to me reading scriptures? That's how you're gonna explain what you did to my mother? Huh? You told me not to leave so you could explain it. I'm waiting. I don't know what you can say, but I'm waiting."

"I have no excuse…"

She interrupted him. "You damn right, you don't. But I'm waiting, anyway."

"You're right. There is nothing I can explain. I guess, what I really wanted to say was: Will you forgive me? I'm begging you to forgive me?"

"You know, people who study the minds of criminals, say that rape is not about sex, it's about hate, anger and control. Did you hate my mother? Did you want to control her?"

He looked down at his desk for a second, then back up at her.

"I'm not sure what I was feeling at that time, but I can say that it wasn't hate. I could never hate your mother. Maybe, I did want to control her. But I know no matter what my reasoning was, it was wrong. I've counseled with my pastor who was my mentor. We've spent hours and hours talking about it, trying to grasp why I would've done such a thing."

"So, do you know why you did it?"

He shook his head.

"No."

"What I want to do is do you like you did her. I'd like to beat you up. Adrian told me what she looked like when he found her. You beat her and left her there, unconscious in a pile of ants. She could've died. Do you know that?"

"Yeah, you right. I didn't think of it that way. It was so close to her house I figured someone would come looking for her if she couldn't make it herself." He walked around his desk and leaned on the desk in front of her. "Besides feeling guilty for what I did to Feen, it has, also, been a punishment for me to watch you grow up into the fine lady you are and never being able to say that you were my daughter. You know I married you and couldn't give you away. That was a hard thing to do. You're my only child, Charlotte."

She was surprised by the tone in his voice when he said that, and for a moment, she looked at him as a human being who'd never had children, wanted one and couldn't claim the only one he had. But then she remembered what Adrian said about how her mother had looked that day and the anger returned.

She asked in a sarcastic voice, "That's right, you did marry Adrian and me. Now I know why my mama cried throughout the ceremony. Knowing the truth must have been so hard for her." She tilted her head to one side and asked, "So, why didn't you? Why didn't you tell me you were my father? You know I loved your mother and all this time. I didn't have a grandmother and I wanted one. I went to her funeral not knowing she was my grandmother."

"I know. But you did get to know her and spend time with her. And I can tell you that she loved you."

"I know. She told me often."

Charlotte got quiet as she thought about Julia. She remembered how she'd always thought she resembled her kids more than she resembled Luke, but she'd assumed she'd just looked more like her father's aunt's children than him. That happened, sometimes, in families.

She got up to leave.

"Wait a minute." He walked up to her and reached for her hand. She jerked it away.

"Don't touch me," she said. "Don't ever try to touch me. You're not my father. Lucien Ford is my father. You are a rapist." The last sentence she spat the words out to him. "If you're looking for absolution, there is no absolution here."

She slammed the door behind her. But as she drove away, she remembered the way his voice sounded when he'd said that she was his only child.

∞

Charlotte went directly to her mother's house and knocked on the door. Feen opened it and smiled. "I didn't know ya were comin' by today," she said.

"Mom, you won't believe who I've been talking to."

Feen smiled a little bit and turned her head to the side and said, "No, guess not."

"I've been talking with my daddy," she said and gave her full attention to her mother's reaction.

Feen said, "Ya talked ta Luke today. Ya been ta Naw Orleen?"

"No, I been to the church and talked with Pastor Francisco." Again, she waited to see how her mother would respond.

She wasn't disappointed. Her mother's eyes and mouth opened wide.

"Ya saw Luke at the church talkin' wit' Rev. Francisco."

"Nooo," she said. "I talked with my father, Rev. Francisco."

Silence.

"Adrian tol' ya. He tol' ya, it was Wickliffe."

"No, he told me to go talk to Rev. Francisco. He's the one who told me he'd raped you and he was my father. Mom, I'm just so angry. Why you never told me who he was? I don't understand how you can go and sit in church and listen to him preach about anything." She shook her head. "I just don't understand why he's not in jail. Did you even ever file charges against him?"

"No, I was too shame. People would say it's ma fault. Law don't care nothin' 'bout colored people killin' and rapin' each other. If it woulda been a white girl, they'd a hang him. But a colored girl, they wouldn't a done nothin' ta him, no how. The church and ma neighbor would a look at me funny. Ma reputation woulda been ruint."

"So, he gets no punishment at all."

"Well, Luke beat him up. Beat him real good, I heard tell," she said. "As fur as me listenin' ta him in church, I stopped goin' ta church fur a time and sometime I walked ta St. Paul. But, it's a long way. When he left town, I come back ta church. Taunt Julia talk ta me 'fore they made him the pastor and I agree ta it. I listen ta the word. Somehow, I'm able ta hear the word and not the messenger. Understand what I'm sayin'."

"I think so. I just don't know if I could've done dat. Not punish him and then go sit and listen to him preach."

"Well, it didn't happen overnight. Took some time and I had ta forgive. It was hard on me. It was hard on Luke. In order ta live ma life, I had ta furgive him." She paused. "I never want ya ta know. I want ta spare ya."

She walked to a window. "I know, Mom. But you should've told me. Especially, after you knew I was bothered by some things. You kept on telling me nothing was different about me when I sensed there was. And he married me and Adrian and you never said a word." Charlotte whirled around to face Feen. "And Taunt Julia. Taunt Julia. You knew how much I loved her and you never told me she was my grandmother. Mom, how could you not tell me?" Her voice had risen to fever pitch.

"I kin see it upset ya, but I did what I thought was best. I cain't say I wish I woulda done diff'rent. I dunno how you'd a handle it den. Ya old enough now ta be able ta handle it." She paused. "Ya know ya gotta make the same kinda decision someday. So, 'member how ya feelin' now and let dat guide ya."

Charlotte looked at her, blankly.

"Ya gotta decide how ya gonna tell lil Luke that Adrian ain't his father."

Charlotte was quiet.

"Yeah, I'll have ta do that. Won't I?"

The thought hit Charlotte hard. It had not occurred to her she was doing the same thing with her son. This knowledge made her more understanding of the decision her mother had made many years before. She nodded her head.

"You know I've been unsure what I was gonna do, but I know, now, I have to tell him. I will decide when the time is right. I can't put my baby through the same thing."

"So, ya tink ya kin furgive me?" Feen asked.

"I understand why you did what you did. I just wish you would've done it differently. That's all. I know you were not trying to hurt me."

"So, do ya furgive me?"

Charlotte walked over to her mother and put her arms around her.

"Forgiveness is not the word. I never held anything against you. I ached for you, because you're a victim. You're my mother and nothing can come between us and stay for very long." She released Feen from their embrace and smiled for a second. "I still wish there was some way he could pay for what he did. Do you think he ever did that to anyone else?"

"No, I don't tink so. Course I dunno. His momma tol' me, he was sorry and he wouldn't do dat ta nobody else."

"Yeah, well, that was Taunt Julia. Mommas sometimes protect their children. Even when they're wrong."

"Seem like he been a good pastor. Preach good sermons. Ever'body satisfied wit' him at church. Never hear no bad report. I let him go fur what he done ta me and I pray fur him ta do what's right. I furgive him."

She believed she'd forgiven him, because he didn't occupy a lot of her thoughts anymore.

~ CHAPTER 42 ~

Adrian knocked on the door, called out her name and walked in. Feen heard him, but was surprised to see him. It had been a long time since he'd visited her alone without Charlotte.

"Adrian, ya jus' missed Charlawt," she said.

"I know," he asked. "I didn't come to talk to her. I came to talk to you."

Her eyebrows shot up, "Oh?" she asked.

"Um hmm," he said. "We haven't talked since you seen Lucien in New Orleans. I just wanted to make sure you alright."

She smiled. "Glad you came over. Take a seat. Want some coffee?"

"Yeah, I'll take a cup," he said and followed her into the kitchen, and took a seat at the table.

"I'm doing okay," she said as she sat the coffee in front of him. "It was a shock so bad that I cain't even start ta tell ya how it feel. I cried so much 'til I cain't cry no more."

She paused a second. She was wrestling with whether she should talk to Adrian 'bout Blain. She'd always been able to share her deepest secrets with him and he'd always given her a kind, listening ear. She was confused and needed to talk to someone.

"Adrian, I wanted ta git ya opinion on sometin'. I know you and Charlotte don't like me goin' over ta Blain house."

She looked at him, trying to gauge his reaction. His face did not change expression.

When she stopped for a second, he said, "Go on."

Looking away from his stare, she said, "I lay wit' him las' night."

Silence. Then she turned to look at him. His eyes opened in a realization of what she had just said.

"You mean, you two…?" he said twirling his index finger in a circle, but not completing the sentence.

She nodded her head.

"Hmm," he said and bucked his eyes.

"Well, I knew ya not gonna like it, but I need ta talk 'bout it wit' somebody. I jus' feel so hurt. Why I'm not good nuf fur Luke ta stay? What wrong wit' me?" she said, as a tear rolled down her cheek.

He moved where she was and patted her on the back.

"I can't say I'm not surprised, because I am." When she'd collected herself, he said, "You talked about your feelings for Luke and how he treated you. Nothing about Blain. This thing with Blain, did you do it to spite Luke?"

Feen turned her head swiftly toward Adrian. She hadn't thought of it that way. Was that the reason?

"I dunno," she said. "I don't think so. I did feel bad and we good friends. He lonely and I'm lonely. But I don't think it's right. Keykey like ma daughter."

"Blain is a good guy. If you're using him to make yourself feel better 'bout what Luke did, that ain't right. I know you been through a lot, but so has he. He watched his wife, slowly, die in front of him, and he now seems to have feelings for the woman who's been taking care of him. You can't use him like that, Feen." When she didn't answer, he said, "Maybe I'm wrong. How do you feel about him?"

She shook her head, "I dunno. I really dunno." She closed her eyes as she thought about the last time they were together. "I care 'bout him a lot. I tink 'bout him a lot. We talk easy together, ya know, like you and me use ta. But sometin' jus' don't seem right 'bout it."

"Well, you need to give it some time. Don't move too fast. Because I don't think either one of your minds is right, now. I think you're both wounded spirits. Wait a while 'fore going any further. Give him and yourself a chance to see clearly."

She nodded her head. "I know you're right. Dat's what I'm gonna do. But 'nuf 'bout me. I heard there's not gonna be a divorce."

She smiled up at him. He smiled back.

"So, Charlotte told you, huh? No, there's not gonna be a divorce. I think you're stuck with me as a son-in-law."

"I want you ta know I'm glad. I could tell she loved ya. Right afta y'all got married, I could see her eyes followin' ya 'round." She smiled as she thought about the times that happened. More seriously, she said, "Ya know I didn't want ya ta marry her. I thought bof y'all would get hurt and I gotta admit, I was a lil afraid of losin' ya as my bes' friend. I felt like I needed ya. Even though I got Teresa and Rae, you diff'rent. You a man and wit' Luke gone, sometimes a woman jus' wanna talk ta a man. Not ta go ta bed wit'. Sometimes, I jus' wanna hear a man voice, a man opinion. Ya were dat fur me. I didn't hafta worry 'bout ya makin' a pass. I could trust ya 'round me and ma gulls, and I could talk ta ya 'bout anytin.' I thought I lost dat when y'all got married."

She kneaded her mouth together and there were tears in the corner of her eyes, "Until today. Tank ya fur being ma friend. I know Charlawt don't understan' our friendship, but ever' now and den, could ya come by and talk wit' me?"

"Sure thing, mother-in-law, sure thing. Our talks meant a lot to me, too. And I miss them, too. I told you a long time ago that you could lean on me. You still can."

She touched his hand to show her gratitude. He stood up and gave her a big hug. "Remember what I said 'bout Blain. He deserves a woman who loves him for him."

∞

It was time for Feen to go to the grocery store. She had finished her list, but had not added anything to fix for Blain. He'd called during the week, but she hadn't decided how she was going to handle the situation. To have an attractive young man like Blain find her desirable had done wonders for her ego. However, she was not sure of her feelings for him and thought she needed to take a step back.

The phone rang. It was him.

"When are you coming?" he asked.

"I thought I would not come by today," she said. "I think we need a chance ta think 'bout what happen."

"What?" Blain screamed into the phone. "What are you talking about? You've come by almost every Saturday for the last two years, and now when we've made a connection, you decide you're not coming by. Are you serious?"

"Yes, I am," she said.

"Look," he said. "We need to talk."

"Alright. Alright. I gotta go ta the store first."

"I'll come by and get you. Take you to the store and you can cook here. And we can talk. If you want to leave afterward, den I'll take you home. Alright?"

"Alright."

He drove up in his blue pick-up truck. He jumped out and opened the door for her. At the sight of him, her pulses quickened. When he touched her arm to help her into the truck, her senses remembered the last time they were together. From his face, she knew he was thinking the same thing.

"You sure you want to go to the store?" he said.

208

She laughed and broke the tension.

"Yes, I wanna go ta the store. Ya know ya don't have nothin' at ya house ta eat fur Sunday dinner."

"Alright, then," he said laughing.

After they'd finished shopping and were in his small kitchen preparing jambalaya, he walked up behind her and put his arms around her waist. She turned and kissed him. Long and deep.

She looked in his eyes and with her hand rubbing his cheek, she said, "Dat's all fur today. I told ya we need ta take it easy. We got a lot ta talk 'bout."

"Such as?" he asked.

"Ya know I jus' found ma husband."

"Yeah, I know that. But he been gone for a long time."

"Yeah, he has. But he still ma husband."

"He was ya husband last week, too."

"Last week, I was still reelin' from the news. Ya were so sweet. Ya made me feel like a woman agin. I hadn't felt like dat in a long time. But ya were married ta ma daughter's best friend. You young nuf ta be ma son. Dat excitin' fur now, but what will ya feel like when I'm old and ya still young. Wit' the energy of a young man. Den you'll leave me and I cain't go through dat agin."

Shaking his head. "That's not gonna happen. There's so much more between us. We're friends, Feen. You been coming here for two years. We been enjoying each other's company for two years. I think of you all the time. I daydream about you. It's not just about your hips," he smiled and she rolled her eyes at him. "It's your voice, your kindness, your smile, your trustworthiness, I could go on and on. I don't see any of that changing. If you're concerned about us being in a sinful relationship, we can get married."

Her face telegraphed her surprise.

"What?"

"Yeah, we can get married. Then if the nosey people want to talk, they can talk and we won't be doing nothing sinful."

"Oh, sweet Baby. I'm so honored and flattered. Ya take me by surprise."

"Well, that solves all of our problems."

"But it don't. Ya still young nuf ta be ma son. I know ya feel dat way now, but I would've never thought Luke would leave me either. But he did and I cain't go through dat agin."

"Whatcha saying? You just gonna give up on life. On lovin'. On being happy."

"No, dat not what I'm sayin'," she said, as she turned back to stir her pot. "I'm sayin' when I let maself git crazy 'bout a man, I need ta feel it got a chance ta work. I cain't go in wit' the deck stack agin me."

He shook his head. "You can't mean that. Why did you let it happen?" He threw his hands up in the air. "If you thought this way, why did you let me think you wanted me?"

Her face smiled, searching for the words to make him understand. "Because I do wantcha. Dat not the issue. Why wouldn't I want a fine, handsome, sweet man like you? Ya ain't been list'nin'. If we git married and I git old, ya feelin' gonna change. Don't ya understan', I cain't go through dat agin. I cain't put all ma faith in somebody and they walk 'way from me. I'm sorry. We's friends. Good friends. I like talkin' witcha. I like cookin' fur ya." She closed her eyes and savored the pleasure she experienced making love to him. "God knows I love lovin' ya and you lovin' me," she whispered. More strongly, "But it cain't happen no more. Ya need a young woman and one will come along."

The front door opened and they heard Lil Rae's excited voice, "Daddy, Daddy, I'm back. Did you miss me?"

Blain walked quickly to her, picked her up and hugged her close. "I sure did. I really missed my girl," he said.

Keykey's sister, Mary Liza, stood behind Lil Rae with a big smile on her face. Her eyes were big as she smiled up at Blain.

Feen took in the scene. She took careful inventory of Mary Liza. She was tall and slim like Charlotte, medium brown skinned with black, thick, long hair like her sister, Keykey. Feen thought she was single and checked her ring finger and she was right. She could tell from the way she eyed Blain that she found him attractive.

Her own heart beat stronger. She knew it was jealousy. If she stayed with him, this is how it would be whenever a younger woman came into his vicinity. She'd be suspicious of their motives.

It was partly because of the age difference, but also, because of what Luke and Wickliffe had done to her. They'd shattered her ability to trust and to take things at face value. One had taken vows with her to love and honor, for better or worse. Yet he'd taken up with another woman. The other had physically assaulted her when she wouldn't forsake the vows she'd made to her husband. Two men she'd trusted had betrayed her.

She stood in the doorway of the kitchen and watched the scene. She wished she'd driven Laura's car, so she could leave.

Mary Liza noticed her and smiled.

"Hi, Miss Feen," she said.

"How do," she answered brightly.

"We had a wonderful time this week. Didn't we, Lil Rae?" she said.

"I'm glad. Look Blain, can you drop me back home? I've started supper for y'all. Y'all jus' need ta watch it."

His brow kneaded up.

"Why are you leaving?"

Feen's eyes looked at Mary Liza, whose eyes were going back and forward between the two of them.

Feen said, "I got stuff I gotta do. I need ta go."

He cocked his head to the side and his eyes narrowed as he looked at her. He knew she didn't have anything pressing to do. Today was Saturday. Their day. To prevent an argument in front of Lil Rae, he took her home.

An awkward silence accompanied them on the ride home. Every so often he'd look at her as she sat focused straight ahead. Their lovemaking the week before had awakened something in him that had been asleep and every time he looked at her, he wanted to pull on the side the road, gather her to him and kiss her until she relented. But he didn't do it. He was a man of honor and would respect her wishes.

"Can I call you?"

"Wait. Wait six months. If ya still wanna call me, den ya kin call me," she said.

She waited for his answer, but none came.

She got out of the truck without looking at him. He sped off, spreading gravel as he did so, without another word. Her heart was beating so hard, she started to sit on the ground to prevent herself from falling. Instead, she stood with her eyes closed in one place for a minute. She took deep breaths until she felt like she could make it to the porch.

Once inside, she fell across her bed. She sensed he'd never call again. All week her mind had been fuzzy with her not knowing what she was going to do concerning their relationship. It had been her decision. She thought she'd made the right one, but it still hurt. The disappointment was almost debilitating. Her little romance was over. What would she do on Saturdays? Thoughts of barren weekends flooded her senses, and the tears came.

~ Chapter 43 ~

Teresa stopped by later that day when Feen was returning from a visit with Rae.

"I saw Blain a few hours ago? What's wrong with him? He didn't wave or nothin'. Speedin' down the road, throwin' rocks all over the place, like he's mad," she said.

She knew Feen brought food to him and Lil Rae. Because of the length of time this had been happening, she suspected more was going on than Feen admitted. She eyed Feen, waiting for an explanation, but Feen didn't give her one. Instead, she walked to her porch.

"Well, I come ta tell ya, Sophia, Rev. Francisco's wife died this mornin'. He was out visitin' the sick, and when he gits back, he found her. Laid out on the kitchen flo. So sad."

Feen felt terrible for the lady, although, she'd never gotten to know her well. She'd not had any desire to know her better. She didn't hold Sophia accountable for her husband's actions, but being around her reminded Feen of what he'd done. Therefore, she tried not to be around her much. But she was sorry she was dead. He seemed to really love and depend on her. Now, it appeared he'd lost both his anchors, his mother and now his wife.

"So, what's goin' on wit' Blain?" Teresa asked.

"I dunno," Feen answered.

"Yeah, ya do," Teresa said. "I been watching y'all fur 'bout two years now. Cookin' fur him and sittin' in church together. Ya like him, don't ya?"

"He too young, Teresa."

"Uh-huh. But ya do like him. I tell you what, he sho is fine," she said with a big grin.

Feen couldn't help but smile back. "Yeah, he is," she said nodding her head and remembering the feel of his arms.

Teresa looked closely at her face and her eyes dimmed.

"Whatcha tinkin' 'bout wit dat dreamy look on ya face."

"Nothin'," Feen said.

"Well, Ella is a lot older than Daniel and they fine. Jus' depend on how deep ya feelin' is. Why don't ya talk wit' her sometimes and see what she gotta say 'bout it? See how they git alone."

"Maybe. But, Teresa, ya know Deacon Brown, that live 'cross the street from Blain would have a fit. It's funny he ain't said sometin' 'bout it already."

"But mos' young guys jus' use a woman older den they is. Ya know, ta git what they want, den they drop dem?"

"Yeah, dat's true. But, Teresa, he ax me ta marry him."

"What? Whatcha tol' him?"

"I'd let him know in six months."

"Well, ya cain't let gossip mongers rule ya life. They not witcha on those lonely evenings. Anyway, I jus' come to let ya know 'bout the pastor's wife."

∞

About two months later, one day when Mose was sober, he went over to Feen's house to repair siding on her hen house. Angie made sure he had cool water to drink. She did this anytime he did chores for

Feen. He'd shown her how to saddle and ride her horse, and she and her mother appreciated that. With Luke gone, she hadn't had a father figure.

The church pianist had given Angie some of her old piano lesson books and had gotten her started on how to use the books. She needed to go to church to practice, and her mother did not want her to go to the church alone. She walked alone to most places, but Feen had been adamant about her never being alone at the church, so Angie asked if she could go with Mose when he went to cut the grass.

Feen said that was a good idea and they went on her horse. Mose sat in the front part of the saddle, and she rode behind him with her arms about his waist.

He worked outside, while Angie practiced. Rev. Francisco had been there when she'd arrived, but he'd left to run an errand.

She practiced for an hour and then read a book she'd brought with her, while she waited for Mose to finish. When she got sleepy, she decided to lay down on a pew.

Her sleep was deep until she felt someone touching her along her legs and awakened to see her uncle leaning over her. At first, she was not afraid. He'd never done or said anything mean or nasty to her before.

"Uncle Mose, you ready to go?" she asked.

"No," he said. "Not yet."

He did not move his hand as she shifted her legs from the pew to the floor and sat up. She was still not alarmed until he sat next to her and continued to rub her thigh. She moved his hand away.

"Uncle Mose, what are you doing?" she said, now anxious.

"Ya so lil and pretty. Jus' like Rae use ta be. Ya look jus' like her. Go on and lay back down. Jus' fur a lil while. I promise I won't hurt ya. It's not gonna hurt a'tall."

As what was happening dawned on her, she jumped up, grabbed her books and headed for the door. He caught and stopped her. His eyes had changed. She thought he looked scared. She wondered why would he'd be afraid of her.

"You cain't leave until you tell me ya not gonna tell Rae what I say."

He seemed to be in a panic state.

So, she was right. He was afraid. He was worried she would tell her aunt. With the marriage problems they'd been having, this would be the end of it. Even in Angie's fifteen-year-old state of mind, she knew a scared man is a dangerous man. His drinking had taken its toll over the years, and he was a fraction of the man he once was, but she knew she was still no match for him.

"Don't worry, I'm not going to tell," she answered with her eyes big.

She was afraid and trying not to let it show. But she could tell from the look on his face it was showing.

"No, ya gonna tell. They gonna know sometin' happen. If not today, den someday, but ya gonna tell."

His grip tightened on her arm as his breath quickened. His eyes scanned the church. She became more and more afraid. What was he looking for? He pulled her to the back to the office near the desk. His eyes fell on a letter opener, then they came back to her.

Now his eyes traveled her body and he got that lustful look again. He shoved her to the floor behind the pastor's desk.

"Don't be scared, Angie. I'm not gonna hurt ya. I promise."

He fell on top of her as she tried to get up. He pushed her skirt up as they wrestled on the floor.

"What's going on in here," said the pastor as she felt Mose lifted off her.

Angie was in tears and could hardly speak. Mose's eyes had that scared look again.

"I'm sorry. She got scared a me fur no reason and I was tryna calm her, so we could go home."

The pastor didn't answer him. His attention was focused on Angie. "Are you alright, Angie?" he asked.

"What some ever she say, she lyin'," Mose said. "I'm not gonna hurt her none,"

Wickliffe's eyes dimmed.

Mose retreated, slowly, looking around as though he was looking for a place to escape. The sound of Angie's weeping filled the room, and Wickliffe's eyes left Mose and switched to her. Mose grabbed the letter opener from the desk.

Angie screamed. Rev. Francisco spun around to face Mose, who stood with the letter opening in his outstretched hand poised to attack.

"Rev. Francisco, nothin' happen. Nothin' was gonna happen. Ya cain't tell nobody."

"I'm not going to tell anybody anything," said the pastor. "Just calm down and put down that letter opener before you do hurt somebody."

"Pastor, Angie gonna tell Feen and Feen gonna tell Rae. Ya don't know dat woman."

Wickliffe took a small step to his desk.

"I understand, Mose. Put it down. I'll talk to Feen. She's not gonna tell nobody."

"She gonna tell."

Wickliffe took another small step to his desk.

Wickliffe said, "Tell him Angie. Tell him you're not gonna tell."

Angie was trembling. She couldn't speak. All of this was too much for her to handle. She stood behind the pastor as she tried to find her voice to tell him she wasn't going to tell.

"I'm ... not ... going ... to ... tell," she stammered.

"Sorry, Angie, I don't b'lieve ya," he said.

Rev. Francisco, with Angie behind him using him as a shield, was behind his desk, directly in front of his desk drawer. He slowly put his hands on the top of his desk. His center drawer was slightly opened.

"Mose, I know you're a good man, who loves his family. Angie is a part of your family. She's your neice, Man. You've known her all her life. If she says she's not going to tell, then she's not going to tell."

Mose began to creep forward from the center of the office toward the area where Wickliffe and Angie stood. Seeing things were about to come to a head, Rev. Francisco reached into the desk and withdrew the small pistol he kept in the office to kill snakes. They'd found a snake in the church a few years before they'd repaired a hole in the floor and the deacons had bought a pistol to keep in the church to take care of the problem.

Mose saw it and turned his attention to Wickliffe instead of Angie.

"Sorry, Pastor," he said.

He raised he letter opener in the air, rushed toward him and stabbed him in the chest.

Angie screamed, "No, no. Shoot him. Shoot him."

Simultaneously, Rev. Francisco fired his gun three times, and they both fell to the floor.

Still crying, she went to the pastor and knelt by his side.

His eyes were opened, "How is he?"

She looked over at Mose, "I think … I think he's dead. His eyes and mouth are opened, but his eyes are blank." Looking back at the pastor. "I'm going to run to the house across the street for help. Hold on, okay?"

"Um hmm," he said.

She hurried across the street to the neighbor's house.

The owner called the ambulance. He and Angie went back over to the church to wait. The scene was as she'd left it. Mose on his back, seeming to be dead and Wickliffe, whose chest was all bloody, was struggling to breath. She owed him her life and she was filled with gratitude. She sat next to him on the floor.

"Rev. Francisco, why didn't you shoot him before he stabbed you?" Angie asked.

"I just didn't think he would do it. I only took the gun out to scare him. I never meant to use it. I never wanted to kill anybody," he said. "Angie?"

"Yes."

"Tell your mama I'm sorry for what I done to her. Ask her and Charlotte to forgive me."

Angie wondered what he had done that he would apologize and ask forgiveness at a time like this. It must have been something that weighed heavily on his mind.

"I will. I'll ask them to forgive you. They'll want to thank you. I owe you my life."

"My job is to protect my flock. I had to do everything I could to protect you." Pause. "You know. I missed Sophia a lot. I didn't know I'd get to see her so soon," he said in a strained voice.

"You'll be alright," Angie said.

His gaze moved from looking at her to something or someone behind her, and he said, "Sophia?"

Angie turned to see who he was talking to, and she saw no one. The neighbor was out front waiting for the ambulance.

He repeated it with his eyes fixed somewhere behind her, "Sophia?" There was a slight smile on his face. His head fell to the side and his eyes closed.

"Oh no, Rev. Francisco," she cried.

She shook him gently, but it was no use. He was gone.

~ CHAPTER 44 ~

The church was crowded. People had come from miles around. Feen and her family arrived early so they could get a seat. While sitting, deep in thought, Blain passed down the aisle, being shown to a seat two rows in front of her by the usher. The sight of him jolted her senses and for a minute, the horrible reason they were here disappeared.

She missed him so much. She missed thinking about what he'd want to eat, how his eyes lit up when he saw her. She, especially, missed him on Saturdays.

He walked straight ahead with his jaws set. He'd dressed in the black suit he'd bought for Keykey's funeral, and he looked so handsome, Feen gasped. As he turned to enter the pew, his eyes met hers and opened wide in surprise. Their eyes held for a short while. Then he turned and took his seat. She must've been holding her breath without being aware of it, because she was relieved when she exhaled. As she watched the back of his head, she felt like leaning across the row between them and caressing his head. The desire was so strong to touch him, her eyes closed as she relived the sensation. Coming back to herself, she chuckled when she thought about what the reactions of Sara and Deacon Thomas, who sitting in front of her, would have been.

She'd given him up for a noble reason, but now she needed him to calm and comfort her in that calm, gentle way he had. She used to have Adrian, but he comforted Charlotte now. Luke was in New Orleans taking care of Clarice's needs, so when she wasn't consoling Angie, she had to encourage herself.

"Momma, are you okay?" Angie asked. "Is Mr. Blain upset with you? He gave you a kinda mean look, just now."

"I'm fine. No, he not mad wit' me. 'Least I don't tink so. Never kin tell, though."

"Why would he be, Momma?"

She patted her on her hands. "He not mad wit me, Baby. He's got a lot on his mind, jus' like we do."

Seeing him like this had brought up different kinds of feelings. She'd assumed after six months was over he wouldn't call her, and it would be over. Now she wasn't so sure. From the way he'd looked at her, she knew it wasn't over yet for him. Not for either of them. Six months was four months away. Would she marry him or have a sinful affair? At one point, she'd thought she'd walk away, now she didn't know.

Service began, and when Angie's part of the program came, she walked to the front of the church with her paper she'd worked on so diligently after she'd been asked to say a word.

"Greater love hath no man than this, that a man lay down his life for his friends. John 15:13. It was me, but it could have been any one of you. If he hadn't been there, I'd be dead. He cared about everyone in this church and the whole community. He, especially, cared about the young people. He wanted them to have an education so they could succeed in life. And he loved his wife. The last thing he told me was how he'd been missing Miss Sofia. That he would see her soon."

At this point, her voice broke and a sob escaped her.

Different ones from the congregation said, "Amen. It's alright, Chile."

"He saved my life," said Angie. "I'll thank the Lord for the rest of my days for Rev. Wickliffe Francisco."

With choruses of Amen, Angie returned to her seat, where Feen patted her on her hand as she sat down.

The organ music filled the church as they rose to sing the congregational hymn before the president of the pastor's association delivered the funeral message.

Amazing Grace. How Sweet the Sound. That saved a wretch like me. I once was lost was lost, but now I'm found. Was blind. But now I see.

Most were too emotional to sing. What a terrible thing to happen, not only at their church, but to the church's shepherd. The song resonated in Feen's head, especially the last part. "Was blind, but now I see." His selfless act of saving Angie and his dying words had accomplished what all his other proclamations of "I'm sorry" had not.

Forgiveness. Over the years, she'd thought she'd forgiven him. But now she knew she hadn't. She'd only tolerated his presence and endured his sermons. She knew because of the sadness she felt at his passing and the gratefulness she felt for him saving Angie. Tears ran down her face. The burden of humiliation for being assaulted by him was lifted. She, finally, sensed the knot of hatred and regret loosen in her chest.

Angie noticed the tears on her mother's face and placed her arm around her shoulder. She tilted her head to the side so that their heads were touching.

"It's okay, Mom. I'm okay."

Charlotte sat on the opposite side of Feen and Adrian sat by Charlotte holding Lil Luke. Laura and her kids sat in the pew behind them. Feen held Charlotte's hand, tightly. Charlotte had not had a chance to get to know him as a father. Now he was gone.

Feen's mind went to Rae. Her strong, faithful older sister, who'd suffered through a lot of hard times, but had remained the one everybody could depend on. She seemed to have gotten to her limit.

She'd crumbled with the revelation her husband was not only dead, but had killed their beloved pastor and had tried to rape her niece.

When she was told, she'd exclaimed, "Ya mean he tried ta hurt my Angel?" In a voice that exhibited her inability to comprehend how this could have happened.

She was having a hard time dealing with the whole matter and was home in bed.

Feen worried about how they'd pay for Mose's funeral, not for his sake, but for Rae's. As far as Feen was concerned, the just thing for him would be to lay him out in the woods and let animals take care of him.

As the funeral message was delivered, she thought about the little boy she'd played with, the teenager who'd flirted with her, and she smiled through her tears. She'd never thought she'd ever get to the point where she could think of that time with good feelings attached to them. The horrible time that followed was still there, but it did not carry with it the same bite of hurt. Now she believed he understood what he'd done to her, that he knew the devastation he'd put on her life; therefore, she could truly forgive him.

At the end of service, as Feen walked out of the church, holding Charlotte and Angie's hands, she stopped in front of the casket, looked down at him and said, "Tank ya fur savin' ma baby." In a softer voice so no one else could hear her, she mouthed, "I furgive ya."

Charlotte, standing by her side, let her eyes move across his face and body, taking in every feature.

"I didn't get to know you, but I thank you for saving my sister." She nodded her head several times. "You've earned my forgiveness, and I believe I would have gotten to the point where I would have enjoyed being your only child. I'm so sorry we didn't get that chance."

~ **Chapter 45** ~

While the funeral was going on in Marksville, Clarice stood in the doorway of their tiny bedroom in New Orleans and watched Luke pack his bags. He'd been distraught when Laura called to tell him what had happened to Angie and to his cousin, Wickliffe.

"Ya know ya ain't been the same since Charlawt found us," Clarice said as she walked around their small bedroom.

"Dunno whatcha mean by dat Clarice. I'm still here, ain't I?"

"Only in body, Luke. Ya min' somewhere else."

"Afta what happen to Angie, I worry 'bout her."

"Luke, we's been here nigh on fourteen years and ya never worry 'bout dem before?"

"Course I worry 'bout dem. I jus' didn't say nothin' 'bout it. No use to worry ya 'bout it. Ya didn't know no more than me how they were doin', so why bother ya 'bout it."

"Well, I wantcha ta love me like ya did 'fore they came," she said.

"Whatcha mean by dat?"

"Talk ta me like ya wanna be here wit' me."

He turned from packing his clothes, walked over to her and pulled her into his arms. She closed her eyes as she lay her head on his chest.

He said, "Ya tremblin',"

"I jus' so scared ya not comin' back. I scared ya goin' back ta her."

"Why ya tink I do dat? Didn't ya hear me tell Charlawt when she came and Feen when she came dat I love ya? Dat ya ma wife. Didn't ya hear dat?"

"Um hmm. I heard. But ya change afta dat. Like ya not here no mo. Ya somewhere else. And now ya packin' ta go ta Marksville. Ya ain't been in fourteen years."

"Ma daughter was mos' raped and she was there when two men die. I gotta go see her. Let her know ever'tin' gonna be alright."

"Like ya done when Feen got rape?"

He turned her loose and stood back with a scowl across his face.

"Whatcha say?" he asked.

Clarice realized she had spoken out loud and her heart jumped into her throat.

"What I say?" she said, stalling for time for a response to come to her mind.

"Whatcha mean by Feen been rape?" he repeated. "How ya know Feen been rape?"

Clarice looked down at her hands. "I dunno nothin' bout her been rape. Dunno why I say dat."

"Ya always say ya saw dem kissin'. Like she met up wit' him on purpose. Now, ya say rape."

Clarice burst into tears. Her hands flew up to her face and she shook her head back and forth.

"I love ya so much, Luke. Please, don't leave me. Please don't go."

"How many times I gotta say I'm comin' back." She continued to cry, so he said, "Look, wanna come?"

She nodded her head in assent.

"Ya kin come," he said, "but I wanna see Angie by maself. Jus' me and her."

"Feen gonna be there. How come I cain't be there?"

225

"Feen her mama. Angie might not want her ta leave."

Clarice could feel the life she had built over the years slipping away from her. She had worked so hard to get Luke away from Feen and his children. Now they were back in their lives, and disrupting the flow of things, like she'd known they would. Every little problem Feen and her children would encounter, they'd be running to him.

She looked around the room for something to put her clothes in. It had been a long time since she'd left New Orleans. Luke was quiet again. She knew he hadn't wanted her to go, but she could not allow this to happen. She couldn't let all the sleepless nights she suffered, because of some of the things she'd done to get Luke away from these people, be for nothing. He was hers now, and he was going to stay hers. She'd do whatever she had to do.

~ CHAPTER 46 ~

It was late afternoon the day of the funeral when Luke came to visit Feen and his children. When he knocked at the door, Charlotte took a deep breath and opened it. Luke waited, not knowing what her reaction would be. She reached out and hugged him. He, immediately, hugged her back, relieved they seem to be on better grounds than they were the last time they'd spoken.

"Daddy, I know," she said.

"Ya know what?" he asked.

"That you're not my father. That Rev. Francisco was my father, and I know what happened."

Luke looked deeply into her eyes. "Okay. I'm glad it's out. Are ya alright?"

"Yes, I'm okay." She pointed to Laura and said, "We've all been talking about it, and I'm coming to terms with it. What I wanted to say was, you never made me feel like I wasn't your daughter or left out in any way. In fact, you always made me feel special, like maybe I was your favorite." She smiled sheepishly at Laura who rolled her eyes at the ceiling. "Adrian told me how you took up for Mom and how you always cared for me. I want to thank you for that."

Luke smiled at her. "No, tanks needed. From the day ya born, you ma daughter. I held ya, fed ya, kiss ya scratches, kiss ya goodnight, took ya ta school, nurse ya when ya sick. I done ever'tin' a daddy do cause ya ma daughter." He nodded his head up and down. "Dat's all there is ta it."

Charlotte went into his arms again and they held each other.

Laura stood, patiently, by knowing Charlotte needed to clear the air, because she'd been angry at him too. Until Adrian explained it had been her mother's choice, and Luke had honored it. Now, Laura waited for her chance to hug him and say hello.

Once that was done, she walked into the bedroom to awaken Feen and let her know Luke was there.

She didn't want to see him. Not now. Her heart was too heavy as it was. How was she was going to act like she's alright?

But she knew he'd driven all the way from New Orleans, because of Angie and Angie would need her father. She didn't know him at all and still felt a little shy in his presence.

Feen turned to awaken her, who'd been sleeping with her ever since the deaths had happened.

"Wake up, Angie. Ya daddy is here."

"Huh?" Angie answered, drowsily.

"Ya gotta wake up, ma baby. Ya daddy is here."

Angie's eyes became big. "What? Why?"

"I'm sho he came ta see if ya alright."

Angie frowned. "Mama, you're coming in there with me, right?"

"Yeah, Baby. Mama's comin' witcha. I'm gonna stay right by ya."

As they walked into the front room, Luke stood by the front door with his hat in his hand. His eyes went to Feen first, and he looked at her as though he was waiting for an answer from her. Seeing him stirred up strong emotions and she felt as though the wind had been knocked out of her again. He looked at Angie, and his expression changed to a look of concern.

"Angie," he said. "I come ta see if ya alright. I wanna know if I kin help ya."

Angie did not answer. She kept looking at him all wide-eyed.

"Angie," he said. "I know we didn't git a chance to talk the other day when y'all came to Naw Orleen, and I know ya don't 'member me from when you's lil, but I 'member you. You were the prettes' baby I ever see."

At that her eyes became even bigger. "Prettier than Laura and Charlotte?"

Luke looked over at Laura and Charlotte, who was sitting on the sofa. They both sat with their arms crossed looking up at him, waiting for his answer. The moment took the tension out of the room for Feen. Now, she wanted to burst into laughter. She was anxious to see how he would get himself out of this situation.

He smiled at his two older daughters as if he hoped they would understand what he was trying to do. He nodded his head, "Yeah, the prettes' lil baby I ever see. Laura," he said, as he waved his hand toward her, "she had the loudest cry I ever heard. Cry all the time. She turned into a pretty lil tike afta she start ta walk. And Charlawt, well, she hardly cry a'tall. Jus' smile all the time. She was the happ'est baby I ever see. Butchu, ya the prettes'."

He stole a look at Laura and Charlotte to see if he had been able to smooth their ruffled feathers.

Laura and Charlotte both smiled and shook their head from side to side.

Angie gave him a big smile. She smirked at Laura and Charlotte as if to say "See."

He walked up to her, put his arms around her and she let him. Feen could see her back was still stiff. She'd just been through a horrible experience with a man she trusted, and even though Luke was her father, he was still a man she didn't know. He released her and looked down in her face.

"It alright. I understan'," he said as he shifted his gaze to Feen. "I understan'," he repeated.

"I'm glad you came, Daddy," Angie said. "Did you know Uncle Mose?"

Luke nodded his head, "Yeah, knowed him good. Sho did. Well, thought I did. Cuz I never thought' he'd a done dat."

Angie started to cry and Luke put his arms around her again. "Gone and cry. Cry all ya want."

Charlotte and Laura got up, went into the kitchen and signaled to Feen to go along with them. She shook her head no.

"I'ma stay wit' Angie," she said, as she sat in a side chair.

Luke and Angie sat on the sofa. "Do ya wanna talk 'bout what happen. Laura tol' me some a it."

"Maybe sometime, Daddy. Not today. I'm glad you came, though."

He wasn't surprised she didn't want to talk about it. He'd gone through the same thing with her mother.

"I had ta come," he said, in a low voice.

"You had to come?" she asked. "Daddy, I needed you today. But, I can't tell you the number of times I've wanted to know you, to talk with my daddy. Why didn't you always feel that way? Why didn't you feel you had to come before?"

As Feen looked on, it took all of her willpower not to jump in and tell Luke some of the things that had happened when he'd been needed. But this was not the place or the time. This time was for Angie to speak her mind, to let him know how she'd been hurt and maybe make peace with him. If she could build a relationship with him, she might get a chance to understand what it was like to have a father. Well, as much as she could, considering he lived in New Orleans.

"Daddy, I didn't even know what you looked like. I could have gone on a field trip to New Orleans and passed you on the street and not know who you were."

Luke sat with his head down.

"I know. I know. I wouldn't know ya either. Ya dunno how sorry I is. I'm real sorry and I wanna make it up ta ya, if ya lemme." He reached into his pocket and came out with a folded paper with a pink hair ribbon inside. "I didn't know if' ya like hair ribbon. Laura and Charlawt use ta like dem, 'specially, in the summertime. They like ta wear ponytails. I dunno the color ya like, but I thought pink a pretty color fur a pretty girl."

Angie smiled and nodded her head, as she took the ribbons out of his hands.

"I like ribbons, Daddy, and I like pink, too."

Charlotte hollered from the kitchen, "Y'all want to eat. Plenty of food left."

Feen looked at Luke, "Ya welcome ta stay fur supper."

"Well, if it alright witcha, I like ta stay and eat wit' ma fam'ly. Ain't done dat in a long time."

His words took her by surprise, and she began to cough. Good thing she didn't have anything in her mouth, because she would've choked on it.

Feen looked at her small kitchen and said, "I don't 'member the last time five people sat 'round dis table."

Laura said, "If I remember right, you like to sit in this chair where you could look out the window."

He smiled. "Yeah, I did, so's I could see what was goin' on in the barn wit' the animals and see the road in case somebody stopped by." Pausing for a moment, he said, "Ya 'member dat?"

"Daddy, I remember everything about you. Don't you know that?" she asked.

A frown came across his face, "I jus' got so much ta makeup fur."

Charlotte said, "No need to worry about it right now. Sit down and eat. We all know it's going to take a while before the anger we feel subsides. But we're willing to hear you out and let you show us you're sincere in trying to make things right."

"'Preciate dat, Charlawt. I 'preciate dat a whole lot."

"Angie needs you," Charlotte said, as she looked at Angie. Pointing at Laura, she said, "Laura had you all of her childhood." At herself, "I had you some of mine and you were a good daddy." Holding his gaze, she pierced into his very soul, and he closed his eyes, feeling grateful she felt that way. "But Angie never had you at all. She doesn't have the slightest idea what it feels like to have a daddy."

The atmosphere was so heavy with regret at the loss of all those years, the times that couldn't be regained.

Luke reached over to Angie and held her hand tightly for a second. He said grace over the food and they ate. The conversation was light. Someone passing by who didn't know the history wouldn't have known the father and husband in this group had deserted them for years or that the youngest child had just been attacked, narrowly escaped being raped herself, while she'd witnessed two violent deaths and that the person murdered was the biological father of another one of them. The surface chatter allowed them to survive those moments, but the pain and hurt were lurking underneath.

After supper, Charlotte and Laura went to their separate homes, after giving their daddy long hugs when they'd said goodnight. Angie looked at him, shyly, and went to bed without giving him a hug.

Feen stood to show Luke to the door and wondered what was going through his head. He'd made a remark about being with his "family" that had puzzled her, but she'd decided to let it be.

"I really enjoyed bein' here witch y'all tonight. Ya know, calm like. I might not deserve it, but it was real nice ta jus' sit and talk," he said as he stood by the door to leave.

"Yeah, t'was nice. Well, jus' cuz nobody was ugly ta ya don't mean they's not still mad atcha. Cuz they is."

He nodded and said, "I know. I know ya still mad wit' me, too. Dat's why I 'preciate ya sittin' down and talkin' wit' me and sharin' a meal wit' me. Really I do."

She stood in front of him, still amazed he was there. All the times she'd thought of this moment over the years, of him standing in front of her. She'd thought it would be under different circumstances. He'd come home like he'd said he would, because he loved her. As if he could read her mind, his eyes darkened and he reached his hand out to her. She stood and looked at it for a minute. She was not sure what he wanted her to do. He put his hand further out and touched her on the arm. She jumped back.

"Luke, whatcha doin'?"

He exhaled and said, "Dunno. Jus' wanted ta touch ya, dat's all. Just wanted ta letcha know I know ya been through a hard time, and I's sorry 'bout dat."

"Ya don't hafta touch me ta say ya sorry. I tink it time ya go. Gone home."

He gave another big sigh.

"Alright. Can I call ya? Cuz we need ta talk."

"We talk tonight. What else we gotta talk 'bout?"

"Angie. How I can help Angie. And Charlawt. How I can help Chawlawt and Laura." He paused. "How I can help you."

"'Preciate dat. Ya kin call me 'bout Angie, Chawlawt and Laura. Not ready ta talk 'bout me witcha.

"I understand. I'll call ya, alright?"

He nodded and walked out of the door.

She watched as he strode to his car. His gait was the same as she remembered. Memories flooded her mind. Their courtship and marriage. Their long talks. She knew she could not let recollections overcome her to the point where she'd forget what he'd put her through. She didn't understand what his motives were, but suspected he'd tried to come on to her. If that was the case, he had some nerve. After all those years and he was still with that woman. She been through too much and had come too far to let him hurt her again. Ever.

~ CHAPTER 47 ~

Clarice stood in the doorway of Teresa's house. "Wonder where he at. Hope nothin' happen ta him. What's keepin' him so long?"

"Clarice, dat his chirren. He talkin' ta his chirren. Ya knowed he had chirren 'fore ya ran off wit' him."

"Yeah, I knowed dat. I know he love his chirren. But he love me too, and it been me takin' care a him. It's time fur him ta come home."

Clarice could feel Teresa's eyes and her disapproval.

"I know ya don't understan'. Ya don't understan' what it feel like ta love a man like I love Luke."

"I know what it feel like ta love a man. Yeah, I do. But dat man married. Was married when ya left here wit' him and he still married now. Ya shouldn't a done dat, Clarice. Ya shouldn't a done dat."

"Wonder where he at," she said as she moved to a window.

Teresa shook her head from side to side.

"Ya not list'nin' ta me. Ya better hear what I say. Dat man married and even though he been gone witcha fur years, he still her husband. And dat's where he at."

Clarice turned around angrily, and said, "He comin' back ta me cuz he love me. Ya jus' wait and see."

"Clarice, I dunno what they talkin' 'bout, but one tin' I know. Dat's her husband. I know how it feel fur a woman ta know her husband wit' another woman. Dat' a hurtin' tin.' I'm a witness."

"Ya want me ta worry 'bout Feen? Feen shoulda took care a him good nuf so's he won't leave. Same as you. Ya shoulda took care a Emile good nuf so he not be wit' Bernice."

Teresa didn't believe what she was hearing.

"Gull, don't talk ta me like dat in ma house. I'll knock ya cross-eyed."

Clarice knew she'd gone too far. Her face got a frantic look as she looked at the clock. They heard steps on the porch.

Clarice ran to the door and opened it for Luke to come in. He entered the room and nodded at Teresa.

"How they doin'?" Teresa asked, trying to calm herself.

"As well as could be 'spected," he answered.

He looked at Clarice. "I come by ta see ya, make sho ya alright. Now, I'm gonna go to Taunt Julia's house. Been a long day. Need ta rest these ole bones."

Clarice's face clouded up again. "I wanna come witcha."

"Ya know ya cain't do dat. Not in Marksville. Ya know we talk 'bout dat on the way here. Ya stay wit' Teresa and I stay wit' Julian."

"I bet Julian would lemme stay," she said.

"I tol' ya, he won't, but even if he would, I done 'nuf harm to Feen and the gulls. Not gonna cast no more shame on dem den I gotta."

"What harm ya doin' dem, by me doin' what I been doin' fur the last fourteen years? Sleepin' in bed witcha."

Luke's eyes shot at Teresa who was standing there, but had no readable expression on her face.

"I'm her husband. Ever'body in town know I'm back. Nuf gossip 'side me addin' ta it. So, I'm gonna go ta Julian. And dat all there is ta it. Don't wanna hear nothin' else 'bout it."

"What time ya comin' tomorra?" she asked, with her eyes wide, anticipating his answer.

"Dunno," he answered. "Have ta help Julian do some work and den I need ta see Angie."

"Ya goin' back over there, agin?" she said, incredulously.

He was quiet for a second. Again, his eyes went to Teresa, who remained observant.

"I cain't keep goin' over dis. I'm tired and I need ta rest. Visit witcha sista. Dunno what time I be here tomorra."

From the tone of his voice, Clarice knew he'd decided what he was gonna do, and anything she said fell upon deaf ears.

"Alright," she said.

Luke nodded again to Teresa, "Much obliged, Teresa. See ya tomorra."

"Clarice ma sista, Luke," she said. "She know she welcome here, anytime."

He nodded again and walked out the door.

Clarice watched him as he drove away and felt he was driving away from her. The pain was so great in her chest, she knew she would die if he left her. Thoughts were flying through her mind on how to stop all this foolishness, once and for all.

Teresa observed her sister. She'd tried to explain to her Luke's obligations to Feen, and his family and Clarice had turned on her. Any woman interloping into another woman's marriage was something Teresa could not understand. She shook her head as she left the room, leaving Clarice looking out the window long after Luke was gone.

~ CHAPTER 48 ~

Walking back to her house from visiting Rae, Feen saw Luke sitting on her porch with Angie, and she got nervous, because she thought about how he was looking at her before he'd left last night. What could he be thinking?

After entering her home, she served supper so they could talk while they ate. She excused herself and went outside to feed her chickens.

Toward her fire pit where she washed clothes, she saw something that looked familiar. It was a homemade stuffed cloth doll, like she used to find all the time, with a needle stuck through the head and another through the heart. She picked it up and looked at it in disbelief. Now it came clear to her. It had been about fourteen years since she'd found one in her yard, or on her porch or under her steps. Now, when Luke came back in town, the hoodoo business started again.

"Momma, where you at?" Angie asked. "Are you alright?"

"Yeah," she said and put the doll in her pocket. "I's comin.'"

Feen opened the screen door to Angie's anxious eyes.

"I'm sorry, Momma, but I got scared. You never take that long to feed the chickens."

"I want ta give y'all time ta talk and git ta know one 'nother."

"We talked plenty, but I got homework I gotta do," Angie said. She looked at Luke and said shyly. "Goodnight, Daddy."

"Goodnight, Angie," said Luke.

They both stood rooted in place.

"Ya kin hug her, Luke."

So, he reached forward and touched his cheek to hers. She smiled at him and went to her room.

"Do ya want me ta go or kin we talk?" he asked.

"We kin talk."

"I thought maybe ya want me ta leave 'fore ya came back in, cuz ya stay in the yard so long."

"So, if ya thought dat, why ya still here?" she asked.

"Cuz I want ta talk ta ya, dat's why."

She shook her head, "Ya know what ya jus' say don't make no sense. Ya ax me if ya kin stay cuz ya thought I didn't want ya ta stay. If ya thought I didn't want ya ta stay, why didn't ya jus' leave?" she repeated.

"Look, we ain't gittin' no wheres like dis. I need ta talk ta ya," he said.

"I didn't wantcha ta leave cuz I gotta talk ta ya, too," she said.

"Oh, really? 'Bout what?"

"No, ya kin go first."

His brow knotted up and dimmed his eyes. She led him to the sofa in the living room.

"Alright, I'll go first." he said.

"Wait, 'fore ya start," she said. When she'd visited Rae earlier, she'd told her that Clarice had come with Luke from New Orleans. He hadn't mentioned it to her, and she wondered why.

"There sometin' else I need to ax ya 'fore dat, cuz I didn't ax ya las' night." She sat facing him on the couch and looking directly into his eyes. "But where is ya stayin'?"

"I'm stayin' at Taunt Julia's house wit' Julian."

"Oh," said Feen. "Dunno why dat surprise me. He ya cousin."

"Yeah, and there never been no hard feelin' tween me and him. Never. He welcome me like a brother. Tol' him I'm sorry 'bout Cliffie and he b'lieve me, cuz I is.

"Would ya believe I sat in dat church and cried fur dat man. Dat man I hated fur so long. Ya know, he tol' me one time, long time ago, dat one day he was gonna do sometin' dat would make me furgive him. He was true ta his word. He save ma chile. I don't jus' furgive him, but I mourn him."

"Yeah, dat's what I mean. I is sorry 'bout him, too." He paused for a moment. "Ya know he did more than rape you."

Feen looked puzzled.

"He rape our marriage, Feen. Ya were diff'rent afta dat. Fur many long years, ya were diff'rent."

She looked at him, really looked at him and saw the pain in his eyes. She knew he'd suffered along with her. But she couldn't help the way she'd felt a long time ago, and she'd tried to make up for her remoteness by doing other things for him, to let him know she really did not blame him for what had happened.

"I know. I still took care a ya, though. Still cook fur ya, still wash ya clothes, did the farm chores when ya couldn't." Her eyes moved away from his face to her hands. "When we's in Naw Orleen, ya say ya were wit' her mos' our marriage."

"Yes, but not 'fore the rape. I was never wit' her 'fore the rape. I know dat's no 'cuse, but never 'fore dat. Ya changed, Feen. Ya didn't want me ta touch ya, and when ya did let me touch ya, ya froze up. Made me feel guilty 'bout touchin' ma own wife."

"Ain't ya sometin'. After whatcha done, ya want me ta 'pologize?"

He squeezed his eyes shut.

"No. No, dat ain't what I meant. Jus' tryna 'splain ta ya what happen, s'all."

"Luke, ya already 'splain ta me in Naw Orleen." When he turned back to look at her, she said, "Where Clarice at?"

He studied her for a second, as she studied him.

He said, "She at her sista. She at Teresa."

"She not stayin' witcha at Julian."

"No. She at Teresa."

Their eyes were locked. His hand reached out to touch her arm and she stood up.

"I'm tied, Luke."

"Alright. Don't wanna outstay ma welcome. Ya say ya had sometin' ta ax me?"

"I found dis in the yard today."

She reached into her pocket and took out the doll. Luke's jaw dropped.

"When?"

"Jus' now. Dat's why I stay in the yard so long. Didn't want Angie ta see me upset. Luke. Luke?"

He was staring at the doll.

"Luke, it's her, ain't it?"

"Dat's what I's tryna tell ya without talkin' bad 'bout her. Cuz she a good woman ..." Feen's hand flew up to stop him.

"Don't do dat in ma house. Don't tell me how good she is. Ya did dat in Naw Orleen, and I had ta take it, but ya ain't talkin' like dat in ma house."

"Fair nuf," he said.

"Not no woman puttin' hoodoo dolls wit' pins in dem in ma yard. Ya gonna come in ma house talkin' 'bout what a good woman she is. Git out. Git out ma house."

"Wait. Wait. Ya gittin' mad. Don't be mad. I'll handle the doll mess. I promise. No mo hoodoo doll. Don't make me go yet." His voice was pleading. "Not when ya mad."

She was puzzled. She couldn't figure out his mood. "What's going on? Why ya actin' like ya care 'bout me and if I'm mad."

"Dat's what I want ta talk ta ya 'bout. We talk 'nother time," he said. "Afta ya calm down some. Now ya all mad and ever'tin.' Ya won't hear what I'm tryna say. I come back tomorra night." He looked away and looked back at her. "I'll take care the doll bidness. I promise."

"Please. Please take care the doll mess. What mo she want? She gotcha. What mo she want?"

Luke regarded her for a second, opened his mouth, then closed it back.

"We gonna talk tomorra. Alright?"

Feen nodded as they walked to the door. He put his hand out to touch her back, but she sidestepped in the other direction.

~ CHAPTER 49 ~

Charlotte asked Angie to come spend the night at her house. She felt, after her ordeal, it would do her good to spend some time with the innocence of Luke and with her. Because of their age difference, Charlotte had been more like a second mama than a sister. Angie would share things with her she wouldn't with her mother.

Luke arrived after Angie had gone to Charlotte's house.

"I cain't say nuf 'bout the good job ya done wit' these chirren," he said.

"Well, I tried ma best. Done like ma momma done me. Made sho they went ta church on Sunday and ta school when it was open." She stopped for a second. "Tried ta live a right life in front dem."

"Well, ya done good."

"Tank ya. We ate already, but I kin fix ya sometin' if ya want."

"No, I'm fine."

They walked into the house and sat on the sofa.

"Now, I'm calm," she said. "Whatcha wanna talk ta me 'bout?"

"Dunno where ta start." He sat fur a long time lookin' at the picture of the former governor of Louisiana, Huey P. Long, their wedding gift.

"Whatcha wanna talk ta me 'bout?" she asked, getting a little impatient.

"I need ta clear the air."

He waited for her acknowledgment.

"Alright," she said.

Her heart was beating in her chest, and she did not know if she'd be able to keep her word. What kind of news did he have to tell her now?

"Feen. I always loved ya. Since we were teenagers. We like friends, not jus' boyfriend and gullfriend. 'Member, dat?"

"Yeah, I 'member."

"Anyway, when ya momma ax me ta marry ya, even though I love ya, I weren't ready ta get married. Cuz I didn't even know if I wanted ta stay here. I knowed ya wouldn't leave here, but I wanted ta go ta Tulsa Oklahoma. Some of the Bontons went up there, and they say lotta work up there. 'Member dat?"

"Tulsa, Oklahoma? No, don't 'member ya talkin' 'bout goin' there. Yeah, I 'member people gone ta Oklahoma, some ta Chicago, some ta California, lotta places. Don't 'member nothin' specific 'bout ya wantin' ta go ta Tulsa."

"Yeah, well, I did wanna go somewhere else. But we got married and it turnt out alright. I was happy and you was happy 'til Cliffie done what he done ta ya." He stopped for a second and took a deep breath. "I felt like I let ya down and all ya feelin' fur me was gone. Wit' the Depression like it was, I could only sell cotton fur much a nothin', and it kept bof us strugglin' ta make ends meet." Their eyes were locked. "Ya hear me?"

"I hear ya, but I was lettin' ya finish like ya ax me. It was hard. But the good times came back. I thought we doin' good, den ya left."

"Do ya 'member what was goin' on den. The dead animals and the dolls always showin' up," he said

"Yeah, but now I tink it was Clarice," she said

"I'm pretty sho t'was her, but I didn't figure dat out til jus' fore I left."

Still lookin' him in his eyes, she said. "Ya left ya fam'ly fur someone ya knowed was tryna ta hurt dem? Is dat the kinda man you is?"

He shook his head. "I'm the kinda man dat wouldn't let ya git hurt cuza me. I knowed I'd done wrong and when I tried ta break it off, …" he stood up, walked to a window and looked outside.

"Whatcha lookin' at outside in the dark?"

"Dunno," he said. "Thought I heard sometin'. Maybe I'm jus' jumpy." He returned to his seat on the sofa. "She not right, all the time. I mean, mos' time she fine. If she tink I'ma leave, she go plum crazy. I cain't 'splain it. Anyhow, I know she wanna hurt y'all ta keep me. Dat's why I ax ya ta leave town wit' me."

"Ya didn't ax me ta leave town?" she said with disbelief.

"Member, the night fore I left, we talkin', and I say it'd be nice ta go ta Tulsa, and ya say dis was home. I had ta do sometin'. I couldn't leave y'all at her mercy. So's I decide ta take her somewhere, sit her up wit' a job, find a way ta put her down easy and den I kin come back. And y'all would be safe. And Adrian was here, I knowed he'd help ya."

Feen couldn't believe what she was hearing. "If all dat's true, why ya tol' us how much ya love her when we went ta Naw Orleen?"

"Like I say, I thought I could let her down easy. But anytime I try ta pull 'way, she held on tight. Wantin' ta kill herself. When y'all came she in the house. I cain't say nothin' else. I guess I coulda tol' Adrian 'fore we went home, but I didn't think 'bout it. Y'all kinda caught me off guard, ya know."

"So, did ya ever love her?"

She could tell he didn't want to get into that part. For the first time, his eyes left hers. But she couldn't forgive him if he didn't tell her everything. He shook his head.

"No. No. I'm sho I never love her, but I like her a lot. 'Specially at first. She need me. Her life was me. And she done ever'tin' ta please me. And at the time, ya didn't want me ta touch ya." Looking back at Feen, he said, "I don't tink it was ever love cuz I never was gonna leave you fur her." He shook his head forcefully, "Never."

"But, dat's whatcha done. If ya never was gonna leave me, why ya done dat?"

"Like I say, I plan ta take her ta Naw Orleen and leave her there. And y'all would be safe from her hoodoo tricks."

"Ya start enjoyin' Naw Orleen too much ta come back?"

"No. She'd get jobs, but she cain't keep dem. Nothin' please her. No kinda work, nothin'. She sit home and wait fur me. I have ta convince her every day I'm not comin' back ta Marksville. I work hard all day long and den gotta come home ta dat. It drain me dry. I didn't know how ta git outta it. I cain't leave her wit' no way ta take care herself. She holler and cry and have bad dreams worse than you use ta have."

"Bad dreams? Why? Did she ever tell ya why?"

"No. The mos' she'd say was it was sometin' she done fur me. I never could figure out what she talkin' 'bout. But I kin say, in fourteen years, the dreams never stop."

"Ya tink it was her conscience?"

"Don't know."

Luke didn't think so. Clarice never had any regrets about their leaving Marksville or of leaving his family to fend for themselves.

They both sat quietly.

"Why ya tellin' me dis now?" she asked.

"Cuz I need ya ta know. Afta I been gone so long, I figure ya found somebody. Maybe Adrian. He always hangin' round ya lookin' atcha all starry eye. When he tol' me ya didn't have nobody, my heart come back ta life. Up til den, I didn't know how dead I was inside."

Feen's heart jumped into her throat. Her eyes got big.

Luke asked, "Is dat true? Did Adrian tell me right? Ya don't have nobody?"

Feen's mind ran to Blain. She saw from the expression on Luke's face he still knew her well enough to know something had happened.

"Oh, so ya do have somebody," said Luke. "Must be sometin' lately, cuz Adrian wouldn't lie to me. But he's not here. I ain't seen nobody hangin' round since I been here. So something not right 'bout it."

"'Preciate ya tellin' me 'bout Clarice. I'm not gonna tell ya 'bout me. Ya left me ta take care maself too long fur me ta start baring ma soul ta ya now," she said. "The strange part, when we were together and not touchin' each other, I never thought you were going somewhere else. Never doubted ya. Ain't dat sometin'? Never cross ma mind. Cuz we had dove eyes fur each other. 'Member dat?" she said. She shook her head slightly as she continued to meet his gaze.

"Ya never wonder?" he asked.

She shook her head again.

"No, I never wonder. Dat's why she was staring atcha at Emile's funeral and why she wanted to be the one to tell ya why I's late comin' back from Teresa's house the night Emile died. But it all became clear when I saw ya in Naw Orleen. Dat's when I realize how stupid I was."

"No, Feen, no. Don't say dat. Ya mind was troubled and ya trusted me. There was nothin' wrong in ya trustin' ya husband."

"Yeah," she said. "Troubled, and I trusted ya. I trusted ya so much. I feel like a fool. I shoulda know sometin' was goin' on."

"Ya had a lot on ya plate and I'm sorry I done what I done. Ya hear me? I'm sorry," he said. He took her chin in his hand. "I always loved ya. Never stopped."

He leaned forward and gently kissed her. The pressure of his lips was so slight, and her heart pounded fiercely. He kissed her again. This time with more force and she couldn't stop herself from placing her hand on his neck and gently caressing him. The kiss deepened, and her mind went to when he'd kissed her for the first time. When she pulled away, they stared at each other.

"Ya know I cain't do dis now," she whispered.

"Lemme stay the night. Angie is not here," he whispered. "And Ya still ma wife."

"I know. But I don't feel like ya wife, anymore. I felt like ya wife until I saw ya in Naw Orleen wit' Clarice. Look, 'preciate ever'tin' ya tol' me tonight. It help ta know the whole story. Maybe somma dis pain in ma heart will ease, but there's too much water under the bridge."

"I jus' wanted ya ta know. I gotta figure out how ta tell Clarice. I'm gonna talk wit' her tonight, and soon as I git her ta 'cept dat idea, I'm gonna be back ta work on ya. Tell ya man, ya husband back. He can go on now."

Feen laughed at that.

"Oh yeah. My husband, huh? Well, we gonna see 'bout dat."

She walked behind him to the door. He whirled around and she bumped into him. When she gasps in surprise, he took her elbows and pulled her into his arms. He pressed his body to hers as he kissed her. She had loved this man so much and had longed for him for so long. Her heart beat so hard, it drowned out everything else. She wanted to push him away, yet her hands stroked his face and ran through his hair. His lips and tongue worked their magic on her, and she felt suspended in time.

Finally, when they released each other, he whispered, "You're still ma wife."

With those words ringing in her ears, and the feel of his lips still burning on hers, she watched him as he walked out of the door to his car.

~ CHAPTER 50 ~

Because of the excitement of kissing Feen and the possibility there might be a chance he could get her to take him back, he passed right by Teresa's house. Once he realized that, he decided to go on to Julian's house and come back to see Clarice in the morning, when he was fresh. He was in too good a mood to argue or to endure the scenes that were inevitable.

Once there, his delight in what had happened made him sprint to the house. Julian noticed his disposition.

He tilted his head to the side and said, "Did you get some good news today?"

Luke smiled, "Ya have no idea. I done sometin' today I been tinkin' 'bout fur fourteen years."

Julian's eyebrows shot up. "Hmm. Something to do with Feen, I presume."

"Ya presume right," he said.

"Want to talk about it?"

"No. You and the whole world will know when it happen." He looked at Julian with a satisfied grin. "If ya don't mind, Man, gonna git me some rest. If ya got some chores ya need done, lemma know 'fore ya leave in the mornin'?"

Julian nodded his head, and Luke walked to his room, cleaned up and went to bed, where he quickly went to sleep.

He saw Feen sitting at the edge of a high ledge by the banks of Red River. Her back was to him. This was a dangerous part of the banks. This part had been gradually caving into the river, so that the edge was sharp and the fall was high. Another piece of the bank could break off and fall into the muddy red waters at any time.

Feen knew not to sit there. He called out to her as he walked faster. It took him forever to get there, because the more he tried to hurry, the more it seemed he was running in place. Finally, he reached her. He kept calling her name, but she would not turn around.

He heard someone behind him sobbing. He turned and it was Clarice. He became afraid for Feen. He wanted to console Clarice, but he was worried about Feen being in such a vulnerable position. Clarice seemed to know what he thought because as she cried, she'd look from Luke to Feen's back, then back to Luke. Her sobs were so loud they shook her whole body. She gave a loud battle cry, "Aaahhh," as she ran full force into Feen's back and they both went sailing through the air.

With his arms outstretched, he ran to catch her, but he was too late. They were gone, and he found himself, also, flying and observing the water below. As he sailed downward, he screamed her name. Feen.

His eyes flew open and he grasped he was in bed at Julian's. He breathed a sigh of relief. It had all been a dream. Until he understood there was someone crying in the room with him. At this he spun around and saw Clarice huddled in a corner.

"Clarice, whatcha doin' here?"

She continued to cry.

He sat and waited for her to stop. He knew from experience that was the best way to handle the situation. Finally, after about fifteen minutes, the tears lessened, but she continued to sniffle.

"How ya git in here? Julian know ya here?"

"Don't tink so," she said. "Ya know he don't lock the door, jus' latch the screen door on the back porch. Took a long tin stick, put it through the hole in the screen and unlatch it."

"Um hmm. I see. Why ya here?"

"Came ta see ya. Ya ma man. My life. Been seeing ya 'mos' ever' night fur the last fourteen years. Why wouldn't I wanna see ya? Why ya didn't come by ta see me tonight?"

"Cuz I'm tied. Was gonna come by ta see ya tomorra," he said.

She sniffled and asked, "When we goin' back home?"

"Let's talk 'bout dis tomorra, Clarice. Since ya here, ya kin stay tonight. But ya gotta go back ta Teresa in the mornin' and den we kin talk."

She stared at him. "What's the matter, Luke? Ya don't want me no more? Ya been over there at Feen ever'day and ya ain't jus' been talkin' ta Angie, either."

From the way she was talking, he gathered she knew what she was talking about. There was a good chance she'd been outside of the house while they were talking.

"Since ya wanna talk 'bout Feen, she found sometin' in her yard. Sometin' she use ta find all the time 'fore we left." He waited to see if she'd answer. She didn't. "Ya know sometin' 'bout hoodoo doll and I know ya know 'bout dead animal under step?" he asked.

"No," she said. "Dunno nothin' 'bout dat." She was no longer crying. Her voice began to take a hard, aggressive tone.

"Don't ya tink it funny it stop when we left and start back up when we come back? Don't ya tink it funny?"

She didn't answer. Silence. "When we gone back ta Naw Orleen? Ya say ya wanted to see Angie, Charlawt and Laura. Ya saw dem all. Now we kin go home."

"Ya put dolls wit' needles through dem in ma wife yard. A yard where ma chirren and grand chirren play. Ya don't seem ta know what's wrong wit' dat."

250

"I wanna go home, Luke. Jus' you and me. Like before. Dat's how I want it."

She walked over in a seductive walk and tried to put her arms around him. He pushed her arms away. Her face contorted in a frown.

"I love ya mo than Feen ever did or ever could. It's time fur us ta go home," she said, her voice was forceful.

She walked around the bed toward the door. He remained seated on the bed, and asked as he turned toward her, "Ya gonna go back ta Teresa?"

She leaned down to the floor, an area he could not see behind the bed and came up with an ax.

Before he could react, she moved toward him, shouting, "I wanna go home," swung the ax and hit him with the blunt side of the blade. Blood gushed from the top of his head, and he fell to the floor.

She stood over him and screamed, "Luke. Luke. Luke, Ya owe me. All I done fur ya. I wanna go home. Take me back ta Naw Orleen."

She remained looking down at him as if she expected him to get up and bring her back to New Orleans.

Julian ran into the room.

"What's going on?" he asked. Julian's mouth flew open when he saw Luke on the floor.

"I wanna go home," she cried.

Her words were so muddled with tears, he barely understood her. Still screaming, she held the ax in her hand over her head and aimed it toward Julian. He put his hands up in front of himself in a defensive posture.

"Hold on," he said. "Clarice, think what you're doing?"

Still crying uncontrollably, she threw the ax at him. He ducked as he heard the crackle of the wood as the ax penetrated the wall behind him. She squealed and ran out of the room.

Luke lay face down on the floor. Blood streamed from his head. Julian's knees buckled, but he steadied himself.

"Pull yourself together," he mumbled to himself, as he felt for Luke's pulse. There was a faint one.

Giving a massive sigh of relief, he said, "Hold on, Buddy." He ran into the living room to call for the sheriff and an ambulance.

∞

When Clarice left Teresa's house to go over to Julian's to see Luke, she'd brought two things with her, an ax and a bottle of lye. She'd been in Feen's yard earlier that night and had heard some of their conversation. She'd left when Luke had gotten up to see who or what was outside. The tone of his voice telegraphed to her he was after something. And she guessed the something he was after was Feen. She couldn't let that happen. She hadn't a specific plan in mind, but she'd known things couldn't continue the path it was going. Luke had to be made to understand she was the best thing for him and going back to New Orleans was what they needed to do.

Now, she was running to the river with the bottle of lye in her hand. Lye. The dolls and animal guts she'd placed over the years had not bothered her conscience. She wished she'd put more to make sure Feen would've become unhinged. It didn't bother her that the dinner she'd laced with rat poison and given to Feen to eat had made her niece, Louisiana, sick or that Feen and her children had suffered the years Luke was gone, not knowing where he was or if he was alive or dead.

What had bothered her for all the years she'd been away was the death of Toyotae. He'd been such a sweet boy. He'd be around church, early, to ring the bell and would help her carry and move things at church suppers or other events when she'd been preparing food. Knowing Feen and her family would be at a church gathering, she'd baked some special cookies. Lye water in small amounts was sometimes used in baking, so she decided to make some with a tremendous amount of lye and camouflaged the taste and smell with vanilla and sugar. At first the cookies would crumble and it had taken her a while to figure out a recipe that would work. On the day she'd brought the cookies, Toyotae had been especially nice to her, helping her break the ice in big chunks with an ice pick to put in the punch.

When his cousin, Charlotte, came through the line, Clarice had slipped three cookies onto her plate. Toyotae fixed himself a plate and left to go sit with her and Keykey to eat. Clarice almost fainted when she saw Charlotte give him her cookies. She'd felt like running to him to take the cookies away, but she couldn't do that. It would let people know what she'd done.

Charlotte knew he loved cookies. She always gave him her dessert when they ate together. Toyotae had become very ill and suffered while he withered away.

She'd had a hard time sleeping at night. He'd appear with his body shriveled up, skin sticking to his skull and huge eyes that shone with suffering. She wished it had been Feen, but Toyotae's huge eyes would not give her peace. She couldn't lessen her burden by sharing this secret with Luke. He'd hate her if he ever found out.

Now she'd killed him, too. The man she loved. Her reason for living. What kind of life would she have without him?

She stood on the bank where fishermen launched their boats. She was so tired and her feet hurt. She'd walked all the way to Julian's from Teresa's. After hitting Luke with the ax, she'd run across the road and over the levee to the river bank. The area she and Luke had made love for the first time was a long way down the river, close to where Feen lived. Maybe if she walked there, she could give Feen some lye.

As she walked the bank, the water became further away, because parts of the riverbank are even with the water; other places are high above the river. She continued to walk until she could no longer just walk into the water. The further she walked the more the banks looked like cliffs.

Good memories flooded her mind. The first time she'd kissed Luke was on River Road right near the river, and she'd made love with Luke for the first time under a tree on the riverbank. She wanted to go there, but that spot was a long way. They'd spent countless hours talking, eating and making love at the hunting shack which was even further down the river.

She decided to walk to the place where they'd made love under the tree. She could rest when she got there. She would wrap her arms around herself and relive the moment when they'd first became one. Maybe if she lay there and concentrated hard enough, she could bring him back to life. After all, she was a hoodoo priestess. She didn't have her candles, herbs or potions, or her mojo bag with bits of his hair and nails in it, and she needed those things for that

At night, the river water looked black. Large waves formed as the water moved swiftly down the channel. Strong enough to carry anything far away from where it entered. She stood on the ledge and looked down through the sharp rock edges that formed the cliff. It was a long way down to the water. She looked at the gulls flying and wondered what it would be like to fly above the river and watch it as it flowed down its route.

She sat with her legs hanging down over the ledge. She stretched her arms out as the breeze touched her face. She got up and walked some more. She was so tired. Luke. She loved Luke so much and she could not live without him. She was thirsty. A little sip of water would help her make it to where she and Luke had made love. She was so tired now. Her legs were weak and she wasn't thinking, clearly. The moon was out, but only a waxing crescent that didn't give much light. She couldn't tell where she was on the river.

She sat on the ledge, again, when it occurred to her she had some liquid. It wasn't water, but it was wet. She could drink it. She wouldn't drink much, just one swallow, something to wet her throat. She opened the bottle and took a huge gulp.

The taste and the pain were immediate. She wondered if the cookies had burned Toyotae's throat. She coughed and her body jerked, violently, sending her off her perch into the open air. Her arms spread out, as though she was a bird and she plummeted downward, taking her secret with her.

~ CHAPTER 51 ~

A doctor stood by the ambulance. Julian got out of his car to speak to him.

"Are you the next of kin?" the doctor asked.

Julian had to think for a minute. "No, I'm not the next of kin. He's married."

"Well, we need to speak to his wife, because we gotta have some insurance information before we can treat him."

"What?" said Julian loudly.

"That's right. If he doesn't have insurance, he needs to go to the Charity Hospital in Pineville."

"Are you serious? He's not going to make it to Pineville."

"I'm sorry, but we can't treat him here without insurance. If you know his wife doesn't have insurance, then we shouldn't waste time. The ambulance can take him on to Pineville right now."

Julian was looking toward the road, desperately searching for Feen. "A lotta people have died on the way to Pineville, Man, that's about forty miles away."

"I understand, but we can't treat him. That's why I'm telling you, y'all need to go right now."

He saw two cars drive up, one containing Feen and Laura, another vehicle with Adrian and Charlotte.

"Wait a minute, here she is. Let me go get her."

After parking their cars, they ran to meet him.

The doctor shook his head, feeling that time was being wasted.

"C'mon Feen. Hurry. Do you have any kind of insurance?"

"Insurance?"

"Yeah. They're not gonna treat him unless he has some insurance."

They were walking briskly to the place where the ambulance and doctor stood.

"Ma'am, I've been telling them, he needs to go to Charity Hospital," the doctor said.

"Call Dr. Frank," said Feen. "Tell him Feen over here and she say y'all need ta treat ma husband."

He looked at her quizzically for a moment. "Call Dr. Frank?"

"Yeah, call Dr. Frank, I say. Tell him Feen over here and y'all gotta treat her husband."

He stood looking at her dumbfounded.

"Sir, did ya hear me? We ain't got time right now. Please, sir, gone and do it."

He turned and rushed into the hospital. They went to the back door of the ambulance and tried to see Luke inside to see if he was alright. The attendant told them that he was unconscious. He lay on the stretcher with his eyes closed and his head bandaged.

Charlotte let out a sob and Adrian drew her to him. Feen got a handkerchief out her purse and buried her face in it.

"Feen, don't cry," came a weak voice from inside the ambulance.

"Oh, Luke," she cried his name. "Yo wake. Thank ya, Jesus."

"Don't try to talk," said the nurse. "Stay calm and quiet."

The attending doctor returned and they hastily admitted Luke to the hospital.

"Ya say he got hit in the head?" Feen asked Julian.

"Yeah, in the head with the butt of an ax."

All their mouths dropped open. Charlotte said, "Oh my God. With an ax?"

"Well, that's what she had in her hand and it had blood on it."

"What happen, Julian?" asked Feen.

"She hit him in the head, that's all I know. Clarice hit him in the head."

"How you know it was Clarice?" asked Laura.

"Because she was there, screaming, crying, all out-of-control."

He turned to go into the hospital through the emergency room doors.

"Where she at now?" asked Feen, as they walked into the hospital.

Laura pulled Julian's arm and he stopped and turned to her.

"Tell us the truth, Julian. If he was hit with an ax in the head, he ain't gonna make it, is he?"

"I don't know, Laura," he said, as he turned his head and eyes away from her sharp glance.

"Wonder what happened," said Charlotte. "I thought they were so in love."

"Let's see what we can find out," said Feen.

After speaking with a nurse, they found out Luke was still alive. They took a seat in the Colored waiting room, which was a small room at the back of the hospital near the emergency room.

"So, the police got Clarice?" Adrian asked.

"No. Well, I don't think so. She wasn't at the house when they came. But, they're looking for her," said Julian. "I think she believes she killed him."

"Why do ya tink that?"

"Because I saw her looking through the window afterward and she was crying hard, saying stuff like 'I wouldn't a kilt ya if ya woulda taken me home.' Luke was just lying there bleeding. She knew she hit him

258

pretty hard. That's what she intended. To kill him. That's what she intended."

"I hope he make it, but you right. I must say, she fooled me. I wouldn't have thought it in a million years," said Adrian.

"I told you I didn't trust that woman," said Charlotte.

"Yeah, you did," he answered.

"Why you so quiet over there, Mom? You know something about this? Something we don't know?" Charlotte asked.

Feen sat with his head down and her eyes closed, praying. She raised her head when she heard Charlotte's question. "Dunno no mo than y'all. I's at home sleepin' when Julian called."

Feen wondered if Luke had talked to Clarice about her going back to New Orleans without him. If he had, she knew that would be very disturbing to her. Maybe causing her to erupt. But aloud, she repeated what she'd said before, "I dunno what happen. Y'all jus' pray he be alright."

Hours passed before a doctor came and told them he'd made it through surgery alright. He was in a coma and would probably be that way for days. They all decided to go home, rest and come back to check on him the next day. They stood in a circle and said a pray for him before they departed.

∞

The sheriff and his deputies searched Teresa's house, yard, and shed to no avail. They broadened their search area to include Teresa's neighbors and friends. The house in the woods where she'd lived before moving to New Orleans, also, got searched. Speculation had begun to surface she'd hitched a ride back to New Orleans and the local police in New Orleans had been notified to check their house there, as well.

Two days after Luke had been assaulted, fishermen found Clarice's body on the banks of the Mighty Red River. She was splayed with face turned to one side as though she were sleeping, except her mouth was opened. Her arms were positioned as though she may have attempted to break her fall with her hands. They ascertained she had fallen from a ledge high above the water's edge. She'd missed the water entirely and landed on the dirt and rocks. She hadn't gotten her wish to fly above the river to follow the gulls.

Teresa claimed her body and because her body had laid out in the elements, a fast funeral was arranged.

~ CHAPTER 52 ~

Feen hadn't confided to Charlotte the weird things that happened around her house over the years, because she hadn't wanted to alarm her. Now, with Lil Luke being the natural son of Ray Dean, whose wife was Clarice's niece and who practiced hoodoo, too, she found it necessary to inform her of those things. She needed to be aware of any danger that might impact her and Lil Luke.

Charlotte sat in her living room trying to come up with a solution on how to let her son know his biological father and at the same time keep Seraphine out of their lives.

When Adrian came home, he found her still mulling over her situation. She conveyed everything to him her mother had said.

"See, that's what I'm talking about," said Charlotte. "That's why I don't like having Ray around my baby, because I believe that wife of his is as crazy as her Aunt Clarice."

"Well, I understand how you feel, but you can't deny a man from seeing his son, because you guess his wife may have problems."

Charlotte's face drew up in a frown. "I don't understand you. Don't you know what that woman did to my Daddy? I didn't know about all this other stuff, about her scaring my momma with dolls and dead animals. She never told me about that before. But some of those people can be dangerous, and I felt that same kind of energy from Ray's wife."

"Don't get upset with me," he said. "I didn't know about that stuff either, and I think we need to talk about it, just not now."

"So, when do you think a good time is?"

"We're all upset about everything right now, and we're worried about Luke. We don't need to add nothing else to the plate right now."

She walked into the kitchen to serve him his supper.

"My gut is telling me this, Adrian."

"Let's wait awhile. Let things cool down a bit before we decide. You're still worried about what happened with Angie, Luke and Rev. Francisco. Shall I go on? Let things settle a bit is all I'm saying."

She still felt they should talk about it now, but she decided to do what he said and nodded to show her consent.

They didn't talk anymore about it that night.

∞

The next day before Adrian got home, she was in the kitchen cooking when she heard a knock on the door and when she answered it, found Ray Dean standing on her front porch, looking at her with a small smile playing around the corners of his mouth.

"What are you doing here?" she said. "I just saw you at school. You didn't act like we had something to talk about."

"I came to see my son." Looking at the expression on her face, he said, "I'm not going to tell him who I am, but because of the recent deaths in this town, it made me realize how fleeting life is. I want to see my son. I want a relationship with my son."

She didn't move, just continued to look at him. Finally, she said, "Why didn't you call first?"

He shrugged his shoulders.

"I know why. You thought if you called I might say no. But if you came over here, I'd probably let you see him. Well, you're wrong. I'm not going to let you see him. I have to think about this."

"I just want to see him. Touch him. I'm not going to stay long. You're going to deny me seeing him?"

Right about that time, Adrian drove up and and at first relief washed over her. She saw his face and his expression was stone cold. Then her relief turned to anxiety. He exited the car and each step he made was purposeful. His chin was out as he faced Ray on the front porch. Ray turned toward him and extended his hand which Adrian didn't accept.

"Whatcha doing here, Man?" he said.

"I'm here to see my son."

"Did you talk to Charlotte about whether you could come over here?"

"No."

"Like I said, whatcha doing here?"

Silence.

"I was telling Charlotte, I'm not here to start no trouble, I just want to see my son."

"I think my wife told you we'd think about how we wanted to handle this. I can tell you right now. This ain't it. Don't ever come to my house without calling or being invited."

Silence.

"I understand. If you think I'm here to start up something with Charlotte, I'm not."

Before he could go any further, Adrian said, "The only thing we have to talk about is Luke. I'm not about to talk about my wife with you."

Charlotte's eyes got big. She'd never heard Adrian speak like that to anyone.

Ray stopped talking for a second, then continued.

"Alright, I understand that. Please consider letting me see him soon. That's all I'm asking."

He turned around to leave.

Adrian said, "I know you're Luke's father, but don't ever come to my house, unless I know you're coming. You got that?"

"No problem, Man. I just want to see my son. That's all I want. I apologize if I overstepped."

Their eyes held for a second, then he walked off the porch, got in his car and drove away.

They stood on the porch and watched him until he was out of sight. He followed her inside.

"I still think we need to wait until things settle down before we decide what to do," he said, taking her into his arms. "When I walked up, I could see you were rattled, but I understand his point."

"You know what I'm afraid of."

"Yes, I do. Let's see how Luke progresses and let your spirit heal from Rev. Francisco dying and all of the revelations that's happened, lately."

He continued to hold her and rub her back as he was talking. She found herself closing her eyes and leaning on his shoulder. It was such a comfort having him in her life.

"I'm just uneasy about that situation. Okay, we'll do it your way. We'll wait before deciding anything. Oh," she said, pulling away from him. "Speaking of crazy women, guess who I saw in town yesterday?"

"I don't know," he said as he walked to Luke's room.

"Wait a minute," she said, before he opened the door. "Before you go in there, I want to tell you something."

He stopped. He knew she was dying to tell him who she'd seen, so he wondered why she just didn't go on and tell him.

"What crazy woman did you see?"

"Annette Jordan."

"Really? Annette ain't no crazy woman. Why you say Annette's a crazy woman?"

"Because of how she acted that night at the dance."

He chuckled and shook his head, "She ain't no crazy woman. I didn't know she was back in town? I wonder why?"

"You don't have to act so excitedly about it," she said, getting a little irritated.

He laughed.

"Are you still jealous of her?"

"I'm not jealous of her. I just wondered if you knew she was in town."

"No, I didn't know she was in town, and you don't have to be jealous of her."

"I said I'm not jealous of her. Like you just said, I wonder why she's back?"

She was getting more and more irritated at his attitude. He was smiling at her, as though he found something amusing.

"Talking about me being jealous," she said. "You seemed to be a little hot around the collar yourself when you found Ray here." She said in her mocking voice, "Don't ever come to my house if I'm not here."

"That didn't have nothing to do with jealousy," he said. "It has to do with respect. Like a song says, 'No man should be comin' 'round my house if I'm not at home.'"

She smiled. "No even my daddy."

"Of course, I don't mean your daddy, or your son. You know what I mean."

"Yeah, I know what you mean," she said, smiling.

He walked to her, pulled her into his arms and gave her a long passionate kiss.

"You don't need to worry about whether Annette's in town or not. You my wife."

She smiled. She trusted him, but she had no reason to trust Annette Jordan, so she intended to find out why she was in town and how long she planned to stay.

"Now, I'm going to my son's room and talk with him," he said. "Find out what kinda day he had. Is that alright with you?"

"Yes sir," she said. "It sure is."

~ CHAPTER 53 ~

The next day, Feen was sitting in a chair by Luke's bedside when his eyes opened.

"Ooh Lord," she said, as she rang for a nurse. "Tank ya Jesus. His eyes open. He 'wake," she said, excitedly.

Because of overcrowding, the Colored patients were kept in a white trailer on the back of the hospital. It was one large room, and the men and women were housed together. The room had wall to wall beds with tiny aisles to get to each bed, and the nurses' station, which was in the kitchen area. Not many people could visit at a time because there wasn't much room in the sea of beds.

Luke lay in bed with equipment connected to him. His head was wholly bandaged and only his eyes were showing and they were closed. There were six other patients in the beds nearest to him, all in various stages of healing. He was the only one unconscious.

As she looked at him, she prayed for him to get better, and that when he did, he'd be cloth in his right mind.

Doctors came and Feen was ushered out of the room. She was encouraged, because he was not dead. It wouldn't be today, but now there was a good chance she'd get to talk with him on another day.

They all visited him daily, not at the same time, but two weeks later, the whole family came to visit. He was conscious and the large bandage had been removed from around his face. A fresh dressing was on the top of his head. He was doing much better and his speech was more precise. Two family members were let in at a time.

Feen and Angie went in first and his face mirrored how pleased he was to see them. Angie was still shy, but she ventured between the beds when he beckoned for her to come to him.

He held her hand and said, "So glad ya come ta see me."

She smiled weakly, "Me too, Daddy. I'm glad I came. I was so scared. Now I know you're going to be alright."

"I sho am, Baby Gull. I sho am."

He looked over at Feen and she said, "We cain't stay long. Two mo people outside wanna see ya. C'mon, Angie. Kiss him and let's go."

Angie leaned forward and pecked him on the cheek. He squeezed her hand and smiled at her.

"Ya come back and see me, ya hear?"

Charlotte and Laura went in when Feen and Angie came out. They stayed for ten minutes and when they exited, Charlotte said, "He wants to talk with you again, Mom."

"He do?" she asked. "Well, visitin' hour 'most over."

"I'm telling you what he said." She had a matter-of-fact look on her face.

"Alright," said Feen. "Y'all gone ahead. I'll be home in a few minutes."

She walked back into the trailer and approached Luke's bed.

"Sometin' worryin' me," he said. "The hospital bill. I know it's gonna be a lot. How I'ma pay fur that?"

"Don't worry yaself 'bout dat. The man dat run the hospital, he a friend a Dr. Frank. He gonna lemme pay on time."

"Aww. I'm sorry 'bout dat. I didn't come back here ta put ya in debt."

"I'm a pay fur it til ya git better. But ya gonna finish payin' it and ya gonna pay me back the money I already spent."

He smiled, "Alright. Sound good. Jus' don't wanna be no burden ta ya." She stood up to leave. "Stay a lil longer."

She met his gaze. "Luke, all that stuff ya say 'fore ya got hurt. Well, I don't wanna hurtcha, but I don't see that happ'nin'."

Luke smiled, slightly.

"I understan' whatcha say. I hurtcha a lot and ya don't trust me. I understan' that. But I'm gonna be 'round, cuz like I tol' ya, ya still ma wife."

He winked at her as he said wife.

Feen laughed. She didn't believe she would ever think of Luke the way she once had. She cared for him and she was still attracted to him, that was true, but he was correct, she didn't trust him. No relationship can grow and prosper without trust. She'd believed him once, because they'd made a vow when they were teenagers, to only have dove's eyes for each other. Sure, he'd left to save her, but he'd cheated on her before that. However, she, also, knew feelings could change. Hers had changed about Wickliffe after he'd saved Angie. Maybe this could change, too, but at that moment, she didn't think so.

She saw a future of his being a dad to Angie, his grown daughters, and a grandfather to their children, but she didn't see him as being a husband to her. She leaned over, kissed him on the forehead and walked out of the room.

As she walked to Laura's car, she had a pep in her step. She'd been on her own for a long time.

She had two choices available to her. Luke and Blain. She didn't have faith in Luke and Blain was at a different point in his life than she was. There was a chance her feelings on the subject might change, because of something either one or both might do. Maybe love was in her future with one of her two suitors or with someone new.

She still had Angie to raise and send to college. She'd concentrate on that. She hummed an old hymn, 'It is Well with my Soul' as she drove home.

THE END

If you enjoyed this book, please leave a review at Amazon.com.

ABOUT THE AUTHOR

Susane was born and reared near Red River in Marksville, Louisiana. Playing along the banks and levees of the river allowed her imagination to soar. Susane's writing exhibits her love for her childhood home as well as the turmoil and dissension that were a part of life in the segregated South.

She attended Grambling College, but obtained a B. S. Degree in Accounting and Teacher Certification in Business Courses from Northwestern State University, Natchitoches, Louisiana.

She has worked in the telecommunications industry, sold real estate, taught high school and owned small businesses, which gives her a wealth of experiences to write about.

The mother of three children and five grandchildren, she is an avid genealogist. She lives with her fur baby, a poodle named Gail, in Texas, and currently working on her next novel.